PELICANS HAVEN
BOOK 2
Now and Forever

Cecelia M. Chittenden

Cecelia M. Chittenden © 2017

Cover Design by C.A. Simonson

ISBN 10: 1545481253

ISBN 13: 978-1545481257

Table of Contents

ACKNOWLEDGMENTS	5
CHAPTER 1	7
CHAPTER 2	27
CHAPTER 3	43
CHAPTER 4	57
CHAPTER 5	73
CHAPTER 6	87
CHAPTER 7	107
CHAPTER 8	125
CHAPTER 9	141
CHAPTER 10	155
CHAPTER 11	171
CHAPTER 12	181
CHAPTER 13	195
CHAPTER 14	205
CHAPTER 15	217
CHAPTER 16	227
CHAPTER 17	237
CHAPTER 18	247
CHAPTER 19	253
CHAPTER 20	259
ABOUT THE AUTHOR	271

Pelicans Haven Book 2 – Now and Forever

ACKNOWLEDGMENTS

Readers of "Pelicans Haven Book One" who shared their comments and ideas helped put this story on these pages. I thank them and hope book two of the trilogy is as good a read as the book one. Many thanks to my friends Sandy Hanula and Beverly Burchett for the hours they spent proofreading and correcting my many errors while enjoying the story. Special thanks to C. A. Simonson for creating a beautiful cover and taking such extra care in the formatting of the text.

Here are a few comments from the readers of Book 1:

"Engrossing portrayal of the post-Civil War south. Bought three copies for my friends. Can't wait for Book Two."

"This is Ms. Chittenden's first novel, and I must say it was very good. It is part of a series. The characters were real and the situations captivating. Well done."

"I loved this book; I could not put it down. I had to know what was happening next, the flow of the book was awesome. I cannot wait for her next book to come out, fantastic writer. I would recommend this book to anyone who likes to read."

"Fun read. Looking forward to book two!"

CHAPTER 1

By six o'clock, the day was promising scorching heat. Dew dampened every surface, and the sweet smell of honeysuckle floated on the breeze. Soon the sun's rays would turn the dew to phantom humidity producing sweat and fatigue on man and beast alike.

Ben slept in his office all night with the door closed. He nursed a decanter of whiskey while agonizing over the crushing blow of his niece's marriage. Now, his first conscious reaction as he woke was the foul, stale taste in his mouth, and stiffness from sleeping hunched at his desk. An overpowering odor of whiskey filled the room making his stomach queasy. Pieces of the decanter he had thrown against the wall the previous day in a fit of anger lay glittering on the floor, and a revealing stain marked the wall. He stared bleary-eyed at the decanter's twin on his desk disgusted he had emptied its contents.

He eased his cramped body up; his injured leg trembled from the demand of his weight. He took a step and heard the crunch of glass under his boot. He looked down, there laid the stopper from the smashed decanter, unscathed. He swung his foot to kick it out of his path and pain radiated up his body. He swore under his breath and made his way to the door.

He needed to ride to New Orleans and see his attorney to deal with his new problem, his niece's marriage to the Yankee Jake Sinclair. The marriage crushed his plans for the plantation.

He changed his foul-smelling clothes, and shaved, but did not take time to eat. Now, along with his pounding head from the liquor, his stomach grumbled from lack of food. He stood in the corridor outside Lawrence Winston's office waiting for the man to appear.

Lawrence rounded the corner stopping short when he saw Ben. "You look like the wrath of God, and smell worse," he said as he wrinkled his nose. "Why are you here so early?" Lawrence paused as he fumbled for his key. "You received your letters from the court and Josh Horn in the mail yesterday, as did I. Come in, let's hear what you have to say, but don't know what you expect me to do. I can reapply for the Guardianship, but it's going to take time."

Ben collapsed in a chair, "That would be useless. My niece married yesterday."

Lawrence paused, his face went blank. "What? Who did she marry?"

"That Northerner, Jake Sinclair."

"The man who brought her father's body home?" asked Lawrence with raised eyebrows.

"The same."

Lawrence gave a snorted chuckle. "The little girl beat you at your own game. Nothing you can do."

"There has to be something."

"No, nothing," said Lawrence.

"I pay you for using your legal genius. I need control of that property. It needs to come to me, all of it. That man will not have control over any of Pelicans Haven."

"Ben this marriage is sudden and unusual, but you have no control, the guardianship is worthless. It's the same as when your father died and you didn't get what you thought you were rightfully entitled to."

"This is different. This girl has no business or sense to continue the work of that plantation."

"That may be so, but it's beside the point. State law says if a woman is married, she has no need of a guardian, and she can inherit. Her parent's Wills are clear; she and her brothers share equally. I had no control over their Wills."

"So Sinclair rides out of nowhere, takes over what my family owned for years, and I sit and do nothing?" stormed Ben, vigorously nodding his head. "That can't happen."

Lawrence looked at Ben with sympathy. "I understand you're frustrated, but her marriage ends any control you might have had."

"Did you get the names of the men I asked you for?"

"I found one man. He knows who you are and where to find you. You won't need him; your plan to tear down the stable is no good now."

"I have something else he can do."

Lawrence looked at Ben curiously, "Something legal?"

Ben looked at the open door and then leaned close as if to tell a secret, "Jake Sinclair needs to meet with an accident."

Lawrence pointed his finger at Ben. "Stop right there. Not another word! You're talking criminal action. As an officer of the court, I can't be involved with anything that even hints at what you're saying."

"Where were your scruples about the guardianship?" sneered Ben.

Lawrence shrugged, "Paperwork gets fouled up in the courts all the time. I spoke to Judge Mayfield yesterday. He's not concerned. This conversation about accidents happening to Sinclair is a concern and stops now."

"You're such a pantywaist, Lawrence. From the beginning, you wanted nothing to do with this. You waded in far enough to get your little toe wet. You sure were willing to take a share of the gold." He paused as a thought struck him, "The gold is still there somewhere, that hasn't changed. I'll increase your share, would that change your mind?"

"Forget about the gold, Ben, my share, or yours. It's over."

"Where does that leave me? I'm still in the same predicament I was before. Lawrence, I'm drowning in debt," whined Ben.

"Ben, listen, I'm sorry, I truly am, but the only thing I will and can do is respond to Joshua Horn's letter. He's Roseanna's attorney now and has asked for the Wills and information about the brothers. I deliberately drug my feet looking for information about Edward, but Josh Horn won't. Now that your niece is married she'll inherit, brothers or no brothers."

"Who is this Horn? Do you know him?" asked Ben.

"Josh Horn, I know who he is. His reputation is good."

"Could we prove collusion between him and Jake Sinclair?"

"That's up to Roseanna."

"Can't I do that, file something, or issue a complaint?"

"If Roseanna thinks they're conspiring against her, I could file a motion against them. She's the one who would make those charges, not you. If you think that's what's happening, express your concern to her and have her come to me. Do you think there is collusion?"

Ben gestured wildly, "This man rides up to the plantation with her father's body and a convenient attorney waiting in the wings. I think my brother told Sinclair everything including about the gold, and he's plotted to get it from a defenseless girl."

"What proof do you have, Ben? The best thing you can do is talk to Roseanna. Maybe you can get her to help you. Get her to understand she may be in jeopardy from these men."

Lawrence's statement fueled Ben's anger. "Go to an eighteen-year-old girl for help! All she knows how to do is powder her nose. You're not taking this seriously, Lawrence. I pay you for advice, and I demand you do something!"

A frown creased Lawrence's brow. "You can't bully me. Your problem is not of a legal nature. There's no basis for anything."

"All the years you've been the attorney for the Ravenna's, now something of importance needs to be resolved, and there's nothing you can do? Bull crap, Lawrence!" said Ben as he stood and pointed his finger at Lawrence, "You're fired!"

Lawrence jumped from his chair, "No, I quit. Get out! Find somebody else to support your schemes. I'm done. Get out, or I'll throw you out!"

Ben stood glaring at Lawrence, breathing heavily. Lawrence returned the stare without wavering. Ben snatched his hat from Lawrence's desk, jammed it on his head, and stormed from the room.

Roseanna woke with a start, sweating and tangled in the sheets. Nine o'clock, she never slept this late. She collapsed back against the pillows exhausted. She had lain awake much of the night worried about her uncle. He had forced her to marry Jake Sinclair by trying to take everything away from her and her brothers, but now the worry of leaving Pelicans Haven, and surrendering her father's assets were gone, but she felt frightened of what her uncle might do.

She had felt relief at the marriage ceremony, but then her uncle came into the house as it ended and reacted dreadfully. He was angry at the sight of them marrying and accused Jake and Randy of taking advantage of her, and refuted the fact they had cared for her father, James when they found him snake bit and ill as they traveled to New Orleans. She owed them her gratitude, especially Jake. His marriage to her made the guardianship invalid, and as a married woman, she was able to inherit her father's assets. Jake had even offered to move her to New Orleans and take her away from her uncle, but she couldn't accept anything else from him, he had his own life, and she would never leave the plantation.

Her own sweet cousin, Nancy, who had happily helped her with the wedding, began to cry as her father became angrier and demanded that she leave the house with him. His treatment of his daughter was inexcusable, and Roseanna wanted to apologize to her again. And what of her Aunt Jane? Roseanna felt her face flush as she thought of her aunt's accusation that a child grew in her belly. She buried her face in the pillow and groaned. Would everyone in the parish have the same thought?

With distaste, she pushed the thought from her mind and hurried from her bed. She stood at the window where a hot wind billowed the curtains. Shade dappled the forlorn and neglected garden. A robin landed below the window. He stood tall as a sentry, cocking his head as he listened for a tunneling worm, then jammed his beak in the ground, and captured his reward.

Her troubles weren't over, and she needed to plan as she waited for her brother, Edward, to return from the war. What happened in the past was gone; the future is what mattered. Somehow, she would start preparing for horses to fill the stable, and she had promised to take care of the rose garden and tend to her parent's graves. There were plans to make and work to do, and work would banish thoughts of her uncle.

A knock at the door interrupted Roseanna's breakfast of biscuits with tea. She opened the door to find Andrew on the doorstep. She rushed across the threshold to greet him, grasping his hands. "Oh, Andrew, I'm glad you've come. Nancy, is she all right?"

Andrew's eyes twinkled as he smiled at his cousin and took her hands. "Nancy is in fine spirits and threatening to run away from home if she isn't allowed to see her cousin."

"I should never have let Nancy be here."

"Nancy's fine and defending her decision to be your bridesmaid. She's been told you're a bad influence, and she will not be allowed to visit."

Roseanna shoulders slumped, "No, they haven't done that." Roseanna started towards the veranda steps. "I need to see your mother."

Andrew grabbed her arm, "There's no need. Nancy asks that I give you a message; she loves you, and they can never keep her from seeing you. She laughed at mother. Now, never mind Nancy, tell me how this happened, you marrying Jake?"

"She's all right then, Nancy?"

"Yes, of course, Roseanna, but will you tell me about this? I paid no attention to Ben yelling yesterday or this morning. Loretta and then my mother told me about your marriage." Andrew shook his head in wonder, "Married to Jake Sinclair. How, tell me?" he said with a playful grin.

"It was the only thing that could stop Ben, but it's all gone wrong."

Andrew drew Roseanna in a hug. "Nothing's gone wrong," he said in a soothing voice, "you've just caused a stir. More like beating on a hornets' nest with a stick," laughed Andrew. "Mother and Ben are beside themselves."

"Did you talk to Ben?"

Andrew laughed, "Not if I don't have too. He was gone early this morning. He stayed closed up in his office all night and in the worst of moods according to mother."

"Andrew, you do understand why I did this?"

Andrew chuckled, "Of course I do. Bravo to Jake Sinclair if he's the one who thought of it. The guardianship is gone, and according to mother you inherit now that you're married."

"Yes, but everyone's angry. I'm, I'm afraid of what Ben will do."

"Afraid of Ben, Roseanna," said Andrew with a look of surprise. "He's just a loud bully. He isn't violent, well except perhaps a cuff to Nathan on occasion. Nothing he can do. There's no need to fear him."

"Do you believe that, Andrew?"

"Of course. Ben will stay angry and pout, but that's all he can do. My mother said she advised you to annul the marriage, and that Jake is a scalawag and a bounder, and you should run as fast as you can," hooted Andrew.

Roseanna sighed, "Andrew stop, don't tease. This is dreadful."

"Roseanna, it isn't dreadful; you've outsmarted not only Ben but Lawrence by having your own attorney. Bravo for Jake."

"Ben said outrageous things about Jake."

"Ben says what suits himself. Don't listen."

"Jake nursed my father until he died and then brought his body home. Jake is none of the things Ben claims, neither is his friend, Randy."

Andrew frowned at Roseanna. "I don't believe what Ben says, ever. Where is Jake?"

Roseanna dropped her eyes and blushed. "He's not here, and he won't be. The marriage is not… it's only to stop the Guardianship."

Andrew stared at Roseanna's flushed cheeks, "I understand. By the way, Ben told mother about the gold."

Roseanna looked up in surprise. "He admitted he knows? That's what this is about, the gold."

"He promised mother that he would finance my return to London with the gold, and I apologize. She thinks she can help Ben now because of me, but I would never accept money from him. I need to tell her about Loretta and me."

"Why don't you, Andrew? You love Loretta, your mother would never argue against that."

"It's risky. Mother could tell Ben, and I need no more of his hatred, my deserting was enough. I won't risk bad treatment to Loretta from him. I need to keep the secret even if Mother would understand."

As they stood on the veranda, the mail carrier, Mr. Plumb, came with letters for Roseanna. He handed envelopes to her with a nod; she returned his greeting and turned back to Andrew. "I meant what I said about giving you the money for London, but where would we search, Andrew. We've looked every place that is obvious, and it may have never been here at all. We just don't know. Come in while I finish my breakfast, there's enough for you, too."

Roseanna tossed the envelopes she held on a table with other unopened mail. "What's this package? I've neglected the mail." She picked up the package wrapped in heavy brown paper and tied with knotted twine. "It's addressed to my father."

Andrew drew a knife from his pocket and cut the twine binding the package. Roseanna sat in a chair and looked at the return address on the package. "It's from Ohio." She took the wrapping from the box and removed the lid. A folded, grease-stained paper lay inside. She handed it to Andrew. "Maybe a letter. Read it will you, Andrew, while I see what's here."

Dear Mr. Ravenna,

My name is Rufus Sparks. I was a guard at a Camp Chase Union Prison in Columbus, Ohio where your son Edward was held. I'm sending his personal effects. Edward was here for over a year and a model prisoner until he tried to make his escape with several others. He was shot and died from his wounds. He and I become friends, and he often told me about his family, and the horses you raised. Forgive me for taking so long to write. Coming home has been difficult for me. Find in this package his bible, his pipe, his watch, the buttons and insignia from his uniform, and the buckle from his belt. I am sure he was a fine soldier and son, and I was proud to call him a friend. I know where his grave is as I marked it myself. If you come for his body contact me, I will assist you.

With best regard,

Rufus Sparks

Roseanna sat fingering Edwards's possession as tears coated her cheeks. "Oh, Andrew, what was he going through? He must have suffered. You've heard about the terrible condition in those camps."

Andrew knelt by her chair and pressed a handkerchief into her hand. He put his arm around her, "Roseanna, I'm so sorry. This war has been tragic for you. Your brothers gone, John and now Edward. It's not right."

"This explains so much, why no one knew where he was for so long. He was captured. All that time in a prison camp," said Roseanna in wonder. "Mother insisted father go and look for him; she wanted to know if he was alive before she died, but father would never have found him," said Roseanna her voice becoming more hysterical. "He may have been dead before my father left. It was useless to go, and then to die from a snakebite. He would still be alive if we had known Edward was a prisoner." Roseanna covered her face with her hands, crying in earnest, her sobs shaking her shoulder.

Andrew tried to console her, "Oh God, Roseanna! You should lie down. Let me help you to your room, or find Mama Teal."

Roseanna gripped Andrews's arms, "I want to bring his body home, Andrew," she said through her sobs. "I want him here with me and my mother and father."

"Roseanna, of course, you do. Let's worry about that later, there'll be time. Let me do something for you now."

"There's nothing you can do."

Andrew stayed by her side until her sobs had subsided and her breath had calmed. "Will Jake come today?"

"No, not today. Andrew, I'm glad you were here with me," said Roseanna gripping his hand and indicating the letter from Rufus Sparks. "I couldn't have faced this alone."

Andrew laid a light kiss on Roseanna's temple. "I'll go now, send Simon if you want company. Rest Roseanna. I love you, we all love you." And he quietly left.

Roseanna stayed in her chair fingering the trinkets from the box and thinking about her brothers and the happy childhood they had shared. She went to her father's office, drew stationary from the drawer, and wrote Rufus Sparks a letter thanking him for being her brother's friend and for returning his things to his family. Roseanna assured him she would come to retrieve her brother's body and would thank him personally. She wished him well and sent her hope that his life since the war would become more manageable.

Her breakfast was cold, but she had lost her appetite. She went to find Mama Teal to give her the news about Edward.

Lawrence's dismissal of his troubles infuriated Ben. The declaration that no legal action could be taken was unacceptable, something had to be done. His head was pounding, and his stomach gnawed from lack of food. The two-hour ride home would wait until he ate.

Finishing a meal at a restaurant, he gawked as Jake Sinclair entered. An elegantly dressed woman was by his side, and a man followed. They walked by his table but took no notice of him. Ben asked the waiter if he knew the men.

"Yes, Sir, Mr. Jake Sinclair, and Mr. Joshua Horn. Never saw the lady before. Would there be anything else, sir?"

"Just the charge, thank you."

Ben watched the three in revulsion. They were in animated conversation, sharing a laugh, probably about the easy pickings in the South, and bamboozling his niece. Would Roseanna know her husband was with this other woman? He couldn't let this man invade Pelicans Haven.

 He rode slowly through the crowded streets. New Orleans was coming alive since the surrender, but his head still pounded, and he had no tolerance for the confusion. Traffic thinned as he reached the outskirts and he rode at a leisurely pace thinking how he would get Lawrence to act against Sinclair. Lawrence was wrong; this was not the time to withdrawal. He rode in the sweltering heat with sweat plastering his shirt to his body and insects droning about his ears adding to his misery.

Begrudgingly he began to think Lawrence was right, and the best action was to talk to Roseanna. If they could agree on how the plantation could be run, and the gold was found, they could equally prosper. Roseanna was headstrong and didn't know her place. Her father, James, treated her as he treated his sons instead of insisting she do the womanly thing and let men take the lead in pressing decisions. Nancy or Jane would never act defiant towards a man. Roseanna insisted on raising horses, which was wrong. As he rode, he planned what he would say but would not admit to his debts. He had to persuade her that his plans for the plantation were vital, and he needed to have his way.

Roseanna found Mama Teal hoeing weeds in the kitchen garden, and Simon watering the tender plants from a cup and bucket. They sat in the shade of a large oak tree and Roseanna read the letter from Rufus Sparks. Mama Teal wailed and covered her face with her apron as Simon shook with sobs and laid his head on his mother's shoulder. Mama Teal recalled what a beautiful baby Edward had been. He never cried and was content lying in his cradle. They talked about both the boys and how proud and handsome they looked in their uniforms as they went off to war, their spirits high. They were eager to face the Yankees convinced they would be defeated, they would come home victorious, and the Yankees would have their tails between their legs. No one thought about the lives and families the war would destroy, only the victory.

Now families victorious or not shared grief and loss. Life at homes around the nation would never be the same.

Finally drained, they sat in silence for a time under the tree, lost in their own thoughts. Roseanna broke the spell. "I must do something. This day has been a waste."

"No needs, it hot, Miss Roseanna. Stay here by me and Simon."

Roseanna reluctantly rose to her feet. "The garden needs work, Mama Teal, I can't sit still."

She gathered a basket and shears, found a wide brimmed-hat to protect her from the sun, and pulled on her gloves. As she worked, she thought about her brother and clenched her jaw each time her tears threatened to fall. She tried to puzzle out how long before the end of the war Edward had attempted his escape. Had he waited he would be released to return home. No one had news about his capture, and she was thankful to Rufus Sparks for writing his letter; otherwise, they would never have known Edward's fate.

Roseanna looked up to see her uncle riding towards her. She thought of her talk with Andrew, how he told her she should not be frightened of Ben, and Jake had told her there was nothing he could do. She turned her back and ignored his approach. He stopped his horse at the white picket fence boundary close to Roseanna. "Roseanna, good afternoon," he said.

Roseanna didn't respond but glanced coldly at her uncle and then back to the rose she was pruning.

"It's hot out today. You should stop and take the shade."

Anger welled in Roseanna. "Now you're concerned for my well being, Uncle Ben?"

"This heat isn't good for anyone, the air is heavy; I've seen men drop in this kind of heat. We'd give the slaves protection when it changed like this. Humidity saps everyone's strength."

"You should go home then, Uncle Ben," said Roseanna, tersely, continuing to work.

He had to clear the air. This girl was his lifeline, the only one available. He'd made mistakes, the biggest when he bought the shares in the slave ship, but he was right about how the plantation could prosper, and needed her to see that. To beg and bargain from this snip of a girl was distasteful, but she was his only hope.

How had it gone so wrong, his brother, instead of him amassing a fortune? James had given him twelve thousand dollars and never batted an eye. Now his daughter had it all, her, and the Northerner. They had everything that could make his life meaningful. He was no longer significant to his niece. Sinclair took that away; he would be the one who controlled her and his brother's assets.

The silence between them stretched on. Ben couldn't find words to say. Finally, he spoke, "Could we sit there on the veranda and talk, Roseanna?" he said in a pleading voice.

Roseanna didn't want to talk; Edward weighed heavily on her mind, she wasn't ready to share the news about him with her uncle, and his behavior at her marriage was still painful. "There's nothing to say, Uncle Ben. We'll talk another time."

"I think it's time, Roseanna, plenty needs to be said. I'll go sit on the veranda. You come sit too when you're ready."

He dismounted, led his horse to the veranda, tied it to a post, and then sat in the shade fanning his face with his hat waiting for his niece to join him.

Roseanna angrily continued to prune, watching from the corner of her eye as her uncle went to the veranda. At first, she made no move to follow, but finally, with a sigh of resignation, threw down her shears and gloves, and joined him. They sat in silence for a time before Ben cleared his throat and began to speak.

"I guess I should start by apologizing for how I acted at your marriage ceremony, but I'm shocked, Roseanna, that you married that man," said Ben, with emphasis.

Roseanna grit her teeth, "You left me no choice, Uncle Ben!"

"You've ruined your life, letting that man come on to this plantation as your husband."

"Is this your apology, to once again say things about Jake? He made it possible for me to keep this plantation and I'm grateful. I'm waiting for an apology from you."

"What did you expect, Roseanna? I tried to work things out with you, but you had a bullheaded attitude and paid me no mind."

Roseanna glared at her uncle and began to speak.

Ben held his hand up for silence. "You hear me out now. Can you do that? Just listen," he demanded.

Roseanna took a deep breath; she wanted to say so much. "Out of respect, Uncle Ben, I will, but I want the same respect from you."

"This isn't easy for me, Roseanna. I'm a proud man, not used to having to explain my actions to anyone, and especially to an eighteen-year-old girl."

Roseanna raised her eyebrows and gave her uncle an icy stare.

"Give me some consideration. I know the way the land lays now, and I'm trying to accept that."

He sat in his chair, then took his handkerchief from his pocket and moped the sweat from his face.

Roseanna drummed her fingers with impatience. "Uncle Ben, make your point."

Ben cleared his throat. "I'll start by saying that I truly believe your parents would want me to step in and make decisions for you."

Roseanna looked at him with disgust; Ben again raised his hand to stop her from speaking.

Roseanna ignored him, "No one gave you any authority, no matter what you believe."

"You know no such thing, Roseanna," said Ben, heatedly. "Just let me talk then you can have your say, can you do that?"

Roseanna glared at him with hooded eyes, "I'm listening," she said crossing her arms over her chest.

"Right before your father left on that damn fool goose chase looking for your brother, Edward, the two of us sat down and talked about what we should do with the plantation now the war was over. We decided to combine our resources and work together to get us both back on our feet. We agreed that his returning to the horses would take too long to turn a profit and that cotton and sugarcane should be planted on the entire place because that would be the fastest way to make a profit."

"We both lost everything because of the war and your father gave me the twelve thousand dollars as his share of what would be needed to start what we wanted to do, hire labor and clear his side of the plantation. I joked with your father about the IOU. I insisted on signing one, your mother was there, she knew this to be true, now they're both gone you have nothing but my word."

"This next will be hard for you, but nonetheless it's true. I've just come from meeting with Lawrence Winston, and he voiced what I have been thinking all along, and that is Jake Sinclair, and this attorney, Horn, are in collusion to take advantage of you. I think your father unintentionally misled Jake Sinclair. He must have been in a great deal of pain, and probably delusional, which made him say things he shouldn't. Because of that, Sinclair came here, influenced your decisions, and turned your head with all the attention he is paying you."

"That's preposterous ,Uncle Ben, and far from the truth. The attention he is paying me is because of you. He knew you were up to no good," said Roseanna in anger.

"Roseanna, Roseanna, please let me finish. Now Lawrence doesn't personally know this Horn fellow, but he tells me that his reputation around the courthouse isn't good. I realize that I was wrong and forced you to marry Sinclair, but your father would be heartsick by your decision and would not want Jake Sinclair to take over this plantation, and I'm certain of that."

"You and I can do what's needed together. This marriage needs to be annulled. It's not too late. Lawrence Winston stands ready to do that for you. He will draft an agreement that you and I can both sign about what needs to be done, what each of us will contribute, and how we will divide the profits. I don't need an agreement because we're family, but I can see that maybe you do. Your father didn't need one with me, but you might given what has happened. I wish your father and I had written something down, then none of this would have happened."

"Is that all Uncle Ben," said Roseanna outwardly calm.

"Not quite Roseanna. I wanted to tell you that your Aunt Jane is ashamed that she suggested that there might be a child between you and Jake Sinclair. She knows that's not true, she said it out of anger and without thinking how hurtful it would be. And Nancy, why of course she should have stood up with you, the shock of the wedding was why we acted so poorly. Neither of us holds any anger towards you or Nancy, we're concerned for you, Roseanna. What is this man you've married going to do next?"

"This last will be hurtful, and I don't mean it to be, but if you're determined, you should know. I saw your husband today in the company of another woman. Doesn't seem a newly married man would be with another woman."

Roseanna hissed in disgust. "You're lying; I don't believe that for a moment."

Ben turned his hat repeatedly in his hands. "I suppose you don't have to believe me, Roseanna, but I'm telling you what I saw. I've said what I needed to, Roseanna, but I need to reiterate that what I have told you is what your father and I discussed before he left. I'm sure you would want to take that into consideration before you make any other decisions."

"You had quite a lot to say, Uncle Ben," said Roseanna, "but let me tell you what I know to be true. First, Jake Sinclair has done none of the things you have accused him of, including influencing any of my decisions. My father never planned or intended to join forces with you as you have suggested. But let's get everything out Uncle Ben, you left out the most important part, the gold."

Ben looked at Roseanna in stunned surprise. "Gold? What gold, Roseanna. I know nothing about any gold."

"Oh, but yes you do, Uncle Ben. I know about it the same way you do, from the bank president, Mr. Cutler. I went to the bank with my father's account book because I didn't understand why there was a large amount of money showing there, but then it was gone. He told me how my father closed his accounts and took the money in gold. Mr. Cutler told you as well, and you never told me because you wanted it for yourself."

"Roseanna, you're accusing me of doing something that I didn't even know about, this gold. Cutler never told me it existed."

Roseanna turned on her uncle angrily, "You've known because—." Roseanna stopped she couldn't betray Andrew. "You've known all along, and you've had the opportunity to tell me, but instead you tried to force me from my home so you could search and take it for yourself. Isn't that why you want Jake gone because you wanted no one to help me or give me advice? Lawrence Winston, who is supposed to be acting in my best interest, knows about the gold too. You speak about collusion, that's what you and Lawrence Winston have done."

"Roseanna, you're wrong. There's no plan with Winston."

Roseanna vibrated with indignation. She tried to moisten her lips, but her mouth was dry, and her throat closed until her voice came as a harsh, raspy whisper. She pressed her hands to her ears. "Stop, Uncle Ben! I won't hear your lies. You did know, Mr. Cutler told you. It doesn't matter because it's not here, there is no gold. Do you remember, Uncle Ben, I told you that Jake Sinclair had brought a letter from my father? My father did write something down, something to my mother. That letter warned her about someone who would do her harm. I was confused about who that could be, but not anymore. My father knew you so well; he knew you would do exactly what you have done. I have heard the stories about how you harassed my mother to the point that my grandfather was going to throw you off the plantation. My father wouldn't have left my mother here with the possibility that you would be her only source of protection and help. They had a plan, Uncle Ben, and you were not part of that plan, he never mentioned you in the letter, not once. After as much pride and success as my father took with his horses, he would not have decided to plant sugarcane. He wanted his wife and children to continue with what built this plantation."

"Roseanna, you want me to accept what you said when your father and I had plans of our own. It's a lie about my involvement with your mother; its hateful gossip."

Roseanna ignored her uncle's protest, raised her voice, and continued to speak. "As far as Jake Sinclair goes, I have the highest recommendation of him from the person I love more than anyone else, my father. His letter to mother told her that Jake was a kind and honest man. Jake helped me make one decision, and that has been the most important one, to seek my own legal counsel. I have total confidence in Josh Horn. I don't believe you saw Jake with another woman, and even if it's true, you have no way to know why. You criticize the way my father raised me, but little did he know he was preparing me to face a persuasive adversary because one day he knew I might have to.

"I'm done now, Uncle Ben, except for one thing. If I inherit, I will have the power to forgive the IOU, and I will do that, but that is all I will ever do for you."

Ben sat stunned his face turning red from embarrassment, shame or anger. Roseanna didn't know which, and it didn't matter. She was done with her uncle. She stood on trembling legs, "I'd like you to leave now. I asked you to tell me the truth, but you haven't. Your apology was just more lies, and there was no sincerity in anything you said. I will thank you, for one thing, Uncle Ben; you've shown me that my father had great faith in me and raised me to stand up for myself. I'm just sorry it took me so long to realize it because none of this intrigue would have happened. Jake Sinclair saw it, and he is the kind of man who respects women as equals, not as pawns who can be manipulated and used."

Ben Ravenna rose from his chair. "Roseanna, you don't trust me, your uncle, and the one who cares for you the most. You must believe that your father and I were going to work together to build a better life for all of us. I'll admit that I do recall Cutler at the bank mentioning something about your father and gold, but I was there on my own affairs and took no interest in what he was saying. Then this stranger you don't know comes along, and you believe every word he says. It proves to me that I have been right about Jake Sinclair all along. He has put nonsense in your head about me. You'll live to regret the day you've let Jake Sinclair drive a wedge in our family."

He looked intently at his niece, took a deep shuddering breath, and left the veranda. The pain in his leg prevented him from mounting his horse; he untied the animal and without a second glance at his niece, limped to his barn. He should have walked away like a dog with its tail between its legs, or felt explosive anger after listening to Roseanna's tirade, but his ego wouldn't allow that weakness. She was the weak one; she was the angry one, with her tantrum, like a selfish child who didn't get her way. He could see by tremors in her hands and the halting sound of her speech. Children who threw tantrums didn't get their way, he'd see to that. He'd get his way; he'd get what he wanted.

He was confident his brother had given Jake more information than he was admitting to Roseanna, but she refused to question his motives. The Wills still not settled, not until the whereabouts of the brother, Edward, was resolved. James' idea of raising the damn horses fed the silly girl's romantic notion and was a waste. So, the gold wasn't found, but he knew his brother well enough to know the truth, it was here and could still be his. He was not discouraged, and not ready to ask Roseanna for help. There was no need. He had time. He needed to persuade his niece away from Jake Sinclair.

Roseanna watched him go and then hurried into the house before he could see her tears.

CHAPTER 2

Roseanna watched at the window as her uncle crossed the bridge to his barn. She was shaking, crying, and hugging herself to stop her trembling. Her uncle was her only family now, but no longer the loving uncle she knew. He pleaded for her to listen, and seemed remorseful and apologetic, but it was an act. He told her nothing but lies. He was wrong about Jake. Jake had asked for nothing and married her to keep her safe from him. Marrying Jake was the only way she could hold on to her home. She trusted him; she was sure of him.

Roseanna collapsed in a chair and wiped her eyes trying to calm her emotions. Did she really know Jake? No, she didn't really know him. Maybe what her uncle said was true. She had trusted him, and she needed to trust someone. She needed someone to turn to, and he was there asking nothing in return. Now she had doubts about everyone, her uncle, and Jake. She paced the house, wandering from room to room clamping her hands to her head to shut out the questions and doubts that rang in her ears.

Edward would not be home and be with her. She was still plagued with thoughts of what he suffered as a prisoner. She heard the stories about the camps and the conditions, no food, or blankets. They were left out in the elements, nothing to protect them during the bitter cold and the scorching heat. Thoughts of his ill-treatment, and then his death during an escape were agonizing. If he'd just waited for the surrender, he would be alive and home with her, and her father, too.

She walked into Edward's room and fingered the items on his dresser, a comb and hairbrush made of Elkhorn, a crumpled packet of tobacco dried out and worthless. She went to his desk where his favorite books were stacked. She looked through them, but none seemed familiar. The drawers of his desk yielded little save a few letters from schoolmates and one from a girl named Beverly, who promised she would wait for him until the end of the war.

Who was she? Roseanna knew no girl named Beverly. It saddens her to know she couldn't even contact the girl to tell her that the promise she had made to

Edward need no longer be kept; he wasn't coming home. Would her brother John know who she was? There was no one to question about the girl; everyone was gone. Roseanna lay on Edwards's bed and cried for all she had lost and finally fell asleep.

She woke as the clock in the hall struck four a.m. Her head was aching, and groggy from lack of sleep and pent-up emotions. The emptiness of the house closed around her, and for the first time the anticipation for the return of her family, her father, and brothers, was gone. The realization that she was alone, and no one was ever coming home struck her; it was real. It was eerily quiet; the only sound the house creaking in the night. She went to her own room, curled on the bed and tried to sleep. Her eyes flew open; she was to see Jake and Josh in the city in just a few hours. Her conversation with her uncle about them came back filling her with dread. Her uncle had come to her when she was depressed and vulnerable, intruding on the grief and her feelings for her brother, but his accusations against Jake now were unsettling. She had defended him, but doubts crept in. She didn't want to believe that her father had sung praises about the plantation so that Jake would think he could profit at Pelicans Haven. Her father's letter to her mother praised Jake. He had helped her father and then helped her. He meant her no harm.

She left her bed and hurried to find her father's letter. It wasn't in his hand, but Jake had said he was too ill to write. She studied the signature scrawled shakily at the bottom of the page, but was unsure if it was her father's writing. Why hadn't her father named Ben as the person who could do her mother harm rather than a riddle that Roseanna couldn't figure out? Why hadn't he said what plans they had?

Tomorrow she would see Jake; she didn't want to face him with doubts, but what if her uncle was telling her the truth about him and Josh Horn? She would see them both; she would go to New Orleans and get the truth. Was there a woman with Jake? What did it matter to her?

She gave up trying to sleep and rummaged through her wardrobe for something to wear; she wanted to look nice for Jake. She immediately dropped that notion and grabbed the first dress that came to her hand. She bathed and dressed quickly, and as she combed her hair, she looked at her haggard reflection in the mirror. Her face looked pinched and dark circles framed her eyes. She tossed her comb on her dressing table and hurried from the room.

She needed to get out of the stillness of the house and be in the company of the people she loved and trusted, Mama Teal and her children. The usual time for her breakfast was several hours away, but she knew Mama Teal's family would be gathered in the kitchen house. As she walked through the door, they looked up in surprise.

They all rose from the table. "Miss Roseanna yous early," said Mama Teal. "I's get your breakfast in the big house."

"No, Mama Teal, I'd like to join you here for breakfast."

"We talkin' bout Mr. Edward," said Simon. "Everybody dyin'. Simon goin' die too?" he asked with tears in his eyes.

Roseanna reached for Simon's hand, "No, Simon, you're going to be an old, old man with a long white beard. You're not going to die. Nobody is going to die."

"Simon don't yous upset Miss Roseanna, yous hush," said Mama Teal in a scolding voice.

"Simon is upset because Edward was special," said Roseanna as she smiled at Simon and squeezed his hand. "Simon, I'm going to the city today. Would you like to come?"

"Simon," he said, gesturing to himself.

"Yes, Simon!"

"And we takes the gig?"

"Yes, we take the gig," said Roseanna smiling at Simon's excitement.

"I's go hitch it," said Simon.

"Yous gets clean shirt and yous shoes," yelled Mama Teal at Simon's hastily retreating back.

By the time Roseanna and Simon reached the city, Roseanna was glad she had invited him. His evident joy at leaving the plantation for the city put Roseanna in a happier mood and distracted her from her thoughts as she listened to his barrage of chatter and excitement over everything he was seeing. She let him take the reins for a time until they reached the outskirts. His chest swelled with pride at the importance of driving Roseanna.

When they reached Josh Horn's office, Roseanna parked the gig at the edge of the street and secured the reins. "Simon you stay with the gig. Don't go off now. I'll be right through that door," she said pointing. "If you need me, you come and find me."

"Where Mr. Jake? When he comin'?"

"He'll come out with me when we're done inside."

"I's stay and wait for Mr. Jake."

"I know you will Simon."

Roseanna went into the offices and sat to wait. Josh came out of his office after a short time and greeted her.

"Is Jake not here? He was to meet me."

"There was business trouble somewhere, he and Randy have gone upriver to take care of it."

Roseanna felt relief or disappointment, she wasn't sure which. How would she react to Jake after the conversation with her uncle? "I hope it's nothing serious."

"I don't know the details, something about the business, but come, I have someone I want you to meet, and who very much wants to meet you," he said with a smile as he took Roseanna's arm and led her to a closed door.

He opened the door to reveal an elegantly dressed woman sitting at a table. She rose as the two entered the room.

"Miss Ravenna, I would like you to meet Miss Gwen Mason," said Josh with a flourish. "Jake, of course, wanted to make this introduction, but I am pleased to do so in his absence."

"Jake has told me about you," said Roseanna as she took the woman's hand in greeting.

Josh excused himself and left the women to become acquainted.

"Josh has already forgotten that you are no longer Miss. Ravenna but now Mrs. Sinclair," said Gwen with a forced smile slowly scanning Roseanna from head to toe.

"I didn't notice, I'm not used to the Mrs. Sinclair myself."

"I was surprised when Jake told me he married. I had no idea he had met someone, and we are in touch quite frequently."

"Your dress is lovely," said Roseanna to change the subject, regretting that she had not taken the time to dress more carefully. "We're behind the times in Louisiana with fashion compared to New York City. It must be fascinating living there."

The stylish dress that Gwen Mason wore had a full skirt made of light blue taffeta with inserts of palest green. There were ruffles and flounces at the bottom of the skirt, and a bustle gathered at the rear. She wore a small hat, nothing like the wide-brimmed bonnets that were common in the parish, but made from the same fabric as the dress, shaped like a triangle with the apex resting on the forehead, and gathered with netting and flowers at the crown. Gwen Mason was an attractive woman with a beautiful complexion, flaxen hair, and blue eyes.

"I find New Orleans lacking in many things compared to New York. Have you been to New York, Mrs. Sinclair? If not Jake will have to bring you the next time he comes. Speaking of Jake, I can't tell you the reason he isn't here, only some emergency. He did at least leave me a note and asked me to offer his apologies to you. He was gone before I was out of bed this morning."

"I'm sure it was important, and it isn't necessary for him to be here with me today."

"Jake tells me you live on a plantation a distance north of New Orleans. I'm intrigued, being a city girl, I've never really been in the country long enough to understand what folks do so far away from a city. Jake is a city boy, too. I wonder what his impressions of the plantation would be."

"He hasn't said, but he says he prefers the pace of New Orleans over New York. And he finds the weather here more to his liking."

"I'm surprised. I've known Jake since we were children and he has never expressed that to me. He was being polite," said Gwen.

The door opened, and Josh Horn came in. "Sorry, Miss Ravenna, I needed a minute to finish with a client. Gwen and I are going to lunch when you and I are finished, and it would be delightful if you would join us."

"Josh where are your manners? This is Mrs. Sinclair, not Miss. Ravenna," said Gwen, lifting her chin with a slight smile.

"Forgive my rudeness, I'm so sorry Mrs. Sinclair," Josh said turning to Roseanna with a slight bow.

Roseanna laughed, "Jake teased me about introducing myself to you. Please, just call me Roseanna, and as much as I would love to join you, I'm short on time today."

"We should get started, so I don't keep you," said Josh. He could see Roseanna seemed troubled.

He escorted her to a comfortable chair in his office. "Now, Mrs. Sinclair, I must tell you that I have heard nothing from Mr. Winston, so I'm not able to give you information about your parent's Wills today."

Roseanna took the letter she had received from Rufus Sparks from her bag and handed it to Josh.

"What's this then," he said as he began to read the letter.

Roseanna waited patiently for Josh to finish reading. "I'm so sorry. We knew he was missing, but to find out these circumstances and his death is distressing and adds to your burden of grief."

"I can't help but think if he had waited until the surrender and not tried to escape he may have come home," said Roseanna, tears clouding her eyes.

"I'm extremely sorry, and it's upsetting knowing he might very well have come home. You wanted news of Edward, but all the same, this comes as an unhappy surprise. Does Jake know?"

Roseanna shook her head, "I just received the letter, he doesn't know."

"This will make the process of clearing the estate faster, but that's not important given your brother's death."

"I'd like to retrieve his body and bring it home, but I'm not sure how I could do that."

"I'll find out how to make that happen. We'll contact the government on a federal as well as state level to see how it can be done."

"I've had a conversation with my uncle, and he suggests that he and I sit down with Lawrence Winston, and discuss signing an agreement or contract that would state how we could run the plantation together. He also suggested that I have my marriage to Jake annulled."

Josh paused before he spoke, "As I said, I've not heard from Mr. Winston. Is this contract that you would sign with your uncle something you would consider?"

"I don't know. What would be in my best interest?"

"Let me give you something to think about, and perhaps that will help you make your decision. Signing a contract with your uncle now would be premature. The Wills aren't settled so there would be nothing you could agree to in a contract, as your inheritance is still unclear. Did your uncle specify his proposal?"

"He didn't go into the details, but I know our ideas are different. How long will it take to settle the estates now that we know about Edward?"

"Again, I can't give you an answer without seeing the Wills and review what Mr. Winston has done as far as settling debts, notifying creditors, transferring property, paying taxes and other details. Most importantly, we need information about your brother, John. The letter from Mr. Sparks goes a long way to settling Edward's death, but we still need verifiable proof about John."

"Of course, and I've heard nothing about John from Mr. Winston. Could we talk about the process of the annulment?"

Josh shifted uncomfortably in his chair. He couldn't allow himself to think how an annulment would devastate Jake who had confessed his feelings for Roseanna, but as his client, she was entitled to an answer to the question. "Are you considering an annulment?"

"You and Jake had the conversation about annulment when I wasn't with you. I want to know what would be involved. We signed some documents before we were married."

"Yes, those papers were Jake's way to protect you both. Annulment isn't one of my specialties; however, one of my firm's partners is an expert. I will tell you it is a lengthy and slow process. A petition is filed with the parish where your ceremony was performed, and multiple forms would need completion. It does dissolve the marriage; in fact, it will appear that the ceremony never took place."

"What reason would be given for an annulment," asked Roseanna.

"It could be on religious grounds or civil grounds. For instance, Jake is Catholic so the church could become involved. In civil grounds there could be any number of reasons such as fraud, force, threat, concealment of information vital to the marriage, or if the parties were closely related by blood, to name a few."

"It would be that complicated?"

"Complicated yes, but needs to be done thoroughly. I would ask again if you're contemplating annulment. We still need time to conclude your inheritance and an annulment now may not be in your best interest, but I can see you're not ready to answer."

"No, I'm unsure what to do. Thank you, Mr. Horn. You've given me much to think about. I should go so you and Miss. Mason can have your lunch," said Roseanna, as she rose.

"Roseanna, give me more time to get a response from Mr. Winston. If the information I need is not in the mail today, I personally will visit him at his office. I'm here to help you deal with whatever decisions you need to make. Can I do anything else to put your mind at ease today?"

"No, you've answered my concerns. Please let me know when you've heard from Lawrence Winston and convey to Miss. Mason what a pleasure it was to meet her."

"I will," said Josh. "Good to see you. I know Jake will be sorry he missed you."

Roseanna paused as she was leaving the office. "I wonder, could I ask you one other question?"

"Of course, anything at all."

"Are you my attorney, Jake's attorney, or attorney for both of us?"

"Ah, you're concerned about conflict of interest. I would understand if you would feel more at ease with another attorney. As it stands, I'm Jake and Randy's attorney, representing their needs for their business. I'm your attorney representing you in settlement of your parent's Wills and your inheritance. The agreement you signed before your marriage protects you from Jake receiving consideration in the resolution of those Wills and protects assets he had before the marriage. You can rest assured that your confidentiality is protected as I resolve issues concerning you. If you have misgivings, I will give you a list of attorneys from other firms that can handle your needs."

Josh paused waiting for Roseanna to respond. "If I could just tell you, Roseanna, Jake hasn't in any of the conversations I've had with him pried or confided any of your personal business, he's not apt, too either. The only discussions I've had with him and Randy Thomas were about the tragedy of your father's death.

"I wanted to be absolutely certain you are taking care of me and no one else even if Jake and I are married, and I have complete confidentiality when I speak to you. If I make any decisions, I will let you know. Thank you for your time."

Roseanna satisfied with her meeting with Josh, went back to the gig to find Simon snoring lightly as he dozed. She gently shook him awake. "We can go now, Simon."

Simon woke with a start, "Where Mr. Jake?" he asked, as he scanned the street for Jake.

"He couldn't be here today, Simon."

"I's wants see him, Miss Roseanna."

"I know, and you will soon."

"Can I's drive, Miss Roseanna?"

"Yes, you can."

Simon sat at attention chattering with joy at driving the gig as Roseanna reviewed her conversation with Josh. She felt confident he would work solely for her benefit. He relieved the doubts her uncle had tried to impress on her about his or Jake's motives or their honesty by his willingness to refer her to a new attorney. There was no reason to doubt Jake's motives; it was only her uncle's lies that had filled her with doubt. The other woman she knew was probably Gwen Mason. She wanted to see Jake, and though she hadn't realized it earlier in the day, she had felt excited she would see him, and now disappointed he wasn't at the meeting.

Meeting Gwen Mason had been a revelation. Jake had stated Gwen was interested in Randy Thomas, but Roseanna noted possessiveness of Jake. Perhaps Gwen's interest in Randy was a ruse, and she was after all in love with Jake. Roseanna had felt jealous; maybe her feelings for Jake were more than she realized. The day was still early, and she would be home before Mr. Plumb, the mail carrier came. She would write Jake telling him that she had missed seeing him and asking when they could be together.

Mama Teal met Roseanna as she returned home telling her that her aunt and uncle learning of Edward's death had come to see her. They asked that she visit them as soon as she returned from the city.

Roseanna walked across the bridge and knocked at the door. Her aunt answered her knock. "Roseanna, we've heard about Edward from Andrew. You should have come to us," she said as she gathered Roseanna in a hug.

"I was too upset to come; it was too much of a shock."

"Of course it was," said Ben as he came into the room. "I'm sorry to have pressed you in our conversation yesterday. Had I known what had happened the conversation could have waited for another time," he said as he hugged his niece.

"You didn't know, but his death doesn't change anything. The things we said had to be said even if the time wasn't right. You're both disappointed that I married, you don't approve. Jake isn't the person you're making him out to be, I hope in time you'll see."

Jane's shoulders slumped, "Roseanna you don't mean that. You can wait to make the decision when your mind is clearer, when you're not upset about Edward. We have your best interest at heart, and you don't want to continue with this mistake."

"It's not a mistake, Aunt Jane."

"I should talk to Jake man to man. Your aunt and I would perhaps change our minds about his character. When will he be here, Roseanna?"

"You're wrong to question his character."

"Now, Roseanna," said Ben, "you can't make these decisions without the proper counsel. We'll go to Lawrence Winston and get his opinion. We'll talk about all our futures. You can at least allow that," he said in a pleading tone.

"I've been to the city today to see my attorney, and I have confidence in him. He listens to what I have to say, and then tells me the options I should consider. I'm not going to need the advice of Lawrence Winston."

"You'll regret this, all of it, especially the nonsense of raising the horses," stormed Ben. "Your father must be turning over in his grave to see how foolish you are. You'll have regrets, Roseanna, I'll see to that," Ben finished.

Jane frowned at Ben and gestured for him to stop talking. "You're not fair to Roseanna. Give her time to catch her breath. She's had so much happen in such a short time. We can talk about this another time, can't we, Roseanna?"

"No, Aunt Jane, I've said all that's needed."

"Roseanna, you need to think of the rest of us. You're selfish. Don't you see how this will be for Andrew, Nancy, your uncle, and I? Think what this could mean to the whole family, the whole plantation if we worked together," pleaded Jane.

"I don't intend to be selfish, Aunt Jane. I'm sorry you think that. I'm doing what my father wanted. Please, accept what I've told you."

Roseanna turned leaving her relatives standing in silence watching her go. "Ben, I don't think she'll change her mind. What can we do?"

"I thought when I talked to her yesterday she understood that I was apologizing, and asking for help. I didn't make myself clear. She has to change her mind. Time is dwindling now there is news of Edward. I'll think of something," said Ben, as he turned and went to his office.

Jane was particularly upset, especially for Andrew. Why hadn't the Moorcroft twins written? She'd sent a second letter. Surely, they didn't still harbor ill feelings for her. She wondered if their mother was still alive, maybe her letter should have gone to her. She should have never brought Andrew to America; she should have stayed in London and faced society. In time all the gossip would have stopped. Andrew would have had a proper place in society, money of his own, and never have had to go to fight the American war, or put up with an unrelenting Ben Ravenna.

Ben was despondent and unable to think clearly about what he should do after his talk with Roseanna. Jane had become a burden, and he regretted telling her about the gold and promising to help Andrew. No one saw his plight; they were blind to what needed to happen. Roseanna was stubborn and ignorant about her future. If he had to content himself with accepting Jake Sinclair, then he needed him to see that Roseanna's stubbornness about the horses was a problem he should face. It was up to Jake to explain the importance of making the plantation support the family. He needed to talk to him man to man. Jake needed to get his wife under control.

He eyed the liquor decanter and then pushed it aside. A rapping came at his office door. "Go away," he yelled.

A voice whispered at the door, "Mr. Ben they a man here for you."

"Who is it?"

"He saying he come for work."

Ben was puzzled until he remembered that he had asked Lawrence Winston to find him men to work at tearing down the stable. He sighed heavily. "I'll see to it."

The man stood slouched on the veranda, his hands in his pockets. "You've come about the work that I needed to be done. I'm sorry to say my plans have changed," said Ben.

"I was told to come, and I've ridden for two hours from New Orleans, and there's no work?"

"Sorry," said Ben, as he reached into his pocket to give the man a token payment for his trouble.

The man snatched the money from Ben's hand and turned to leave.

Ben watched as he walked towards his horse. He thought about how he could use the man to move his plans for the plantation forward. He was desperate to get Roseanna to realize that crops should be planted and time and money should not be wasted raising horses. He was angry and frustrated that she couldn't see what made perfect sense to him.

"Wait," said Ben, calling the man back.

"What?"

"There is something you can do."

"What is it?"

"I need a stable burned. It sits behind the house across the creek. It's not mine, so it's a risk."

The man looked in the direction that Ben pointed. "How much?" he asked.

"A hundred dollars."

"In advance."

"No, when the job is done."

The men huffed, "You're asking me to burn someone else's property, and you expect me to show my face back here to get paid. Find somebody else."

The man turned to leave.

"Wait, a hundred dollars in advance," said Ben.

"Can I have other men with me?"

"I don't want to know the details; I don't care how you do it, but don't torch the house."

"When do you want it done?"

"I don't want to know," said Ben, as he dug in his pocket for the money and paid the man.

This was wrong, but Ben was beyond seeing right and wrong. He wanted his way and control; burning the stable would stop the notion of the horses.

"Pleasure doing business with you," said the man. He pocketed the money and left.

Ben watched as he rode away. He should call him back and tell him to keep the money but not to do what he asked. No, Roseanna's insistence about the horses had to stop. This might be the way to do it.

At the end of the day, Roseanna and Mama Teal stood on the veranda watching the evening sky. "Look like a bad storm brewin'," said Mama Teal. "Air still, like it dead, nothin' stirrin'. Gonna blow a big storm."

Roseanna looked at the sky; it had changed from dull silver to a muted black as the sun went down and clouds had begun to gather. "Someone mentioned a storm coming off the gulf when I was in town today. You can feel it, Mama Teal."

"Yes. Not no hurricane, but it a big one comin'."

"Simon had so much fun going to the city, Mama Teal," said Roseanna with a grin.

"He minds his manners?"

"Of course he did. He loves driving the gig."

"What gonna happen to that boy when I gone, Miss. Roseanna?"

"You're not going anywhere, Mama Teal. Edwards's death has made all of us sad. No one else is going to die. You have a long life ahead of you, and if anything should happen, Simon will be here with me as he always has been. He's part of the family."

"That give me comfort, Miss Roseanna. I's say goodnight now. Yous sleeps tonight and won't be worrin' over Mr. Edward."

"Thank you, Mama Teal. I'll sleep very well and won't worry about anything. Good night."

CHAPTER 3

Roseanna watched as Mama Teal left the veranda and rounded the corner of the house. Her worry for Simon's welfare concerned Roseanna. She needed to keep a roof over her head and take care of Mama Teal's family. Their daily needs were being taken care of with the little money she had, but soon it would be gone. If she had her father's gold, she could plan, but searching had failed. Andrew's suggestion that her brothers might know the location may be accurate, but with Edward gone so was that hope. She would go to the bank, speak to Mr. Cutler, and ask him for advice. Once the wills were settled, a loan could be made against the house or land. She wanted to bring the horses back to the plantation, and a mortgage could make it possible.

Nathan walked out of the gloom of the twilight and nodded his head in greeting. "Miss Roseanna yous be having work for Nathan?"

"Aren't you working for Mr. Ben, Nathan?"

"Yes, ma'ma but he don't pay me none."

"Are you still set on going north?"

"That's what I's wantin', but don't gots money, Miss Roseanna. Mr. Ben, he feed me, but I's needin' money."

"There may be work sometimes Nathan, but not now."

Nathan nodded in agreement. "I's could do any work, Miss Roseanna."

"The brambles and seedling trees need to be cleared from the pasture for horses. It'll be hard, and I would expect you not to wander off but stick to the work and get it done."

"I's ready Miss Roseanna, I's ready now."

Roseanna smiled, "I'm ready too, but we need to wait."

"I's ready, Miss Roseanna. Yous call for Nathan."

"I'll remember. Have a good night, Nathan," said Roseanna as she rose from her seat.

"Night Miss Roseanna," said Nathan. "They a bad storm a-comin'," he said as he wandered away.

Roseanna stood at the edge of the veranda watching the sky in the south. The distant subtle flash of lightning flared on the horizon as the storm moved closer. Where was Jake? Had he returned from his trip upriver in time to escape the storm? Roseanna hoped he was not in danger.

After having trouble sleeping the night before she was ready for bed, but first, she would write to Jake telling him she was sorry to miss him at Josh Horn's office earlier in the day and ask when she would see him. She hoped it would be soon.

Gwen Mason and Josh Horn sat in the lobby of the St. Charles Hotel in New Orleans. It was seven o'clock in the evening, and Gwen's anxiety about Jake and Randy was growing.

"Gwen, stop fretting. I'm sure all is well."

"I know, Josh, but I can't help but worry. This storm is coming, Jake may be caught and not able to get back to the city."

"The storm is predicted to be bad; it could cause trouble for everyone. I've been here long enough to know that when a storm hits the port, it can do a lot of damage. Jake and Randy know too, and their business is doing so well; I'd hate to see a setback."

"It's amazing how quickly they've gotten the business on its feet. Now with the new property, they can build their warehouses and dock and do even better."

"The river is deep enough there to support the ships as they hoped?" asked Josh.

"Yes, Jake just received the findings. You prepared the documents for the sale, and now they've gone in the mail for the owners signature."

"I'll miss seeing them around town, not that I saw them that much, but we did spend some of our evenings together."

"Jake told Roseanna he preferred New Orleans to New York. He'll be in the wilds of Louisiana where the new property is, but that seems to be what he and Randy want. I wonder if Roseanna knows him as well as she seems to think. I've been to the new property, and there is nothing around for miles."

"The plantation where Roseanna lives is close to the new property, Jake will like that."

"Oh, I hadn't realized," said Gwen. "I hope he hasn't bitten off more than he can chew with this marriage. I was surprised to meet her. I don't know what I expected; she's certainly attractive, but plain and unsophisticated."

Josh gave Gwen an astonished look. "She's neither. She is different from most women here, she's intelligent, and someone has seen to her education. She's different compared to what you're used to, and Jake cares for her, he told me that himself."

Gwen raised an eyebrow. "Hmmm, we shall see, I'm not so sure. This marriage was too quick, and everyone seems unwilling to tell me why."

Gwen paused hoping Josh would be forthcoming with information about the marriage, but to her disappointment, he wasn't.

"Jake deserves the best; he has much to offer a woman. I've had no time to talk to him, and I've spent very little time with either of them. They've been busy since I arrived, and now they've been gone for two days. I was hoping we could spend time this evening. I miss them in New York."

"I'm more than happy to stand in for them, Gwen," said Josh taking her hand in both of his.

Gwen gave Josh her most engaging smile with a flutter of her eyelashes. "Josh, you've been wonderfully sweet. I've very much liked spending time with you, but I do want time with Jake and Randy."

"I'd like to show you more of the city. You'll see we have most everything New York does just on a smaller scale and look who just walked in the door," said Josh gesturing.

Gwen turned to see Jake and Randy being assisted out of their wet, dripping rain gear by a valet. They made their way across the lobby.

"Jake, you look exhausted!" said Gwen.

Jake leaned to kiss Gwen's cheek, "Exhausted and starved," he said. "Have you had dinner?"

"No, we've been waiting for you," said Josh. "Must have been quite an emergency to keep you gone so long.

"One of the ships with our cargo went aground. Ripped a hole in the bow. We offloaded our merchandise and then spent time waiting for another ship to re-load. Now, another crisis, this storm is wrecking havoc at the docks, and our merchandise is sitting on the wharf. It has to be moved before it floats away in the tide, which by all accounts is going to rise to flood levels."

"Has to be moved and quick," said Randy.

"Can't one of the boats pick it up?" asked Gwen.

"They're not coming down river into this storm; everyone's going upriver to get away from it, and they're not stopping to load cargo. Traffic going north on the river is thick and clogged, it's slowed everything down. We have to move it to a warehouse," said Jake.

"We have a place to put it; we just need to find enough men to do the work," said Randy.

"Josh did Roseanna come to see you?" asked Jake.

"Yes, she was here."

"Did you meet her, Gwen, and give her my letter?"

Gwen reached into her reticule and handed Jake an envelope. "Jake I'm so sorry. We were visiting, and it slipped my mind."

Jake tucked the envelope his pocket. "Wasn't important," he said brushing Gwen's forgetfulness aside. "How was she, Josh?"

"She's received a letter about her brother Edward. It's not good news."

Jake exhaled in a groan, "That can mean only one thing, he's not coming home."

Gwen turned to Josh with a startled look, "You never told me. That explains why she looked so frail."

"Not my place to say, Gwen. But Jake would want to know."

"What else, Josh?" asked Jake with concern.

"That's the most important thing. Roseanna needs to be the one to tell you about the rest of the visit."

Jake turned to Randy. "I need to get up to the plantation. How long do you think it will take to move this merchandise?"

"Four or five hours."

"I'll start without you, Randy. You eat and rest," said Jake.

"What and miss all the fun?" said Randy. "No, I'm ready."

"Jake you've been working so hard and by the time you get this shipment moved it will be midnight. This storm is about to hit; you need to wait for the storm to pass before you go riding to wherever it is this girl lives."

"Storms not going to bother me, I need to see my wife," said Jake dismissing Gwen's concern.

"I'm not much good at this kind of thing, but let me lend a hand."

"Thanks, Josh, we could use the help," said Jake.

The three men started planning how to accomplish the work ahead of them. Gwen was left on her own to deal with the absence of the men as best she could.

Roseanna was dreaming. The horses were running. She heard the sound of their hooves pounding the earth. She woke to pitch-blackness. It wasn't a dream, horses were running. She threw off the covers and ran to the window. Riders were kicking up their mounts as they cut across the yard brandishing torches. They wheeled their horses and retraced their path leading through her mother's rose garden crushing the plants and destroying the picket fence. They raced out of sight towards the back of the house.

Roseanna snatched a quilt from the bed and threw it around her shoulders as she ran downstairs. She went to the pantry where her father's shotgun stood, loaded and ready. She snatched the gun and ran into the yard.

Mama Teal, Loretta, and Simon huddled together in their nightclothes watching the spectacle of the riders. The riders yelled as they circled the pasture and disappeared behind the stable.

"Mama Teal take Simon and Loretta and go inside," screamed Roseanna.

Moses suddenly galloped out of the darkness, coming from the stable. Simon ran after the horse, "Moses comes back! Comes back!" he yelled.

Loretta ran after her brother shouting his name. Simon fell, and the riders charged towards where he lay. Loretta reached her brother pulling him from the path of danger as he scrambled to his feet.

Mama Teal ran after the two. "Comes here, comes here!" she yelled waving her arms.

The riders reappeared from behind the stable, charging back and seemingly taking no notice of the people in the yard. They wheeled their mounts and turned towards the main road away from the plantation no longer carrying their torches, done with their senseless work. Moses whinnied at the commotion of the other horses and galloped after them as they disappeared into the night, the sound of their hooves fading into the darkness.

The scent of smoke caught by the wind filled the air as tongues of flame lit the blackness of the night. Roseanna dropped the shotgun, and the quilt fell from her shoulders as she rushed towards the stable. The stable doors stood open, and fire rapidly lit the interior. The hay ignited and flashed quickly to the loft where bales were stored. Smoke poured from the eaves. Roseanna backed away from the scorching heat and could do nothing but watch in shock with Mama Teal and her children.

The flames crackled and popped devouring the building, and soon the sound of glass breaking was heard as the heat destroyed the windows.

Simon was crying, Mama Teal took his hand and pulled him away from the stable and towards the house. "Where Moses gonna sleep Mama? They burn his house. Where Moses?"

Roseanna stood in disbelief. Who would do this? The fire burned hotter and brighter until the building was completely ablaze. She moved away as the winds from the approaching storms pushed the heat and the dancing flames toward her. Suddenly, the roof collapsed with a whoosh creating a shower of sparks and flame. The framework of the walls now stood like skeletons.

Andrew ran up to the group, his hair in disarray, his nightshirt hanging from his trousers. "My god, Roseanna! What happened? I heard horses running."

"Look what they've done," said Roseanna, as she watched the blaze destroying the stable. "It happened so fast, the hay just fed the flames."

"Who were they?"

"I don't know."

"Ben! It has to be Ben! How could he? He is determined to stop you from raising horses," said Andrew.

Roseanna could hear Simon crying and calling for Moses. "Come on, Simon, we'll find him. He probably hasn't gone far. Let's look."

Roseanna retrieved the quilt placing it around her shoulders and walked to the front of the house as everyone followed. She slowed her pace and stopped as she came to the rose garden. She could see the damage to the fence. In the morning she would get a better view of the plants, but what she saw now was total devastation.

"Oh, Miss Roseanna, look whats they do to you's mama's garden," said Mama Teal.

Roseanna didn't respond but turned and hurriedly walked towards the lane leading out of the plantation. Moses had followed the other horses, but she hoped he hadn't gone far. She reached the main road, and there stood Moses, grazing at the entrance to the plantation.

"Here's Moses, Simon." She walked to the horse, took hold of his bridle, and patted his nose. He reared up still excited by the commotion. Roseanna pulled tight on the bridle to keep the horse from bolting. "Come on, Moses let's find you a place to stay."

"What we do wiff him Miss Roseanna?" asked Simon as he trotted beside Roseanna.

"Roseanna let me take him and put him in the barn at Ben's," said Andrew.

"No, he can go in the empty slave cabin for now," said Roseanna as she guided the still nervous horse towards the cabins. "I don't want him at Ben's."

"Do you think he did this?"

"I don't know, Andrew. Why, why would anyone burn that stable?"

"We should get the authorities?"

"What can they do? The damage is done. I don't even know who they were. They came so fast and then disappeared. I don't want to believe Ben would do this. It's senseless," said Roseanna.

The fire continued to burn, flaring up whenever a gust of wind fanned the flames, or it found new fuel. The wind blowing from the south kept the fire away from other structures but ignited a large tree that stood at the side of the stable; it blazed in a golden globe.

Simon and Andrew helped to shelter Moses than gathered shovels and filled buckets with water to be prepared in the event the fire spread.

They all stood watching as the flames licked at the remainder of the roof and walls. Now there was no shelter for horses. The expense of rebuilding a stable was yet another obstacle to overcome for Roseanna.

Ben, if he was responsible for this had made the task go from difficult to impossible. If that had been his intent, he had succeeded. Andrew was convinced Ben was accountable and Roseanna could find no words to deny the accusation.

By dawn, the smell of burning wood filled the air, wisps of smoke rose from the rubble as the last of the fire found fuel. Hay bales smoldered, small tongues of flame erupting and then disappearing as the fire burned deep into the core. Piles of charred rubble lay smoking in the center of the stable while the structure at one end, the tack room, still stood, heavily damaged but withstanding the brunt of the flames. The fire had leaped from the stable and consumed some of the railings in the pasture. A thin layer of smoke hung in the air dissipating slowly into the stormy morning sky.

Roseanna stood at a distance surveying the ruins her jaw clenched in anger. She wrapped herself in a waterproof coat that had been her father's as the rain were beginning to fall. Moses was spared, and Roseanna was thankful. Ben did not come to ask about the blaze forcing Roseanna to believe that Andrew's accusations against him were probably correct.

By late in the day, and with the help of the rain, the fire had burned itself out. The sky turned an ugly shade of gray as threatening dark clouds moved towards the plantation from the south.

Gusty winds blew and rain fell in torrents then stopped as waves of the storm passed leaving the air still, oppressive and threatening. Then a steady wind blew, at first rustling the leaves on the trees and then setting the branches to dancing as they bent from the strain. Debris flew through the air, petals from the destroyed rose garden scattered across the yard.

Roseanna shuttered the house tight against the storm as night descended. The intensity of the wind increased as lightning split the darkness and thunder collided violently over the house. The rain came thick and heavy beating at the windows. Torrents of water ran through the yard and across the lane. The creek ran swift getting close to the top of its banks. Roseanna lay on the couch in the parlor dozing fitfully. The fire the night before had left her jumpy and scared and now the storm had her nerves further on edge.

Roseanna walked to the window to peer out at the storm when she saw a rider entering the lane. They were coming back. Panic struck her. This time she'd be ready.

Running to the pantry, she grabbed her father's gun. She looked through the window; a flash of lightning illuminated a single rider. He stopped at the burnt out stable, turned the horse, and headed back to the front of the house at a gallop.

Roseanna ran to the front and looked out the window. The rider hurriedly dismounted and ran towards the veranda. Roseanna stood back from the door and raised the gun, the door opened, banging against the wall from the force of the wind. The figure dressed in black pushed through the opening. Roseanna pulled the trigger, but the intruder grabbed the barrel and forced it upward. The momentum threw Roseanna and the intruder to the floor as the noise from the shot reverberated in the house, and the smell of gunpowder filled the space.

"Jake, oh my God Jake!" cried Roseanna. "I could have killed you!" She reached for his face, "Are you hurt," then she started to cry.

Jake angrily wrestled the gun from Roseanna and threw it across the room. "Are you trying to kill me?"

"Jake, Jake, no! I thought you were those men coming back! Why are you sneaking around at this hour of the night? I could have killed you!"

"I'm not sneaking around," said Jake furiously, "and what the hell happened to the stable?"

"I didn't know who you were. I thought they were coming back."

"Who?"

"Men that burned the stable!"

"You're not making sense."

Roseanna scanned Jake, "You're sure you're not hurt?"

"No, but I do have a knot on the back of my head," he said as he gingerly rubbed his head. "I hit the floor pretty hard."

"It's raining in, I need to close the door," said Roseanna as she got her tears under control.

Jake began to chuckle. "This is the last thing I expected when I left New Orleans, being shot at by my wife.

"That's not funny, what do you expect when you come riding up in the middle of the night scaring the daylights out of people, and what are you doing out in this storm?" said Roseanna as she pounded at Jake's chest with her fist. She scrambled to her feet to close the door. "You should have waited until the storm passed."

Jake roughly grabbed Roseanna, placed his lips on hers gave her a long lingering kiss. "I was hoping you'd be glad to see me, not shoot me," said Jake as he held her close.

She clung to Jake. "I'm so glad to see you." She trembled at how close she had come to shooting him. Again, she assured herself Jake was not hurt. "Do you realize how close I came to shooting you? I was terrified."

"You're terrified," said Jake in awe, "I'm a little shaken myself."

"I missed you at Josh Horn's. What happened you weren't there?" she asked as she allowed Jake to continue the embrace.

"Nothing, it's under control; one of the boats sank with our merchandise on it."

The clock in the hallway struck the hour. "It's one o'clock in the morning. Why didn't you wait until daylight?"

"I wanted to see you. Josh told me about Edward. I'm sorry I wasn't there to hear it from you. I didn't want to wait."

"Edward," said Roseanna with a sigh. "Jake he could have survived if he hadn't tried to escape. This is hard for me. Why didn't he wait?" said Roseanna, new tears forming at the thought of her brother.

"He was a good soldier, Roseanna. He did what he thought was right."

"I know, but Jake he could be here today and my father if we had known where Edward was. They both would have survived and been here," said Roseanna.

"We'll never know what he was going through. He was being honorable and trying to fulfill his duty, Roseanna. Had he been successful he would be here; he took the risk, he wanted to come home."

"I know, Jake, but he should have waited. Trying to accept that no one is coming home is hard."

Jake hugged Roseanna tight and kissed her forehead. "I need some dry clothes and so do you. How about food, is there anything to eat?"

"Yes, of course. And you're staying; you're not going out in this storm again."

"Didn't intend to."

Some of Roseanna's father's clothing gave Jake the clothes he needed, but the pants were too short. There was not much in the pantry for a meal, so the two bundled up against the storm and ran to the kitchen house where they found food and set the coffee pot to perking.

"Tell me about the stable, Roseanna."

"Andrew thinks it was Ben, and I agree. His way of telling me I won't raise the horses."

"When did this happen?" asked Jake.

"Late last night, there were riders carrying torches. They raced around the house and the stable and trampled mother's rose garden. I got the gun but never had an opportunity to fire at them, they were here and then gone just as quick."

"You're not staying here by yourself Roseanna. When I go back to the city, you have to come with me. You can't be here alone."

"I can't, Jake, I won't leave Mama Teal and Simon. If Ben thinks I'm gone, he'll just cause Mama Teal trouble. Andrew said I should tell the authorities, but I don't even know who it was. I can't accuse Ben. I have no proof."

"We do need to let the authorities know, and you're right, there's no proof Ben is responsible. I'll pay Ben a visit while I'm here. We'll see what he has to say for himself, but I agree with Andrew, Ben had a hand in this."

"Ben came to me several days ago and apologized for causing me so much trouble, especially about Nancy standing up for me at our wedding. He tried to convince me he and my father had agreed to rebuild the plantation together and the money from the IOU was money my father had given him to start the rebuilding. I didn't believe him and told him so. My father would never have agreed. Aunt Jane told me how selfish I was, I should be ready to help the whole family and the plantation. I told them I was determined to raise horses and then the stable burned. How can I help but think Ben is responsible?"

"You do what you see fit with the place, Roseanna, that's not selfish. Ben Ravenna needs to get this through his thick skull. I intend to see he does," said Jake.

Roseanna found a bed for Jake, and they both retired for the night. Roseanna exhausted from her sleepless nights after the news of Edward's death and the fire fell instantly asleep. Jake being in the house made her feel safe. She was pleased he had come to see her, and she fell asleep with a smile on her face.

Jake, a few doors down the hall lying in bed thinking how close his new bride was and how he wanted to remedy the misfortune of the distance between them. He could tell Roseanna was pleased to see him and that gave him hope.

The burning of the stable was grave. Jake needed to confront Ben Ravenna and the threat he had created for Roseanna. Thankfully, no one was hurt, but Ravenna would be told that no more incidents would be tolerated. Jake yawned mightily, rubbed at the knot on the back of his head, and drifted off to sleep.

CHAPTER 4

Jake rose early to find the worst of the storm had moved away from the plantation. A light wind and gentle rain were all that remained. From the window, he could see the remains of the stable and was curious to inspect the burned out hulk. He quickly dressed and went downstairs.

Mama Teal was in the dining room setting the table for breakfast. She looked up in surprise as he entered the room.

"Laudy, Mr. Jake, yous done scare me. When yous come here?"

"Morning Mama Teal. I came about the time the storm was at its worst. Roseanna still sleeping?"

"Yes, sir. That's being yous and Miss Roseanna at the kitchen house last night. I's be thinking I's has give Simon piece of my mind if he be taken food."

"Not Simon, me and Roseanna. I could use your help with water for a bath this morning and towels. I'm going to be here for a day or two. Roseanna put me in her father's room last night. Would you ask her if that's the room she wants me to use?"

"Yes, yes. I's get Simon for the water and I brung yous towels and such and gets yous a room ready. Yous be eatin' with Miss. Roseanna or you hungry now?"

"I'll wait for Roseanna. Tell me about the fire, Mama Teal."

"Oh, Mr. Jake it be scary. Thought Simon goin' get runned over wiff them horses 'cause he be running after Moses right where they was a coming."

"Did you know the riders, Mama Teal?"

"I's sees nobody, it over right quick," said Mama Teal, snapping her fingers. "Miss Roseanna's daddy so proud 'cause he fixes the stable nice and it gone now. Yous think Miss Roseanna goin' puts it up again, Mr. Jake?"

"I hope so Mama Teal. Having the horses around is what makes her happy. I'm walking over to Mr. Ben Ravenna's, but I won't be long. That should give Simon enough time to fetch the water."

"I's tell him, Mr. Jake.

"I'm taking Roseanna into the city with me. She's concerned about you and your children after the fire."

"She not be, Mr. Jake. Andrew stickin' close to Loretta…" Mama Teal slapped a hand across her mouth. "I's not 'pose to say nuthin' about that. It just Simon who don't know nuthin'. He is talkin' like he always do to everybody."

"Roseanna will feel better about leaving knowing Andrew is here. She'll talk to you, too. We both want you to be safe."

"I's not ascared, Mr. Jake. It be fine."

Jake pulled on his rain gear and walked out on the veranda. He eyed the damage to the rose garden. The fence he could repair, but the plants were a different matter. Gardening was not within his abilities. The storm had left its mark in the yard, debris were scattered everywhere, Spanish moss, broken branches on the ground some broken but still dangled in the trees. He crossed the bridge between Roseanna's house and Ben Ravenna's stopping for a moment to look at the fast-moving, swollen creek where debris were caught against the bridge pilings. He knocked on the door at Ben's home.

A young black woman named Cindy answered his knock. "Yes, Sir? Help you?"

"I'm here to see Mr. Ravenna."

"Won't you come in?"

"No, I'll wait."

As he waited, Jake eyes scanned the massive fields where cotton should be growing. Ravenna had to be hard up for money, not that he was concerned. Ravenna like other Southerners was suffering because of the loss of the war and their slave labor.

Ben came to the door with a napkin tucked in his shirt collar like a bib.

"Why Mr. Sinclair," said Ben, giving Jake a hearty greeting. "I didn't know you had come up from the city to visit Roseanna. I was just ready to sit down to breakfast," he said indicating the napkin. "Would you join me?"

"No, thank you."

"At least come in for coffee," said Ben, with a smile. "I just the other day said to Roseanna that you and I should get together and have a talk about the plantation and here you are. What a perfect opportunity."

"What I have to say won't take long, and the only person doing the talking will be me. There's nothing for the two of us to discuss. The property belongs to Roseanna, and she will make any decisions regarding its use. We'll discuss your role in the burning of the stable."

"My role?" said Ben, gesturing to himself, the smile leaving his face. "You're mistaken, very unfortunate, but had nothing to do with me."

"We won't debate your involvement, but understand there'll be no more incidents."

"I had nothing to do with that fire, Sinclair. I've warned Roseanna repeatedly about men looking to cause trouble in the South since the end of the war. I'm never without my derringer for protection," said Ben, as he patted his chest where the gun was kept. "A man can't be too careful these days."

"Trespassing by you or anyone you know, on my wife's property except to use the bridge to access the main road, won't be tolerated. Should there be any kind of incident a gate will go up on Roseanna's side of the bridge secured with a strong lock to prevent any passage to her property."

"You can't do that. The bridge is the only way off my property; I use it every day. You can't deny me access."

"Oh, but I can and will. You could take your horse across the creek, which would be risky as the bank is steep. If you fell off your mount and into the water, which by the way is quite deep after last night's storm, no one would care. My concern is for your wife and daughter. It would be impossible to get a buggy or wagon across the creek without the use of the bridge which would create an inconvenience for them."

"You bastard! How dare you threaten me? You're accusing me of something I had nothing to do with."

"Not a threat, a warning. Nothing should happen to my wife or her property. Understood?" Jake didn't wait for Ben to speak. He then turned and walked away.

"I could build a gate on this side too, Sinclair," yelled Ben at Jake's retreating back. "It would keep the likes of you away from my property."

Jake casually walked towards the bridge. He hadn't gone far when he heard the satisfying sound of the door to Ben Ravenna's house slamming. Jake whistled tunelessly under his breath. "Looks like he got the message," he thought.

Ben entered the dining room swearing loudly and gesturing with the napkin he had pulled from his shirt collar.

"Ben," said Jane with distaste, "please stop yelling."

"Sinclair, that man Roseanna married, thinks he can tell me what I can and can't do on my own property," stormed Ben. "He had the nerve to accuse me of setting the damn stable on fire and saying he's going to put up a gate on the bridge to keep me off Roseanna's property."

"He can't do that," said Jane indignantly.

"He can if he wants, Mother. After all, it is Roseanna's to do with as she pleases," said Andrew.

"That's right, Andrew. Stick up for that Yankee," said Ben, disgustedly.

"I'm not sticking up for him, Ben. I agree with him. If he wants a gate at the bridge, he's entitled."

"And prevent me from accessing my property? It'll be a cold day in hell when he gets away with that. I'll tear the thing down the minute he puts it up."

"You told him you had nothing to do with the stable fire," said Jane. "That's a terrible thing, but why would he blame you?"

"Yes, Ben, why would he blame you?" questioned Andrew with a grin.

"Andrew, you think the fire was my doing, is that what you're saying?" said Ben heatedly.

"It looks suspicious considering you're the one who thinks Roseanna has no business raising horses. Jake Sinclair and Roseanna must share the suspicion," said Andrew as he spread jam on his toast.

"The Yankee probably did it himself so he could blame me and push Roseanna farther away from her family."

Andrew gave a devious laugh. "Hardly the truth."

"Get out of this room, Andrew," yelled Ben. "I'm not going to be accused in my own home."

"No, Andrew," said Jane, "You stay right where you are. Andrews is entitled to say what he thinks." Jane turned to Andrew with a stern look. "You apologize to Ben; he didn't set the stable ablaze."

"I don't want an apology from him, and I don't care what he thinks. If he doesn't leave, I will," said Ben as he stormed from the room.

"Andrew don't antagonize him," said Jane in a harsh whisper as Ben left.

"I'm not going to patronize him, Mother. You know what he's done to take what's rightfully Roseanna's away from her. To suspect him of having that stable set ablaze is not out of the question."

"He tried to help her and to help all of us. You need to see the good in what he's tried to do."

"When has he helped her? By trying to force her from her home, and take the gold her father left. That's all he's ever wanted from Roseanna, the property, and money."

"What if he does Andrew? Can't you see how much the money would help us all, Roseanna included? She is selfish. As Ben said, it makes far more sense to plant crops on the land than raise horses. What happens to Roseanna isn't my concern if she fails to take her uncle's advice. Ben will never agree to help you get to London if you persist in being so disagreeable with him. I thought we agreed it was in your best interest."

"He would never help me even if he could."

"He's tried in his own way, Andrew."

"He's made no effort on my behalf, he's fallen far short, and you know it."

"You don't help when you're so defiant, Andrew. Why don't you try to see things from his viewpoint?"

"I don't like his viewpoint for one thing, and you have to admit the stable fire didn't just happen from some group of strangers. Someone arranged that fire, and I think Ben did."

"Don't say that Andrew, you have no proof. And as to the gold, Ben would give you the money to go to London. He said he would, and I would insist he did."

"There's not any gold. So what's the point of even discussing it?"

"I want you to go to London, Andrew. Your future should be there with the Moorcrofts. I don't know why they don't answer my letters and help you?"

"You have your answer, Mother, by the fact that they don't answer. I've asked you before why there's been no contact with them. What do they hold against you, or is it Ben they object to?"

"Andrew some things are better left unsaid, it has nothing to do with you."

"Why won't you tell me? What difference can it make?"

"I've told you there's nothing. It's not important. What's important is that I'm certain you are the only surviving Moorcroft and as such, their inheritance should come to you, its English law. It's important for you to meet your uncles so they can see what a fine young man you are."

"No, you're asking me to run away from Ben. This idea of my going to London was because of what you wanted. You need to understand why I agreed with you. It's not because I want to go; it's because of Loretta. I love her, and we want to be together. The child she lost was mine. We want to have more children and get married, and you've told me that in London a black and white together is not a taboo as it is in the south."

"You can't marry that woman Andrew! I know about you and her. Don't say you're in love with her, it's not acceptable. You have no truth the baby was yours. It must have been Nathan's; he goes to her, too.

Andrew was shocked, "Why did you never say anything to me? Especially when you knew she lost the baby. She has never been with Nathan; it was a lie to keep Ben from knowing the truth. The baby was mine."

"Then I'm glad the baby died, Andrew," said Jane cruelly. "I see you at night going to her, but I thought just for what a man needs, not because you loved her. Forget about her and the baby. Don't ever let Ben know you're lying with her. It would be the final straw for him. She's not important. You're what matters. You have to go to London."

"She's the only thing I care about, the only thing that makes me happy. I only want to go to London because I can be with her. Don't you want me to be happy?"

"Andrew of course, I do, but I won't stand by and let you throw your life away over a Negro woman. Ben must never find out about your relationship. You will give him more reason to take his anger out on you. Promise me you'll stop seeing her. Go to London find someone there who is in your social class. I will get Ben to give you the money, but you must promise not to let him know about the baby or your relationship with Loretta. Break with her, Andrew. The rest of your life depends on inheriting your uncle's wealth. Right now Ben is the only way I know to get you what you deserve."

"I won't leave Loretta, and damn Ben Ravenna and how he feels about Negros. His opinion means nothing to me. I'll get to London but not for the reasons you think but to be with the woman I love." He rose from the table and stormed from the room.

Roseanna and Jake were enjoying a breakfast of fried eggs, ham, and biscuits when Andrew bounded into the room. "Jake," he said "I only knew you were here because of Ben ranting at the breakfast table about you accusing him of burning the stable," said Andrew in greeting as he shook Jake's hand. "Welcome back."

"I imagine I spoiled his breakfast. Ben and I had a discussion about the stable and I hope he takes our talk to heart," said Jake.

Roseanna looked up in surprise. "You've seen him already this morning, Jake? What did he say?"

"That he had nothing to do with the stable burning just as I suspected he would."

"I don't want to accuse someone without proof," said Andrew, "but in this case, I have no doubt it was Ben. He said you're going to put a gate on Roseanna's side of the bridge."

"Jake," said Roseanna with surprise, "you didn't threaten him with that. Jane and Nancy need to use the bridge."

Andrew laughed, "The man is finally getting a taste of his own medicine. He needs to take responsibility for someone's welfare besides his own."

"I was harsh," said Jake, "but I don't think we'll have any trouble with Ben Ravenna for the foreseeable future. Your aunt and cousin won't have to swim across the creek, Roseanna," said Jake with a smirk of humor, patting Roseanna's hand.

"I should hope not," said Roseanna. "I can just imagine how he reacted."

"As Andrew said, not well."

"A taste of his own medicine," said Andrew.

"Andrew," said Jake. "Do you know anything about building?"

"Took engineering and architecture in school, but not really outside of helping raise a few barns and cabins over the years."

"Would you be interested in working for Randy Thompson and me?"

"What would you need me to do?"

"The warehouse we are building is going to need a supervisor to hire workers and to keep things going while the two of us are in the city. Is that something you would be interested in doing?"

Andrew straightened in his chair. "If you're serious, Jake, of course."

"You know locals who would be willing to work. Property needs to be cleared for the buildings, and that can be done while the architect finishes with the plans."

"I'd be more than interested. I could find the labor here in the parish. When would you need me to start?"

"Right away. Go out to the land, and look around. You'll see how much needs to be cleared and how many men you'd need for the work. Roseanna and I are going into the city for a few days, and after I meet with Randy and the architect, I can give you a better idea of all that needs to be done."

"Andrew this is wonderful," said Roseanna. "If you save what you earn, you might be able to go to London after all."

"London is a pipe dream, Roseanna," said Andrew dismissively, "but I'd still want to go, and I know Loretta would go with me," said Andrew.

"Find the men to do the work while Randy and I straighten out more of our plans. That would be a tremendous help for us," said Jake.

Andrew stood and shook hands with Jake. "Thanks for this Jake. I won't disappoint you."

"One other thing before you go, Andrew. As I mentioned, we are going to the city for a few days. Roseanna is concerned about Ben and leaving Mama Teal and her family alone, especially after the fire."

"No need to worry. I'll be here, and I'll look out for everyone."

After breakfast, Roseanna and Jake went to walk the fence of a little-used pasture to be sure it would be secure for Moses. Since the fire at the stable, Moses had been confined and unable to exercise. The pasture hadn't been used since before the war but was still intact needing only a few repairs.

"Nathan can do this. I promised him work and he should be glad to do this for me and also the fence around the rose garden."

"What about the stable?" said Jake? "You need to rebuild?"

"I don't have the money, Jake. It's going to have to wait until I hear from Josh about the Wills. I don't think there's any money coming, but I know there are property taxes and the inheritance taxes to pay that Josh told me about."

"I'd pay for it, Roseanna. Money isn't a problem for me."

"I can't let you, Jake. You and Randy have so many things you want to do with the new buildings. You need your money."

"My grandfather settled money on me when he died, more than enough to build the new facility with no help from Randy. He wants to pay his own way so he is a true partner. I've waited for him to start the project until he's saved what he needs."

"Even so, Jake, there are no horses to put in the stable so it can wait until I've decided how I can go forward, or if I go forward with the horses. Good for Randy, he'll be a full partner. And he and Gwen, are they getting together?"

"No, that's in the past for Randy. What did you think of Gwen? She's really something, isn't she?"

"She's lovely," said Roseanna. "We didn't have much of a chance to visit; I was dealing with the news about Edward. But I thought Randy and Gwen had an understanding."

"Randy and I talked about Gwen while we were on our way upriver the other day. He cares for her but doesn't see the two of them getting married. Gwen is domineering and ambitious. With the right man that would work, but Randy is just not interested in being led around by the nose, which is exactly what Gwen would do and has tried to do. In truth, Gwen wouldn't be happy either. Randy is not interested in running with the social crowd, and she lives for that. He needs someone more like himself. Gwen would never be happy in Louisiana, especially out here in the country and away from the city living at the new facility. She'd be pushing Randy all the time to go back to New York. He's not interested."

"I feel bad for both of them," said Roseanna. "I mean if they care about each other they should be able to work something out."

"They're in agreement. Don't feel bad for Gwen, she always lands on her feet and has a string of suitors in New York that would step up to the altar at the snap of her fingers. She's a good businesswoman. Gwen needs to find someone who needs her support to further his career with her social connections. All of that is in New York for her; Louisiana will never be able to satisfy her, just be a place to visit. As to Randy, he'll find what he wants one day. He likes his life here it suits him. He would never return to New York."

Jake wanted to add that Randy would be happy when he found someone like Roseanna, but it could wait for another time. The more he was with Roseanna, the more hope he held they would have a long future together. Jake cared for her with no doubts about what he wanted for their future, but she needed time to accept all that had happened in her life since the war. He would be patient and give her time.

"When would you want to leave, Jake?"

"As soon as you're ready. I need to get with Randy to finish our plans."

"First thing in the morning after breakfast would suit me," said Roseanna.

The weather had cleared entirely, but the humidity rose to an unusual extent from the rain that had come from the storm. As night approached, and the sun set, the fullness of a new moon spread a silvery light over the plantation casting heavy dark shadows around the yard and fields. Roseanna and Jake sat contentedly on the veranda listening to the sounds of the night. The chirp and hum of insects, a croaking frog, and in the distance the hoot of an owl. The smell of honeysuckle lay heavy in the air.

"The moon is so beautiful," said Roseanna. "It's like a huge candle in the sky."

"We call it a lover's moon where I come from. There's magic in the moonlight," said Jake.

He stared at Roseanna where she sat beside him. The moonlight glowed in her hair and softened her profile. The intimacy of sitting here with her made his desire for her grow. He longed to take her in his arms and…

"Do you think life on a plantation would suit you?"

"What? Sorry, Roseanna, I was dreaming. I do and considering the new business will be built in a remote spot I'd better like it. The living quarters will be above the offices with a balcony overlooking the river, peace, quiet and nothing to hear but the sound of the water lapping the banks." said Jake.

"I don't imagine you've spent much time in the country where it's so quiet being from New York, Jake."

"It was very quiet when I was out scouting during the war. You hear every sound and hope it wasn't you that created it or you'll be discovered and shot," said Jake with a smile.

"You've never talked about the war."

"I don't need or want to talk about it, and few men will. There's no point in reliving the horror by talking about what they experienced. As to time spent in the country, I did for a couple of summers in Atlanta at my aunt's plantation. My aunt lives in New York now with my parents. She was alone in Atlanta, and for safety during the war, she moved north. The plantation is still there, but no one has lived there for years. Being a teenager, it was boring with nothing to do. I always missed my friends in the city who I thought were having fun without me. Now I realize they were as bored as I was and probably wishing they were in the country where I was."

"I never remember being bored; there was always so much to do with the horses both work and pleasure. Maybe because I was born here and used to the lifestyle, there's really not much I felt I was missing."

Jake stifled a yawn. "How is it that there is just the one lane going across the plantation and there isn't a lane Ben uses for his property?" asked Jake.

"It's been that way from the beginning, since before my grandfather owned the plantation. When he died, he divided the plantation between his two sons, my father, and Uncle Ben. I suppose Uncle Ben or my father never felt the need to change things so Ben would have a lane accessing his property, he always used the one that crosses both properties. The bridge is wide for the wagons when the cotton is harvested to cross the creek to the mill. It's always worked in the past. Uncle Ben must be furious with you for suggesting you would put up a gate."

"Let's hope he gets over the fury and just learns to respect the fact that half of this plantation is yours and he has no say in how you see fit to use it."

"I'm glad you were here, Jake. It's different when you tell him he can't take what he wants for granted. He still sees me as a little girl he has to make decisions for and who doesn't understand the way things should be done."

"I think he'll start realizing you'll be making decisions that are in your interest, not his."

"Thanks to you, Jake. I never thought of a gate," said Roseanna with a laugh. "I hope this is the end of his interference. I'm not a little girl anymore."

Jake winked, "I've certainly noticed."

Roseanna blushed and changed the subject. "I'd like to see your new property. I'm glad you've given Andrew a chance to work with you. He'll do a fine job.

When will it be ready?"

"Don't know. But when I meet with Randy and the architect tomorrow, I'll have a better idea."

Jake stifled another yawn. Roseanna giggled. "Speaking of being bored, Jake. You should turn in."

"Sorry, Roseanna," said Jake as he squeezed the hand he had been holding. "I'm not bored, but I haven't had much sleep of late. Would you mind if I left you in this beautiful moonlight and went to bed?"

"I wouldn't mind at all. You'll be rested for our trip, and I need time to pack my things."

Jake rose from his chair and bent and kissed Roseanna's cheek "If you don't mind I will turn in. Goodnight, Roseanna," he said as he caressed her cheek. "Thank you for an enjoyable day. I'll be right as rain in the morning, I promise."

Roseanna lingered on the veranda after Jake had gone to bed. It was wonderful to have him here with her. She thought about the time they would spend together in New Orleans, just the two of them away from the plantation. She sat reminiscing about Jake and what a difference he had made in her life. It was becoming hard to remember her life before the war, it seemed so long ago. Her parents and brothers here with her, and the horses and what a beautiful existence they had. It all seemed so distant now, so much like a dream.

It troubled her to realize she had difficulty remembering her parent's, and her brother's faces. Were they all really gone? How could that be? She no longer felt like a pampered child, which she admitted she had undoubtedly been. Her father spoiled her even when her mother protested, and she smiled to herself remembering her mother's outrage at her father treating her just as he had his sons. She knew her parents would like Jake and see the good in him. He would be welcomed into the family, and they would be proud of the man he was. Maybe her fortunes were turning; maybe she and Jake had a future together. Each time she was with him she wanted to be with him more. She wondered if Jake saw a future for them.

No more dreaming in the moonlight, she needed to be ready for the trip to the city. What would she wear? She ran up the stairs to her room and looked at the clothes in her wardrobe. She remembered the smart dress Gwen Mason had worn and was envious; she had nothing that would compare. She wanted to look nice for Jake. Her wedding dress would be a good start. She pulled her carpetbag from the wardrobe and laid the clothes inside, being careful to keep them neat. She finished packing but was restless and excited about the trip.

She could hardly wait for morning. She wondered if Jake was asleep. She tiptoed down the hall to her father's room where Jake slept and pressed her ear to the door. Roseanna heard only silence. She turned the knob and quietly, gently pushed the door open a crack. Moonlight flooded the room making it as bright as day. Jake lay on his stomach, one knee bent towards his chest, his arms curled above his head. He faced away from the door with the covers flung from the bed. He wore nothing but his long johns. His bare back and arms tan from the sun stood out against the whiteness of the sheets with well-defined muscles. His torso tapered to a narrow waist and to legs were long and sturdy.

Roseanna took a deep breath and felt her face flush at the sight of him. She quickly closed the door, and with her hand still on the knob, she pressed her other hand against her mouth. There was a hollowness in the pit of her stomach, and her chest heaved with her breathing. She had seen men in their long johns before many times; she had two brothers who had never been modest walking about the house in nothing but their long johns. Their lack of clothes had never troubled Roseanna, but somehow this was different; this wasn't the same. She was very much attracted to this man.

Jake stirred in his sleep. Something had awoken him. He raised his head and looked around the room. Then his head dropped to the pillow, and he was instantly asleep again.

Roseanna ran to her room, extinguished the lamp, and crawled into bed. She closed her eyes, and all she could see and think about was the sight of Jake lying in the moonlight.

CHAPTER 5

Fresh from her bath, Roseanna slipped her dress over her head and looked at herself in the mirror. She was pleased with the results; the dress, though not new, was crisp and fresh. It was the last one her mother had sewn for her. It was made of pale lavender cotton with small pearl buttons from throat to waist. Lightly gathered in the front, with a denser gathering in the back to give the effect of a bustle and with a collar made of lace. Roseanna added a favorite cameo brooch at her throat passed down from her grandmother. She tugged at the long full sleeves, straightened, and buttoned the cuffs at her wrist, which were trimmed in the same lace as the collar. She twirled in front of the mirror to see the dress swirl and went to find a small hat she and her mother had made to match the dress.

As Roseanna adjusted the hat in the mirror, she heard voices in the yard and looking out the window saw Jake. He was in his shirtsleeves; his coat folded on the grass. He was talking to Simon and Nathan about repairing the garden fence. Roseanna watched as he moved about the yard. She admired his appearance. He was a handsome man. She bit her lip feeling ashamed for spying on him as he slept last night. She wondered what she would have done if he had awoke and saw her. Finished dressing, she went to the kitchen house to find Mama Teal.

"Mr. Jake what's we gonna do with the broke wood?" asked Simon.

"We'll burn it, Simon. First thing is to separate the broken boards from the others," said Jake, as he demonstrated with a hammer knocking the wood apart. "We'll save the pickets that aren't broken and use them again. It'll be back just the way it was when we're done."

"It's gots to be white," said Nathan in a slow, disinterested drawl.

"Yes, Nathan we have to paint, and Miss Roseanna will have to take care of the plants because I don't know what needs to be done," said Jake.

"I knows. Miss Annabel say I's the best with the flowers," said Simon proudly. "Me and Miss Annabel does work digging and all and once Mr. James help, too."

"I helps, too. Sometimes I does," said Nathan when Simon gave him a surprised look.

"Miss Roseanna will truly appreciate both of you helping," said Jake.

"We goes fishin' when we done?" asked Nathan.

"Only if the work is done," said Jake.

"My mama cook the best fish and hush puppies," said Simon, as he grinned at Nathan.

"She a good cooker," agreed Nathan.

"I's hitch the gig Mr. Jake?" asked Simon.

"Thanks, Simon. I would appreciate that."

"Can yous horse pulls the gig, Mr. Jake?"

"Nope. She's just saddle broke."

"I teach her, Mr. Jake," said Simon with excitement.

"I'll think about it Simon, you can take care of her while I'm away."

"Yes sir, Mr. Jake," said Simon as he ran to hitch the gig.

"Morning Miss Roseanna yous look mighty fine," said Mama Teal with a smile when she saw Roseanna dressed in her finery. "Mr. Jake gonna like how you lookin'. He like a tonic, yous always happy when he come round," said Mama Teal as she bustled around the kitchen.

"Am I, Mama Teal?" questioned Roseanna.

"Yes, child, yous is. He good for you. It like your daddy and Miss Annabel when they gets together, yous could just see the sparks aflyin'," said Mama Teal with a giggle and a bright smile.

Roseanna was unsure how to respond to Mama Teal's observation. "I don't understand what you mean, Mama Teal."

"Mr. Jake look at you Miss Roseanna the love just pour outs him. Yous being blind, that man in love. Now, I's see yous act exactly like him," said Mama Teal with a laugh. "Yous needs to see for your own self, Miss Roseanna."

Roseanna was embarrassed, but she knew Mama Teal was right. She felt different when Jake was around. Shaky, and jittery, and last night when she had spied on him while he was sleeping, she admitted to herself she wanted to touch him and run her hands over his smooth tanned back. Embarrassed at her own thoughts, she quickly changed the subject. "I don't know if I feel right to go to the city and leave you here after what's happened with the stable."

"Oh, don't yous be worry none. Mr. Andrew here. They not come back 'cause they finish what they wanted to do."

The door opened, and Jake came into the kitchen house. "Good Morning," he said with a bright smile.

"Mornin' Mr. Jake," said Mama Teal returning his greeting.

Roseanna flushed at the sound of Jake's voice; she rose and quickly turned to hide her face.

Jake looked puzzled at Roseanna. "Did I interrupt something?" he said to Roseanna's back.

Roseanna regained her composure and turned to face him, "Of course not," she said smiling. "We were just discussing my concern over leaving Mama Teal."

Jake looked at Mama Teal, "Mama Teal are you frightened?"

"No, Sir, Miss Roseanna worry bout nothin'."

"It's not nothing, Mama Teal as you put it. I just want you to be safe. The fire at the stable was serious," said Roseanna.

"You look lovely today, Roseanna," said Jake as he searched her face.

"Thank you, Jake," responded Roseanna pleased he had noticed. "Shall we eat here or in the dining room Mama Teal?"

"Dining room all set. I's there right quick with your food."

Mama Teal turned to hide her grin; she knew the signs watching these two young people. They were getting close to having a real marriage. Miss Roseanna just needed a little push, and Mr. Jake was apushing. She hoped what she had said to Miss Roseanna would make her see Mr. Jake wasn't going to go down on one knee and beg. He told Miss Roseanna how much he cared for her every time he looked at her. Miss Roseanna going to have to be the one that tipped the kettle and made this happen that for sure. This trip to New Orleans was exactly what would work. They needed to be alone together to get over the bump, and everything would come out fine.

Breakfast over, Roseanna rushed to finish last minute packing as Mama Teal came into the room to clear the table.

"Don't worry about Roseanna while we're in the city, Mama Teal. I'll take good care of her," said Jake.

"I's knows, Mr. Jake. She be a good girl. She raised up right, but sometime she needs a mama, and I's wants do that."

"You do a fine job, and I know Roseanna cares for you and your children."

"She take good care of us, and we gonna do same for her."

Simon had the gig waiting, and Roseanna and Jake were on their way to the city. As they entered the main road, Jake cast sidelong glances at Roseanna waiting for her to speak. All he could see was the top of her bonnet as she stared at her hands folded in her lap, her chin almost pressed against her chest.

Roseanna was thinking about what Mama Teal had said to her. Jake cared for her, and she could see the longing in his eyes. Roseanna admitted to herself she was longing for him, too. What was she suppose to do or say to him to make everything right between them?

Jake drove the gig at a good pace towards New Orleans. Wanting to break the silence between them, he spoke to Roseanna, "I thought maybe you weren't feeling well today, Roseanna, you've been very quiet."

"Have I?" said Roseanna as she finally turned to look at Jake. "It's nothing; I'm just concerned leaving Mama Teal for the next couple of days."

"Andrew knows we'll be gone. Mama Teal feels good he'll be around. She's quite the lady, very wise."

"She's wonderful," said Roseanna. "I don't know how I would ever manage if she weren't with me, and Simon and Loretta, too."

"Mama Teal is pleased you're going to the city for a time."

"I have to admit, I'm excited to be going. I can't recall the last time I was away from the plantation for any time. It would have been before the war started. We had so much fun when we went," said Roseanna, smiling at the memory. "The whole family would go, and it was a treat to stay overnight. We all had different things we wanted to do and the boys and I would argue about what we would do first. Then daddy would step in and end the argument and tell us exactly what the schedule would be," said Roseanna with a laugh.

"I suppose you wanted to shop for girl's things and the boys wanted to go and look at things for them. I imagine your father had important things to attend to. He must have been at wit's end over the arguments. What about your mother?"

"She was more concerned about who would wander away and get lost, or make sure we were clean and presentable, and of course minding our manners while we were out in public."

"I hope this trip brings back some fond memories for you. We'll have to try to find your favorite places. There's so much change in the city since the end of the war. Things are getting back to normal, and new buildings and businesses are going up every day."

"I wonder if the things I remember are still there. Jake, I do feel jittery leaving Mama Teal."

"Roseanna stop worrying, she'll be fine. Now, wait until you see the St. Charles Hotel. It's very grand. You must remember, its been there for years. The service is excellent, and the rooms are beautiful. Good restaurants in the hotel and other restaurants up and down the street, with nice shops in the hotel and others close by. You'll enjoy shopping."

"It's been a long time since I went shopping," said Roseanna feeling the enthusiasm of having some new things. "Could I really go shopping?"

"We can find time to do anything you want. I need to meet with Randy, Gwen, and the architect and get things settled with the blueprints so we can start the new building. It shouldn't take long; most of the planning is done. We just need to see the final drawings and give our approval. I'm looking forward to getting you and Randy better acquainted, and Gwen Mason for as long as she'll still be here."

Roseanna wasn't sure she wanted to spend time with Gwen Mason. "I would like getting to know Randy. He'll be around the plantation once you've moved the business."

"Yes, but you don't need to wait, Randy and I meet every morning for breakfast. I'm going to get you the prettiest room they have at the St. Charles where Randy and I have been staying. How about a room with a view so you can watch what goes on in the street, and I'll come and knock on your door in the morning to wake you, and you can join Randy and me for breakfast…"

"No," stammered Roseanna hardly above a whisper.

Jake turned to look at her, "You don't want to join us for breakfast?"

"I don't want my own room."

Jake drove on for a short distance not registering what Roseanna said. Then he realized with a start and quickly pulled the gig out of traffic and stopped.

"Are you saying what I think you're saying?" he said in a hesitant voice.

"We're married; we should be in the same room," said Roseanna, as she looked at her shaking hands clenched in her lap, her face the color of a ripe apple.

"Of course we should. It's a splendid idea. No argument from me," babbled Jake stumbling over his words. He paused and studied Roseanna. "Are you sure, Roseanna?" he asked concern creasing his brow.

Roseanna turned to meet Jake's intense gaze, "Yes, isn't that what you think?"

Jake laughed heartily. "That's exactly what I think," he said as he reached for Roseanna's face and gave her a kiss.

Roseanna pushed him away. "Jake! What are you doing, what will people think?" she said as she nervously looked at the other travelers.

"They'll say look at that very happy man," said Jake. "And I truly am," he said as he leaned close to Roseanna and caressed her cheek. He smacked the reins on Moses' rump and steered the gig back into traffic.

Jake pulled the gig to the entrance of the hotel and assisted Roseanna to the lobby. He found her an advantageous seat giving her a view of all the activity while he arranged for their room.

Roseanna watched smartly dressed women as they paraded through the lobby, they wore clothes similar to those Gwen Mason had worn. She became conscious that the dress she wore was no longer in style. The war had changed things, and so had the fashions. Now her desire to shop became a need. She would find a reputable dressmaker in the city.

Groups of men gathered throughout the lobby, all of them talking, smiling and greeting each other as they shook hands. Roseanna remembered that before the war the St. Charles had been a great meeting place for politicians and businessmen, and from the looks of the circles of conversation around her, it hadn't changed. There were also men in military uniforms, some appearing to be recuperating from wounds received in battle. The atmosphere was busy and bright.

Jake stood in line at the hotel desk. He glanced at Roseanna as she waited. To him, she stood out as the only women in the crowd. He was aroused with excitement that they would share a room, and neither knew nor cared how she had made the decision. He admired her courage for telling him.

"Mr. Sinclair, Good Morning, Sir," said the desk clerk. "I have messages for you."

Jake took the offered messages. "I'd like to make arrangements for a suite for my wife who is in the city with me today, one with an excellent view of the street."

"Of course, Mr. Sinclair. We have suites which will allow her a perfect view."

"My wife is particularly fond of roses. Could you make sure there is a bouquet in the room for her?"

"Right away, Mr. Sinclair."

"Could you have our baggage taken to the suite, we have business out of the hotel this morning."

"Pleasure to have you and your wife with us, Mr. Sinclair. Please let us know if there is anything else we can do to make her stay more enjoyable," he said with his best smile as he snapped his fingers at an alert bellhop to follow Mr. Sinclair to collect his luggage.

Jake came to Roseanna with a smile, "Would you like to stroll on the street?"

"Yes Jake, I would like that. I have to tell you I remember being in this lobby before and sitting with my mother when my father met with someone who was buying horses. I remember feeling so important and special. Afterward, we went to a sweets shop, somewhere close by, where my brothers and I had candy and fizzy drinks while my parents had coffee."

"Maybe we can find it. Would you like to see our offices where Randy and I work? It's a few blocks down, and we'll pass some shops on the way." Jake consulted his watch. "Randy, Gwen, and the architect should be there discussing the new building. They should be meeting about now."

Jake proudly took Roseanna's hand and placed it on the curve of his arm. They walked several blocks down the street, turned a corner walked another block and entered a multi-storied red brick building. Climbing to the second floor, Jake led Roseanna to a stout oak door, the top panel having frosted glass with the words "Sinclair and Mason, Imports and Exports."

As they entered Gwen, Randy, and the architect were huddled over blueprints for the building. A discussion seemed heated between Gwen and Randy.

"Jake," said Randy, "you're just in time to help settle an argument," he said as he got to his feet.

Gwen and the architect also rose to greet Roseanna and Jake. "Roseanna you've met Gwen and Randy, and this is our architect Richard Phillips," said Jake.

"Roseanna I'm glad you're here," said Gwen. "We're having a discussion about the living quarters, and Randy seems to think we don't have to pay any attention to outfitting it like a proper place to live. I'll be coming down periodically to stay, and Randy seems to think I could hang a hammock between two trees and be perfectly comfortable. We need a woman's point of view."

"It's not quite that bad, Gwen," said Randy. "I would rather put the money into the business rather than making a comfortable place for you to use when you visit," he countered pointedly.

"Randy," said Gwen, crossing her arms over her chest, "you're forgetting, you're staying at a very comfortable hotel, and someone comes in every day to make up your room. You go to a restaurant, someone sticks a menu under your nose, and you order what pleases you. You won't have those luxuries out in the wilds of Louisiana," said Gwen triumphantly as she sat down.

"She's right Randy," said Jake. "You need to outfit a kitchen, and we'll need furniture, and unless we're going to take care of household chores, we'll have to hire people."

"Thank you for taking my side, Jake. There will be decent furniture, not just any furniture if I have to buy it myself," said Gwen defiantly. "What do you think, Roseanna?"

Roseanna looked at the four faces waiting for her to speak. "I tend to agree with Gwen." Gwen flashed Randy a triumphant smile. "But Randy I would be more than happy for you and Gwen to come to the plantation and look at an attic full of very decent," she said with emphasis looking at Gwen, "usable furniture you can have. Except for a stove, I could also find what you need for your kitchen. Certainly would be plenty of women in the area who could do the household duties and cooking for you."

"Very generous of you Roseanna, if you're sure you can spare the furniture," said Randy.

"I can not only spare it but would be glad someone was able to get some use out of it. It's sat in the attic for years."

"We don't need to rush into getting furniture, Randy. There will be plenty of time," said Gwen not pleased with the idea of cast-off furniture.

"I think we have spent enough time arguing over furniture. It's made me hungry," said Randy. "Why don't we break for lunch? I for one am starving. Richard, will you join us?"

"Thanks, Randy, but I'd like to make the changes to the blueprints and have them ready for you this afternoon. Could we meet after you've had lunch?"

"Jake can you be back and meet with Richard later today?" asked Randy.

"I can, and we need to get this finalized as I'm leaving the city tomorrow," said Jake. "If that's settled let's adjourn."

After lunch, Gwen as she wasn't needed in the final meeting with the architect, graciously consented to introduce Roseanna to her favorite dressmaker. She assured Roseanna the woman knew the latest fashion style in New Orleans.

"When will Jake bring you to New York to meet his parents?" asked Gwen.

"We won't be going to New York; our first trip will be to Atlanta. Jake promised his aunt to see about her property there, but with the new building getting started, we'll have to postpone travel plans. Jake wrote to his parents and invited them to visit the plantation so his father can see the new property."

Gwen gasped, "Oh, my dear," she said, as she suddenly stopped on the sidewalk and took Roseanna's hand. "What will you do?" she asked with a look of deep concern on her face. "I hope you're prepared to entertain them at this plantation where you live. His parents are quite wealthy and used to the finer things in life. If I were here, I could help you prepare. Is there someone in the....village, or wherever your home is located, to give you some guidance? Dear me Roseanna, what was Jake thinking to invite them?"

Roseanna gave Gwen her most engaging smile. "I'm certain we can manage but thank you for your concern and advice."

Roseanna didn't explain how Pelican's Haven had entertained many dignitaries and prominent people who had come to purchase her father's horses before the war. Pelicans Haven had been the site of many parties and galas. It was well equipped to entertain Jake's parents. Most importantly, Gwen didn't know about Roseanna's most trusted asset, Mama Teal.

"How brave of you Roseanna," said Gwen patting Roseanna's hand. "All the same I will tell his parents you are country folks and not to expect too much. But I'm sure you will make them as comfortable as possible."

"Thank you, Gwen. Jake apparently doesn't share your concern, or I'm sure he wouldn't think of having them stay at the plantation," said Roseanna with her most polite smile.

"You have more faith in men's ability to understand these things than I do. No matter, you will just have to make the most of it."

Jake, Randy, and Richard Phillips after a short discussion agreed on the blueprints and completed the task with signatures from all concerned.

"What's the next step, Richard?" asked Randy.

"Getting in the pilings for the dock," answered Richard. "I have someone in mind to do the work. My firm has used them before; they do excellent work. If you allow me to make the arrangements, he can start right away."

"We'll rely on your expertise for that," said Jake. "I've hired a man to start with the clearing of the lot unless you have another idea, Richard."

"Oh?" questioned Randy.

"Sorry, Randy, I haven't had the chance to tell you I hired Andrew Moorcroft."

"Roseanna's cousin?"

Jake nodded in agreement, "He's local so he can start finding labor to do the clearing if you're in agreement Richard."

"Sounds fine to me," said Richard. "He'll be invaluable for finding what we need. You should yield quite a bit of lumber for your building from the stand of trees on the land. There is a man who can set up his sawmill on the property for that purpose, and someone in mind to lay the foundation for the building. Then we can start the actual building. Can the man you've hired read a blueprint?"

"Yes, he studied engineering in school," said Jake.

"You'll need copies of the blueprints. I'll get them to you in the next day or two. Shall I send them here to the office?" asked Richard.

"Jake should have them as he is going to be the one that pretty much runs the project. Send them to him at a plantation called Pelicans Heaven."

"Pelicans Heaven?" asked Richard with surprise. "That's the Ravenna Plantation."

"Yes," said Jake. "You know it?"

"Very well. I built a house there for Benjamin and Jane Ravenna. It was one of my first commissions, and of course, everyone in the area knows about the fabulous horses raised there by James Ravenna. What's your connection there, Jake?"

"My wife, Roseanna, is James Ravenna's daughter."

Richard laughed, "Shows you what a small world it is. If that's where you'll be I can bring the plans to you when I come up with the gentleman who is going to sink the pilings for your dock," said Richard as he rose to leave the office.

"My wife will be excited to talk to you about what you remember, Richard. Her father passed away recently. Send me a note when you're ready to meet, and we'll plan to have you stay at the house. The property is very close to the plantation, it will be convenient for all of us."

"Thank you, Jake," said Richard as he shook hands with the two men. "I'm looking forward to this project and talking to your wife. Are they still raising the horses?"

"Not at the present time. Hopefully, that will change in the future."

"Beautiful animals," said Richard Phillips. "When I was there building the house, I would go and watch as they trained. Your wife must have been a little girl back then. I remember several young boys, but don't recall any girls. Well, I must go as I have other appointments. Thanks for allowing me to build for you, I'm looking forward to the project, and I hope you will be pleased."

After Richard left Randy and Jake talked excitedly about how well the plans for the property were moving along. "I think this calls for a celebration, Jake. Can I make reservations for dinner for Gwen, you and Roseanna and myself?"

"Not tonight, Randy. I have something special planned for Roseanna; it's just going to be the two of us. We can celebration another time," said Jake. "Let's meet in the morning at the usual time and tie up any loose ends before Roseanna, and I head back to the plantation."

CHAPTER 6

Jake woke, stretched his tall frame, took a deep breath, and smothered a yawn. He blinked, focused, and turned his head to glimpse the face of his wife in the morning light that bathed the room. A smile played on his lips, and his heart tripped in his chest. She lay facing him, one hand pressed between the pillow and her cheek, her knees drawn towards her chest. He supported his head on his hand and watched her sleep, and marveled she was with him. How beautiful she was. Her face was tranquil in sleep, her rose-colored lips slightly parted, her lashes fanned on her cheeks long and glossy, her hair, dark and mussed, spread against the pillow.

He remembered their night together and immediately his passion soared giving him an urgent need to wake her. The sheet that covered her was pulled high revealing one naked shoulder. He moved closer and ran his fingertips over the rise of her hip and down the length of her thigh. Gently, softly he traced his finger along the curve of her cheek, then down her throat to her breast watching her face for signs she was waking. She stirred, but still slept. Gently pinching the sheet between his thumb and forefinger, he eased it down the length of her arm exposing her naked breast and midriff. Her eyes fluttered open meeting her husband's gaze. She smiled shyly and whispered his name. He reached and gathered her into his arms. Randy would have to wait.

Very early in the morning Simon and Nathan resumed the work of tearing down the garden fence. They started the work the day before with Jake before he and Roseanna left for the city, but the afternoon had become very hot, and Mama Teal told them to go and swim, and they could finish the work in the morning before Mr. Jake, and Miss Roseanna returned from the city.

In the morning the work would be finished in a few hours and the rest of the day they could fish and swim. They argued about which activity they should do first. Nathan said they would be hot and sweaty after working and should swim first. Simon, who loved his mama's fried fish and hush puppies wanted to fish first to guarantee they would have fish for Mama Teal to cook. Nathan, after some thought agreed, fishing should come first. By mid morning, the work complete, Mama Teal came to inspect the project.

"Good, yous gots it done," she praised, smiling at the two. "You gots time afore lunch to go fishing. Maybe yous gets lucky, and we get fish and hush puppies, then I's has time for supper for Miss Roseanna and Mr. Jake 'cause they be back today."

With a whoop of joy, the two collected their fishing gear and dug for night crawlers. At last, at their favorite shady spot along the creek, with worms threaded on their hooks, they cast their lines in the slow-moving water. They munched corn bread and fished in companionable silence waiting for the fish to bite.

"Nathan," said Simon, "yous and Loretta still go north wiff no baby?"

"I's gots me other plans," said Nathan in his deep, gravelly voice.

"Loretta mad if yous nots take her."

Nathan laughed. "Loretta gotta fess up 'bout me and her."

"She my sista. Yous be good to her."

"Never my baby," said Nathan shaking his head negatively.

Simon looked puzzled at Nathan. "What yous saying?"

"Saying I's never lay with Loretta. I's gots a gal across the field name Sarah. I's gonna take her."

"But yous the baby father, Nathan, and Loretta, the mama."

"If you'd see that baby it had blue eyes. Do I's gots blue eyes, Simon," said Nathan laughing heartily. "It ain't my baby."

Simon jumped to his feet, his fishing pole clattering down the creek bank. He stood looking at Nathan a scowl on his face. "That baby not has blue eyes."

"Look at me Simon I's gots blue eyes," said Nathan giving Simon a wide-eyed stare.

Simon, his mouth slack, bent forward and stared intently into Nathan's eyes. Nathan laughed and smacked his knee. "Simon you gots to stop being stupid. Onlyest reason Loretta say I's the daddy was so nobody get mad 'bout who is the daddy."

"Who the daddy?" questioned Simon.

"Simon yous look, see who gots blue eyes, that the daddy. That a secret I's gots to keep." Nathan looked around being sure no one was about before he spoke again. "I's had me 'nother secret gonna make me rich. Gets me clothes, a horse to ride, everythin'."

Simon stared at Nathan in disbelief. "Yous not gonna, Nathan. Yous gots no money."

"I does," said Nathan insistently. "Well, soon. Mr. Ben goin' give me lots of money. He promised."

"Why he gives yous money."

"Simon I's already say can't tell 'cause its secret. You got a secret, Simon?"

"No," said Simon abruptly. "I's not gots secrets."

His response surprised Nathan. He looked at Simon curiously. "You does, Simon."

"No! No! No! Not telling."

"Yous does have a secret. Come on, Simon. Tell me. Simon gots a secret, Simon gots a secret," chanted Nathan in a teasing tone.

"No," said Simon angrily.

"Yous gotta gal friend? That yous secret? What yous be doin' with a girl," said Nathan laughing and lewdly rolling his eyes at Simon.

"Don't like girls. Only Miss Roseanna, Mama, and Loretta."

Nathan laughed with a sneer. "If yous knows the best thing 'bout girls yous like them lots."

Simon regained his dropped fishing pole, threaded a worm on the hook, and cast the line in the water.

Nathan eyed Simon, "Yous ready to say yous secret?"

"No!"

"Here what we do, Simon. I's tell my secret then yous. That what we gonna do."

Simon ignored Nathan and studied his hands where they tightly gripped his fishing pole.

"Here my secret," said Nathan. "It 'bout Mr. James. He go lookin' for Mr. Edward, yous member Simon. He gots lots of gold then he hides it. Mr. Ben, he wantin' it and he say Nathan I's give you some ifs yous finds it."

Simon sprang to his feet and began running.

"Simon where yous goin', come back," yelled Nathan. "I's gives you some yous helps me find it."

Frowning Nathan stood and watched Simon disappear. "That boy funny in the head, he runnin' like a scaredy cat."

Nathan sat down and continued fishing muttering about Simon's behavior. Feeling drowsy he yawned and stretched out on the bank of the creek scratching at an insect bite on his arm. But with a start, he bounded up into a sitting position. He realized what Simon's secret had to be. He sprang to his feet, dropped his fishing pole, and ran to tell Ben Ravenna.

Randy waited patiently as the waiter seated other patrons. He scanned the restaurant looking for Jake, but it seemed he had arrived first. The waiter greeted him. "A table for one Sir?" he asked.

"I'm meeting Mr. Sinclair. Do you know who he is?"

"Yes, Sir. I'll let him know you're here when he comes in."

"Then a table for two," said Randy.

Randy was getting impatient for Jake to arrive as he sat over his second cup of coffee and had finished with the morning paper. He occasionally scanned the room for Jake and checked his watch thinking he had misunderstood their meeting time, then looked up and saw Jake walking towards him.

"Good morning Jake. Did you oversleep, or am I early?"

"I'm late, sorry. Too much wine with dinner last night," said Jake as he studied the menu.

"Wine can have that effect on you sometimes. A little under the weather?" asked Randy with a raised eyebrow.

"No, I feel great," said Jake as he continued to study the menu.

"Your evening with Roseanna was a success?"

"Yes," said Jake with a smile. "Great evening, a fine dinner, a real treat for Roseanna. She hasn't been in the city for a long time. She's enjoying revisiting places she remembers from when she came with her family before the war. It was good to see her relax and enjoy herself."

"She should come in more often. New Orleans is returning to the city it was before the war. What's on the table for discussion this morning?" asked Randy changing the subject.

Jake tossed the menu on the table, "Something serious concerning Roseanna. The stable at the plantation was torched."

Randy raised his eyebrows and looked at Jake, "What do you mean torched?"

"Riders carrying torches in the middle of the night set it ablaze."

"Anyone hurt?" asked Randy with concern.

"No, thankfully."

"How bad was it burned?"

"Pretty much destroyed."

"The uncle?" questioned Randy.

"Can't say for sure, but who else would have reason to torch it," said Jake with a frown. "He's caused enough trouble for Roseanna and has gone on record as saying she won't raise horses again. Blaming him would be obvious. I need to be concerned for Roseanna. Now that everything with the new building is moving along so quickly, would you agree with me handling the new place while you attend to business here in the city? I can then be with Roseanna at the plantation."

"Not only agree but insist. One of us needs to be there, and it would make sense if it were you."

"I'll come to the city when you need me and bring Roseanna with me. She's concerned about Mama Teal and her family. Andrew is there watching out for them while we're away, but she's still anxious."

"Jake, we'll work out what needs to be done, no argument from me. Roseanna has to be your main concern. Did you confront Ravenna?"

"Of course, and he denied it."

"No surprise."

"Josh needs to finish up with Roseanna's parent's Wills and let Ravenna know that he's out of the picture. He needs to go on record with Ravenna and his attorney, with a very strongly worded letter reiterating the man has no jurisdiction over Roseanna or the property. The gold that is supposedly hidden somewhere on the property is what's driving him, and the man is obsessed with anyone else having any ownership or control because of it."

"Do you think a letter will stop him?" asked Randy. "Could he be dangerous?"

"If he had anything to do with the burning that stable, he is dangerous. This business about the gold may continue until it's either found or proved to be a fabrication."

"Do you think it's there?"

"There's no way to prove anything. Roseanna's father and mother knew and possibly her brothers. The bank president is the only person who seems to think it exists. Ravenna wants that gold if it's there and he's desperate to have it. My presence on the property doesn't sit well with him, he feels threatened if I'm there but I need to be on that plantation."

"No arguments from me, it's the right thing to do."

"I knew you'd understand. If we keep moving along at the same pace with the new site, we'll both be out of the city. It's going well, don't you think?"

"Yes, and there is good news. Gwen and I, and by the way Josh Horn," said Randy raising an eyebrow, "who joined us for dinner last night, he is smitten with Gwen," chuckled Randy. "We went back to the office after dinner and found the signed sales agreement from the owner had come in the mail. Gwen is taking the first boat upriver today so she can get a check to him. Then it's all done and legal. We are the proud owners of the property."

Jake stood and reached his hand across the table, a big grin on his face. "Congratulations, Partner!"

Randy stood and tightly grasped Jake's hand. "Partner! I like that word! Not bad for an old farm boy!"

"And a boy born with a silver spoon in his mouth," laughs Jake.

"We'll do well, Jake, I know we will. I appreciate you waiting until I could pay my own way."

"That's what we agreed to do," said Jake.

"We need to see Gwen off, her boat leaves in about an hour and what about Roseanna?"

"She went shopping; I'll fetch her at lunchtime."

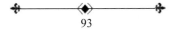

Roseanna lingered in bed after Jake left. She had lain awake watching him as he dressed earlier, marveling at how easy it was to be with him. She had felt embarrassed watching as he shaved but she couldn't draw her eyes away. His back was turned to her as he faced the mirror. He wore no clothing but his long johns and she was mesmerized by the play of the muscles in his back as he slid the razor over his face.

Occasionally he had met her eyes in the mirror and smiled, stopping several times to come to Roseanna where she lay in bed. They shared passionate embraces and deep kisses. Finally, he was dressed and ready to meet Randy.

One last long lingering kiss before he left. "We'd best stop, or I'll never meet Randy," he had groaned.

"I wouldn't mind, but I'm sure Randy would," responded Roseanna with a laugh as she had hugged Jake close to her.

"I'm in love with you Roseanna, you know that?" as he said as he stared into her eyes and tenderly brushed the hair from her face.

"And I love you, Jake," said Roseanna snuggling close. "Oh, I do, I love you," she had said surprised at her emotion.

"I'll come and fetch you for lunch. Be careful if you go out. Watch what's happening around you. This part of the city is pretty civilized, but there some that are not."

"There's a dressmaker just down the street. Gwen introduced me yesterday. I'm to go back today so she can take my measurements. I won't be long, and I'll come back and wait for you in the lobby."

"I have to leave right this instant," said Jake as he looked at his watch. "Enjoy buying your new clothes. After I talk to Randy today, I think we can be together at the plantation all the time. We'll finish what needs to be done here in the city and after lunch gather our things and be home before nightfall."

"I can hardly wait, Jake. I want us to be together all the time."

"I want that, too."

Now Roseanna hugged the pillow that Jake had used in the night, the smell of him lingered, and she buried her face in the scent. She was happy, so happy for the first time in what seemed such a long time. She closed her eyes and visualized how Jake had appeared as he dressed before the mirror. She felt an exciting, aching sensation in her stomach wanting him again.

She was happy, almost giddy. Nothing could be more beautiful than being with Jake; he made her feel complete. She was sad that she couldn't share her happiness with her parents and brothers. She wanted her family to know and love Jake the way she did, and she knew they would. Her eyes filled with tears of happiness as she cuddled the pillow. She laughed at herself, and her own happiness then hurried from the bed and dressed to explore the streets and the shops and to be ready for lunch with Jake and Randy.

Nathan was both excited and scared as he knocked on the door of Ben's house. Excited because the gold could be found, but frightened because he had betrayed Ben's confidence. The black girl, Cindy, answered his knock and told Nathan to get on because Mr. Ben was not to be disturbed and she wasn't going to fetch him.

"Yous better 'cause whats I's gots to tell him cain't wait, and he be mighty mad when he find out yous not get him."

"I ask Miss Jane first," said the girl looking down her nose disdainfully at Nathan doubting he had business with the master.

Nathan waved his arms frantically. "No, no. Yous goes gets him. Tell him I's know where it's hiding. Go gal 'cause yous goin' be mighty sorry if yous don't."

Cindy, undecided if Nathan's warning was a fact, and fearing Mr. Ben's displeasure for intruding in his office, hesitated at the office door. She timidly knocked and was told to enter.

Nathan paced nervously on the veranda waiting for Ben to appear.

"Nathan what's this about," said Ben as he came onto the veranda.

"Mr. Ben, Simon, he know," said Nathan excitedly. "'Cause he tells me he has a secret and then he runs away."

"Do you think it's about the gold, Nathan?"

"Yes sir, Mr. Ben. I's brags about goin' north, and yous give me money."

"And what else?"

"Simon says why Mr. Ben gives yous money and…," Nathan paused; knowing he had to tell Ben he had betrayed their confidence and fearing his wrath. "Now Mr. Ben not gets mad at Nathan but I tole him 'bout the gold, how yous give me some if I's find it," said Nathan waiting for Ben to unleash his anger at him for divulging the information.

To Nathan's relief, Ben just gave him a thoughtful look. "What happened then, Nathan?"

"He run when I's asking about the gold Mr. Ben. He don't talk no more," said Nathan emphatically.

Ben ignored Nathan. Simon knowing where the gold was made sense. James and Annabel could not have handled the weight of the gold by themselves, and as James's sons had gone to fight, someone would have needed to help. Simon would have been the choice. Simon worshipped James, and because of his loyalty, he would never reveal the hiding place.

"You did a good thing coming to me Nathan. I need to talk to Simon. Go find him, tell him I have a surprise for him. Bring him to the overseer's house. I'll wait for you there."

"Yes Sir, Mr. Ben. I's gets him now," said Nathan. He smiled at Ben and then ran to find Simon.

Gwen was at the dock dressed in her finery watching as the last cargo was loaded on the boat she had booked to sail. Josh Horn, looking very pleased, was at her side. She scanned the crowd for Randy and Jake but didn't see them. The passengers were beginning to make their way up the gangway, and she was losing hope that Randy and Jake would see her off. Finally, she saw them pushing through the milling crowds, cargo, and stevedores as they hurried towards her.

"Gwen," called Randy frantically.

"I thought you would miss seeing me. We only have a few minutes, and then I have to board," said Gwen. "Josh was so sweet to escort me down. Don't know how I would have managed without him," she said, giving Josh an adoring smile.

"Sorry, Gwen. I've been running late today," said Jake.

"I'm so glad you're here, Jake. Could we have a word in private?" she asked. "Randy and Josh will excuse us I'm sure," she said giving the two her most alluring smile.

Gwen took Jake's elbow. "Jake I just wanted to talk to you about Roseanna. I was prepared to dislike her when I heard you had gotten married, but she is perfect for you. I never knew the kind of woman you would want until I saw the two of you together. I've never seen you so content, happy, and sure of yourself. I just wanted you to know I like her even though we are different. I can hardly wait to see your parents and tell them how lucky you are to have found her. Please be happy, give Roseanna my best, and tell her that I hope she will let me come to the plantation for a visit. You are special to me, Jake; I want you to be happy."

Jake gave Gwen a hug, "I'll tell her you wished us well and without question she will be pleased to have you visit."

"Thank you, Jake. I need to ask you if all the drama is over for Randy and me. We did talk, and both know we will just be friends. I hope he isn't upset."

"That's between you and Randy. He's fine as far as I know. You have a safe trip back and tell my folks that I am looking forward to their visit; I want them to meet Roseanna and see for themselves what a fine choice I've made. My father is going to be pleased with the progress we're making."

"They'll be happy, Jake. They're proud of you."

Then with a final hug for Jake and a kiss on the cheek from Josh Horn, Gwen waved as she boarded the boat, and Jake went to fetch Roseanna for lunch.

Simon was pleased when Nathan told him Mr. Ben had a surprise. "Why Mr. Ben goin' gives Simon surprise?" He hurried beside Nathan as they crossed the bridge to the overseer's house.

"He not say, Simon. He just say hurry alls I know."

"Mr. Ben not my friend, Nathan."

"Don't know Simon, just say for Simon come quick."

The two entered the overseer's house where heat and a musty unused scent rose, and dust motes floated through the sun that streamed through the windows. Ben was there with a smile waiting for Simon. "Well, Simon," "you've come for your surprise. First, we have to talk. You sit right here in this chair," he said indicating a chair and waiting for Simon to seat himself. "Here's what I have for you," said Ben extending his arm so Simon could see into his hand.

Simon stared at a bright shiny coin in Ben Ravenna's palm. "That for Simon, Mr. Ben?"

"Yes, Simon it's for you. Usually, when you get money, you have to work, but not this time. I'm just going to ask you a question and when you tell me the answer this gold coin is yours."

"Mr. Ben I's work for Miss Roseanna."

"I know Simon. Now I'm going to give you the money, and you don't have to work. Do you remember when Mr. James went to find Edward?"

"He not comes home, and Mr. Edward not comes home. They still gone," said Simon still looking at the coin.

"No, they won't be coming home, Simon. You helped Mr. James hide something, didn't you? It was gold; you know where the gold is don't you

Simon?"

Simon took his eyes away from the coin and began to shake his head. "I's not tell Mr. Ben. Mr. James he say nobody 'cept Mr. Edward and Mr. John."

"That's because Mr. James didn't know Edward and John wouldn't be coming home. So, Simon, nobody knows where the gold is but you. Miss Roseanna needs the gold, so we need to get it for her."

"Miss Annabel know. She help hids it."

"Miss Annabel is dead Simon as is Mr. James. So you're going to have to tell me where the gold is."

"No, Mr. Ben. Waitin' for Mr. John and Mr. Edward."

"Simon, John, and Edward are dead just like Mr. James and Miss Annabel," said Ben patiently. They're not coming home. You're the only one that knows about the gold. You tell me where it is, Simon, and get this gold coin," said Ben, laying his hand on Simon's shoulder.

"I's hungry Mr. Ben. Mama gets my lunch."

"You can go for your lunch Simon when you tell me where the gold is."

"Can't 'cause I's promise, Mr. James," said Simon pulling away from the hand on his shoulder.

"A promise is special Simon, but sometimes the promise has to be broken," said Ben as a pulled a chair close to Simon and sat down facing him. "Now with Mr. James and Miss Annabel dead, the promise isn't a good promise anymore."

"Yous got blue eyes, Mr. Ben," said Simon excitedly as he stared intently at Ben.

"So I do, Simon," said Ben.

"Yous the daddy of Loretta baby?"

"What are you talking about?"

"Nathan he say that Loretta baby gots blue eyes. So yous the daddy," said Simon, smiling.

Ben turned to look at Nathan who stood behind the chair Ben sat in. He was caught frantically waving his arms and shaking his head negatively at Simon to be quiet.

Ben looked at him sternly. "Nathan, what's he talking about?"

"Don't know Mr. Ben. He just talks crazy."

"Is he Nathan? Why would you tell him the baby had blue eyes?"

"I's not sayin' that Mr. Ben," said Nathan fearfully.

"Yes, Nathan yous do," said Simon emphatically. "You say yous not the daddy. Baby gots blue eyes."

Ben stood from the chair and approached Nathan. "Tell me right now, what's this business about that baby having blue eyes," he demanded angrily.

"I's fibbin' to Simon Mr. Ben," said Nathan fearfully, stepping back away from Ben. "That my baby," he said staying loyal to his sister and Andrew.

Ben stared at Nathan. "We'll go into this later. Don't let me find out you're lying to me," he said poking his finger at Nathan's chest.

"No, no. I's not lying, Mr. Ben."

Ben stood silently staring at Nathan and then returned to his chair facing Simon. "You're not telling me what I asked you, Simon. I'll repeat what I asked you. Where did Mr. James hide the gold?"

Simon squirmed in the chair, fear showing on his face. "I gots to go find mama," he said as he started to rise from the chair. "Mama has lunch."

Ben raised his walking stick and pressed the tip against Simon's chest forcing him back in the chair. "Not just yet. You haven't told me what I asked you."

Simon looked at the stick his eyes showing his fear. "I's done talking Mr. Ben."

"You're done when I say you're done. Tell me where the gold is, Simon."

"No, no, no! I's promise Mr. James," he said as his face crumbled and he began to cry.

Ben applied more pressure to the stick.

"Ouchy, that hurt Mr. Ben," said Simon through his tears.

Ben removed the stick from Simon's chest. "You're making this more difficult than it needs to be Simon. Stop blubbering like a baby and tell me where the gold is."

"I's not 'spose to tell. Can't, can't," said Simon his voice faltering and his hands shaking.

Ben struck a sharp blow with the stick to Simon's thigh. Nathan watching from behind Ben's chair winched at the sound of the blow.

"Owee!" cried Simon. "Mama, Mama help me!"

"Tell me, Simon!"

"I wants Mama," said Simon crying harder.

"Grown men don't cry for their mothers, Simon. You want your mama, tell me what I want to know, and then you can go to your mama."

"Please don't hit Simon! I's a free man. Yous can't hit a free man!"

Ben pressed his advantage with Simon and brought the stick down for another blow. Simon cried harder and tried to rise from the chair. "Sit down Simon. You're not leaving this chair until you tell me where the gold is. You're pig-headed!"

"I's asking Mr. James can I tell yous," said Simon as he half rose from the chair.

Ben put the stick back against Simon's chest and pushed him back in the seat, "Nathan get some rope. We're going to tie Simon in this chair until he tells me what I want to know."

Simon struggled against the stick. Ben struck another blow to Simon's kneecap. Simon's head dropped to his chest, and he cried making a blubbering sound.

"Mr. Ben," said Nathan as he came to Simon's side with concern for the pain Simon was feeling, "he tells me won't yous Simon?"

Simon continued to cry, and would not raise his head to look at Nathan. "Simon," pleaded Nathan, "yous tell me won't yous now Simon, so Mr. Ben don't hit yous no more."

Simon would not respond and continued to cry. Nathan moved away from the chair frightened for Simon and agonizing over how this would end.

Ben poked Simon's chest again with the stick. "Do you want me to hurt you, Simon? I'll stop when you tell me where the gold is hidden. This will help Miss Roseanna. You want to help her, don't you?"

"I's telling Miss Roseanna, Mr. Ben," said Simon through his tears.

Ben rose from his chair. "Nathan do as I told you and get some rope. We'll just see how long Simon can sit here tied to that chair before he tells me what I want to know."

Nathan moved quickly across the room and knelt by Simon's chair again. "Simon don't yous make me tie yous up. Don't be dumb. Tell Mr. Ben," he said anxiously as he grabbed Simon's hand.

"No. I's. Can't. Tell. Mr. James say never say." He continued to cry. Nathan don't let me get tied!"

"Nathan do as I told you, get some rope. He'll tell after he sits here for a time," said Ben.

"I's got to pee, Mr. Ben," moaned Simon.

Nathan left the house and quickly returned with a length of rope, then stood to wait for Ben to tell him what to do.

"Go ahead Nathan," said Ben gesturing towards Simon, "Tie his hands good and tight behind that chair and then tie his legs.

Reluctantly and slowly Nathan did as he was told and securely tied Simon to the chair as Ben watched all the while hoping Simon would fear being bound and tell him where the gold was.

Ben stood up and walking around the chair inspecting Nathan's work. "I'm going to go have my lunch Simon," said Ben. "I'll come back when I'm finished and see if you're ready to tell me what I want to know."

Ben stood for several minutes waiting for Simon to speak. Simon hung his head, crying, refusing to meet his stare. As Ben turned his back and left the house the sound of Simon's wailing filled his ears.

Nathan squatted by the chair where Simon was tied with his hands behind his back. "Simon, why yous make me does this? Why yous not tell? Yous a dumb boy!"

Simon gave a long anguished cry. "I's pee my pants. Mama gone be mad 'cause I's not 'spose to do it!"

Nathan winced, wringing his hands. He wanted to untie Simon but knew he would suffer Ben's wrath. He stood watching and listening, trying to find a way to help Simon. "Simon tell, alls yous gots to do is say!"

Simon ignored the plea and continued to hang his head and cry. Nathan nervously watched pacing back and forth in front of the chair where Simon sat. "Simon tell me now where's at and I's untie you and Mr. Ben gets the gold we goes fishin'," begged Nathan as he squatted in front of Simon.

Simon stopped crying, hung his head with his eyes closed and wouldn't look at Nathan. Knowing he was the cause of Simon's distress and overcome with guilt, Nathan left the house closing the door behind him.

Jake rushed to the lobby of the St. Charles Hotel expecting to see Roseanna waiting for him. He was puzzled when she wasn't there. Thinking she must have returned to the room, he took the stairs two at a time to the suite on the third floor.

Roseanna heard his key in the lock and jumped from the chair where she had been sitting and flew into Jake's embrace as he entered the room. He could see that she had been crying "Roseanna what is it, what's happened?"

"It's nothing, I'm being foolish," said Roseanna. She laid her head on Jake's chest and clung to him.

Jake pushed her away so he could see her face. "Tell me what happened, why are you so upset?"

"We signed that document the day we were married. It upsets me to even think that I agreed to sign it," said Roseanna.

"I don't understand, Roseanna."

"I don't want our marriage to start with a document talking about divorce and annulment," Roseanna said sheepishly.

Jake pulled her close to his chest "That piece of paper was never for me, it was for you to give you peace of mind over what your uncle was saying about my coming to Pelicans Haven to take advantage of you and your mother. That's all it was."

"I don't want to think about it. I'm so happy."

"I'm happy too, Roseanna. You know I fell in love with you the first time I saw you. Do you remember? You came into the stable to see Moses, I was there, and we talked. Then the next morning we sat on the steps of the veranda and talked and I knew I loved you then. You were the woman I wanted."

"How can you say you fell in love with me then? You didn't even know me."

"It didn't matter. I knew you were the most beautiful, sad, wonderful girl I had ever met."

"I love you so much, Jake," said Roseanna as she pressed herself tight against his chest. "I've been blind not to see it."

"Don't doubt that the day I married you I knew exactly what I wanted and it was you."

"I love you more than I knew I was capable, Jake."

"So are you done crying?" asked Jake with a smile.

Roseanna laughed. "I'm silly, and I'm done crying. I'm just glad we're together."

Jake gave Roseanna a gentle kiss. "It is wonderful isn't it, and we can have Josh tear those documents to shreds."

"Yes, yes we can," said Roseanna.

"Much as I would love to spend all day right here with you, we can't. Randy is waiting for lunch; I've kept him waiting for me once today. Don't think I should do it again."

"Oh, I'm so sorry. Yes" said Roseanna as she grabbed her bonnet, "let's go meet Randy."

CHAPTER 7

New Orleans was a booming town once again now that surrender had come, and Roseanna enjoyed revisiting the places she remembered as a young girl and delighted in the new things, but now she was happy to be on the road towards home. She leaned her head against Jake's shoulder and clutched his upper arm with both hands as they moved along in the gig.

"I truly enjoyed seeing the city Jake and want to go back. The shops were full of wonderful things, so many things I could buy for home. I could buy fabric to make clothes for all of us. Mama Teal needs new clothes especially, and I want to surprise her with something new. And Randy, I see why you think so highly of him, I can see why he is your friend. He has wonderful qualities, much the same as you."

Jake smiled at Roseanna and chuckled, "Does this mean you like me?"

"I've liked you from the first moment I saw you," said Roseanna with a smile and then with a serious expression. "Jake, the document Josh had us sign, I want it destroyed."

"It means nothing to me, and if you want it destroyed, we'll let Josh know."

"I want it destroyed."

"An annulment would definitely be out of the question, now," said Jake with a grin.

Roseanna blushed. "You have Mama Teal to thank for that."

"How did Mama Teal get in the middle of this?"

"She pushed me in the right direction and made me see what was as plain as the nose on my face."

"I like Mama Teal more and more every day," quipped Jake.

Roseanna grinned and snuggled closer. "You really should, she is smitten with you, too."

"How it is there doesn't seem to be a father around for Loretta and Simon?" asked Jake.

"I once asked my mother that question, and she told me to mind my own business. When I was older, she told me there were two fathers. Loretta's father was a free man, but she didn't know who Simon's father was. You can see looking at them, Loretta so dark and Simon light-skinned, and a huge man, two fathers, makes sense. I remember Loretta's father, or at least I think I do. She is older than I am, and I remember a man being around when I was small. He stayed in the cabin with Mama Teal and was always with Loretta. He must have been educated; I used to sit with him and Loretta while he read to her. Loretta has quite a few books in her cabin, and my father always gave her books. She's intelligent and can read and write. Simon is about my age or a few years older. I have no recollection of a man who could have been his father. Mama Teal never mentions any man. The plantation has many stories to tell from all the years the Ravennas and others have lived there."

"And there's a source of stories I forgot to mention," blurted Jake. "Richard Philips has a connection to Pelicans Haven. He designed and built Ben and Jane's house."

"What! That's an amazing coincidence," said Roseanna as she looked at Jake in surprise. "What did he tell you about the plantation?'"

"He remembers it well, especially the horses. He said he would watch your father training."

"I don't remember when the house was built. I must have been very young."

"He remembers young boys but no girls."

"My brothers, and of course Andrew. The three of them are all about the same age. I wonder if Andrew will remember him. I can't wait, when will he come?"

"Soon and I invited him to stay with us. He wanted to know if the horses were still here."

Roseanna frowned, "Sadly, no."

"Not now, but we can change that, Roseanna. When you're ready I'll help."

"I know you would, Jake," said Roseanna. "I have to think through what I would need to do."

"How would you start? You have old Moses here. Could he be your start?"

"Moses has excellent bloodlines, but he's not proven. He's never run a race in his life. He wouldn't be of much value except for what he is now, a pet," laughed Roseanna.

"How would you get started if not with Moses?"

"I have all my father's records. He kept complete records of whom he bred to whom and where they were sold. It will take time and searching through the thoroughbred registries and a lot of letter writing to find out how each of them has progressed. Before the war father spent most of his time keeping records and corresponding with his buyers. I would need to find mares, great mares with proven bloodlines, they're the most important and then, of course, the availability of stallions for mating, also with great bloodlines."

"Eleven months to wait for a foal to be born, right?" asked Jake.

"Yes, and so I would need to decide if I would want my own mares, or just find the right foals to train and start building a stable from there. My father would say, after spending almost a year waiting for the birth, and two years working with a foal, that it didn't have the fire to run. It's a gamble with the horses. Not impossible but would take time; years just to get where I would have foals to train. I'll be an old woman before I could build a stable of racers."

Jake threw his head back in a loud laugh. "Roseanna you're just eighteen years old, a long way from being an old woman and every business is a gamble."

"Building a top-notch stable would take a lifetime. My father inherited what he had; he just continued the work others started. Then too, the plantation is in such disrepair since the war, and then there's the stable destroyed by the fire. Too much to think about sometimes, Jake."

"Things can go wrong, and it sounds complicated with a lot of work to be done, but that shouldn't stop you. Think about going ahead, it's important."

"I do think about it, and it is important to me, Jake, very important. I want to do it for my father."

Ben finished with his lunch, hurried back to the overseer's house to see if Simon was ready to tell him what he wanted to know. Simon surprised Ben with his stubbornness. He wasn't weak minded and cowardly but had a streak of something unexpected. Call it what you will, loyalty, faithfulness, devotion, but whatever it was, Simon, in small part, had won Ben's admiration. He envied his brother to have someone in his life who was so devoted. Nathan, who had been his constant companion since he and Ben were boys, bowed, scraped, and tried to please but it was an act out of fear not sincerity, and Ben knew it.

Nathan sat on the porch of the overseer house despondent over having told Ben about Simon's secret. He faced losing his friend and now Ben's anger if he did anything to help Simon. He begged Simon to tell, but he was being stubborn and continued to refuse.

Ben suddenly appeared on the porch and Nathan jumped to his feet. "Mr. Ben, Simon not goin' say where it at so I's let him go now."

"You'll do no such thing," said Ben, with a look of astonishment, "He'll sit there until he talks."

"Miss Roseanna gonna come. She mad 'bout tyin' Simon up, Mr. Ben."

"She's gone to the city with her husband, Nathan. Isn't that what you told me?"

"Yes, I's say that. She comes home lookin' for Simon."

"Let me worry about Roseanna. You stand to gain from this Nathan; don't you want the gold I said I'd give you?"

"Yes, but Mr. Ben, Simon not gonna say."

"He'll talk, you'll see."

Ben had to decide what his next step with Simon should be. He knew the walking stick pressed to Simon's chest had been painful, not excruciating, but painful. The blow to his thigh had been hard, and the injury would show. He needed to be careful and keep his temper under control, he wanted no proof he hit the man.

Ben walked into the house and stood before Simon where he sat tied to the chair. The heat and the smell of Simon's sweat, mixed with the odor of urine in the closed up house was overpowering. Simon's body glistened with sweat, and his clothes were soaked clinging to his skin.

"Simon I've just had me a very fine lunch. You know the little gal works in my kitchen, Cindy is her name, is a fine fisherman," said Ben as he pulled up a chair and sat facing Simon. "This morning she went fishing and caught a fine batch of bass, and she fried those up for Miss Jane and me with a whole mess of hush puppies. I had her fix a plate for Nathan, so he had a fine lunch, too."

This last was a lie; Ben Ravenna had no interest in feeding Nathan. If Nathan had food from Ben's table, the kindhearted cook secreted the leftovers to him.

Simon sat silently averting his eyes as Ben talked. His eyes were puffy from the tears he had shed, and his nose had run mixing snot with the sweat and tears covering his face. "My mama gonna come get me, Mr. Ben?"

"No, Simon. Your mother will never trespass on my property. She wouldn't come here unless I say. Don't wait for her," he said with a negative shake of his head, "she's not coming. Best tell me what I want, and we can be done with this."

"Miss Roseanna she comes," said Simon emphatically.

"She's gone, went to the city. Remember Simon, she's gone."

Simon had no response to this; he hung his head and refused to look at Ben.

"I'm full from my lunch. Might need to take myself a nap so you need to tell me where the gold is hidden or I'll go and get my nap and you can just sit tied to this chair until I return."

Simon did not respond.

Ben took his walking stick and laid it very gently on Simon's thigh. "Where is the gold, Simon," he said, emphasizing each word with a strike of the stick, the blows getting successively harder.

The pain gnawed at Simon, he brought his chin down to his chest a grimace on his face. "Not hit me, Mr. Ben. I's can't say. Mr. James says," said Simon dissolving in blubbering tears and struggling against his bindings.

"Simon you know Mr. James is dead. He got snake bit and died. We put him in the ground. He isn't coming back."

Simon cried loudly, "Gives me water Mr. Ben. Please water!"

Ben's patience was spent, "You want your lunch, you want your mama, you want water," he mocked in a singsong voice. "You give me what I want, and you can have your lunch and water and anything else you want including that fine gold coin I showed you. First, I get what I want! Don't be pigheaded Simon! Make this easy, tell me where it is."

Simon sobbed, "I's can't, Mr. Ben."

Ben watched Simon cry, than in disgust he got up from his chair with such force the chair fell over and clattered to the floor.

Nathan, who had stayed on the porch, heard the crash and cringed with fear at what Ben had done to Simon. He came out of the house and stomped away without a second glance at Nathan. Nathan felt tears prick his eyes. He walked to the door afraid to look, but he peeked in to see if Simon was still alive and in the chair. Simon looked at him as tears streamed down his face and then turned his head away.

Nathan thought of setting him free and then running away. He'd leave the plantation and go north as he always said he would, but he feared Ben Ravenna would come after him and that stopped the idea. Nathan was beside himself with anxiety. He sat on the porch and lowered his head on his crossed arms.

"We're about to find out if Simon and Nathan finished with the fence," said Jake as he guided Moses into the lane of the plantation and the rose garden came into view.

"Looks like they finished."

"That would be Simon's work. He's a good worker and loves the garden. He and my mother would spend hours working there. He knows as much about the care of the roses as she did. Now that the fence is repaired, he'll know exactly what needs to be done with the plants. He takes so much pride in the garden, well, and the horses, too. He'll hear the gig coming and be waiting to unhitch. He always hears me when I come home and is waiting for me."

Jake pulled the gig to the back of the house by the burned stable, but Simon was not there. "He probably went fishing," said Roseanna as she climbed from the gig. "I'll go let Mama Teal know we're home."

"I'll unhitch and take the bags in the house," said Jake.

Jake released Moses from the gig, led him to the pasture, then gathered the bags and took it into the house. He started to mount the stairs with his burden, but stopped and left them the foot of the stair. No more separate bedrooms, he'd wait and have a discussion with Roseanna about which bedroom they would share.

Roseanna came in the back door of the house, her face flushed from the heat. "No one's around, that's unusual."

"Not in the kitchen house or the cabins?"

"Roseanna shook her head, a puzzled frown on her face. " I wonder where they could be. Mama Teal is always around and Loretta, too."

"Any sign of Andrew?"

"No, I didn't see him either."

"Maybe Andrew went to the building site, and they all went with him. Let's have another look, and if we don't find them, I'll ride out there. Maybe a picnic by the river or something," ventured Jake.

"I hope you're right, but Mama Teal knew we would be home by evening. I don't think she would leave, she'd be making our dinner."

A search of the cabins and the main house revealed no one. Roseanna was concerned. "This never happens. At least one of them is always here. I'll walk to Uncle Ben's and see if they know anything."

"I'll go. We don't want any trouble from that quarter."

"We'll both go," said Roseanna.

The two crossed the bridge, knocked at the door, Roseanna's anxiety, and concern mounting.

Nancy answered. "How pleasant to see the newlyweds," she said offering a big smile. "Come in and visit," she said stepping back from the door.

"We can't right now Nancy. We've just come back from the city, and no one is at home. Is Andrew at home or have you seen Mama Teal?"

"I haven't seen Andrew for a couple of days. Isn't he working for you now Jake? Maybe that's where he is. I haven't seen anyone. I'd ask my folks but Mother is napping, and Daddy isn't in the house."

"Have you seen Nathan?"

"No, but you know yourself Roseanna there's nothing unusual there. No one knows where Nathan is half the time, especially if there's work to be done."

"I don't know what to think," said Roseanna turning to Jake.

"I'll ride to the building site. It'll take an hour for the round trip. They'll be here when I get back. Try not to worry Roseanna," said Jake as he hurried to saddle his horse.

"Roseanna you stay with me," said Nancy. "I want to hear about your stay in the city."

"Maybe later, Nancy. Right now I need to go home and see if Mama Teal is there."

"I'll come and help you look. Mama Teal wouldn't just be gone. I'm sure there's a simple explanation why she's not there."

"This is not like her to be gone, or everyone to be gone."

"How are things with you and Jake, Roseanna?" asked Nancy.

Roseanna blushed, and couldn't meet Nancy's gaze. "It's wonderful being with him."

"I was right! I knew this would be a perfect marriage for you," said Nancy, with a happy laugh. "Now if I could just find the same for me!"

"You will, Nancy. I'm sure you will."

"Look!" said Nancy pointing towards the north fields. "There's Mama Teal. I bet she's been up to your parent's graves."

The girls sprinted across the field to meet Mama Teal as she hurried towards them.

"Mama Teal you're bleeding," said Roseanna as they reached the woman. There was blood from a wound on Mama Teal's face.

"It nothin' Miss Roseanna," said Mama Teal as she touched her cheek. "I's scratching it on a tree branch. I's look for Simon, he gone."

"What do you mean, where is he."

"Don't know, child. He gone since early. He and Nathan gone fishin' after the garden fence be done. He not come to eat or nothin'. Loretta lookin' too."

"Is Nathan missing?" asked Nancy.

"Miss Nancy I's can't find him nowhere's."

"They've just wandered off, Mama Teal. Maybe looking for a better place to fish. At the lake maybe," said Nancy.

"Ain't fishin'. Me and Loretta find they fishin' poles, they bucket, and they worms on the bank. We done walked the lake, they not there."

"Could they be with Andrew?" asked Roseanna.

"No. Andrew, he gone early after breakfast. Simon wants go, but Mr. Andrew say not till the fence be done, so they here then and they gone to fish after that. I's scared Miss Roseanna they drown in the creek," said Mama Teal with tears in her eyes.

"No, no, Mama Teal," said Roseanna as she embraced the woman. They're both good swimmers. They're always swimming in the creek and the lake," said Roseanna.

"Maybe this time they not swim so good," said Mama Teal continuing to cry.

"I'm going to go find Daddy," said Nancy. "Maybe he knows something, Nathan could be with him," she said as she turned and ran back towards the house.

"Come on Mama Teal, let's wash your face and see how bad this cut is," said Roseanna as she guided her towards the kitchen house.

"Miss Roseanna I's not done with yous supper. You and Mr. Jake goin' be hungry."

"Mama Teal don't you even worry about Jake and me. Let's get you taken care of and find Simon," said Roseanna as put her arm around Mama Teal and patted her shoulder.

Roseanna took Mama Teal in the kitchen house and sat her at the table. She bathed the cut on her cheek with a cloth. "This is a deep cut we need to put something on it."

"No, Miss Roseanna, leave it be. I's just wantin' find my boy."

"We'll find him. Look, there's Loretta," said Roseanna as she looked out the window.

From the look of concern on Loretta's face, Roseanna could tell she had not found her brother.

"Miss Roseanna you back. What happened to Mama?" said Loretta as she entered the kitchen house and swiped at the sweat on her forehead with her hand.

"It nothin', Loretta. Yous not find yous brother?" said Mama Teal.

"No, Mama. It's Nathan," said Loretta angrily, "he made Simon go somewhere with him, and they just forgot about the time, or they lost, that's all. Your face hurt Mama?"

"No. It be fine. Where we gonna look?"

"I don't think Simon would leave without letting you know, Mama Teal. He's never done that before," said Roseanna.

"Nathan probably made him go," said Loretta.

"I'll saddle Moses and go to the main road east towards the church. I don't know where else to look. Mama Teal, you stay here now and let me look. You can let us know if he comes back."

"I'll come with you Miss Roseanna," said Loretta.

"Stay with your mother, Loretta. She's upset, and we shouldn't leave her alone. I won't be long."

Roseanna hurried towards the pasture for Moses. She skipped the saddle and rode bareback towards the main road. She wasn't sure how far to go. Did it make sense they would be on the road or would they be walking through the trees? She kept thinking Nathan was with Simon, but maybe Nathan was off somewhere on his own, and just Simon was missing. She hoped Jake would come back soon.

Mama Teal said Andrew had gone to the building site alone. Simon didn't know where the site was. Had he gone to look for Andrew and gotten lost?

That made no sense because Mama Teal found both fishing poles on the creek bank. The two had to be together, but where were they?

She rode as far as the church with no sign of them. She stopped at the Reverend River's house to inquire, but he had not seen them around the church or pass by on the road. "I can help you look, Roseanna, if you need me," he said.

"I appreciate that Reverend, but I don't know where to tell you to look. They must be somewhere on the plantation. I'm going back and search again. Jake and Andrew will be searching too. I'll send someone if we don't find them and maybe you could get others to help."

"I will, and I'll be here all evening if you need help," said the Reverend. "Take care, Roseanna."

Roseanna rode back the way she had come searching the woods as best she could from the road. She reached the kitchen house to find Mama Teal and Loretta still waiting.

Nancy came in and said she couldn't find her father, and her mother had not seen Andrew, Simon, or Nathan. "My father is missing," said Nancy, "Now I'm getting scared. Where could they all be?"

"Mama Teal, did you search for them over on my uncle's side of the property?"

"Oh no, Miss Roseanna. Mr. Ben be mad for goin' over his side."

"I'll go. Nancy come with me and help," said Roseanna.

Before they could leave, Jake and Andrew came through the door. "You haven't found him?" asked Jake.

"No, Jake. I'm scared. Mama Teal and Loretta have been looking for him since before lunchtime. Nathan is missing, too. What could have happened? Simon's never gone off like this before," said Roseanna. "Nancy and I are going over to look through the buildings at Ben's."

"Did you talk to Ben?" asked Jake.

"He's not home, Jake, and my mother doesn't know where he is," said Nancy."

"Andrew and I will go. We'll take the horses and look through the woods on the other side of the property, too. He'll turn up. We'll find him."

Jake and Andrew left the kitchen house and trotted towards their horses. "Andrew you start up the north side around the lake, the family burial plot, and the woods. I'll go around to the barn, slave cabins, and the woods on the south side. Where the hell have these two gotten off to," said Jake, his own concern growing.

The riders left, Andrew in one direction and Jake in the other. Andrew slowly followed the path beside the creek, which ran close to the edge of the bank. He looked down at the flowing water hoping he didn't find a body floating there. He then turned his mount and headed into the woods at the top of the property calling Simon's name.

He rode slowly, winding his mount between the trees and avoiding the hanging branches as best he could. It was cool and very quiet in the woods and Andrew could hear the echo of his own voice as he called for Simon. The only sound he heard was the blowing of his horse and an occasionally scurrying through the undergrowth of a squirrel or rabbit. Andrew made his way to the edge of the property then came out of the wood and rode slowly towards the family burial plot.

Jake took the lane out of Pelicans Haven and rode to the west along the main road until he came to a break in the trees. He led his horse through and threaded through the trees calling Simons name. He cleared the trees, entered the plantation on Ben Ravenna's property, and rode through the acres and acres of the fallow cotton fields. In the distance, he saw the slave cabins, and as he approached, he saw a man prone on the ground under the shade of a tree. He recognized Nathan. He quickly rode towards him.

"Nathan," called Jake. "Nathan get up."

Nathan sat up and looked up at Jake astride his horse. He sprang to his feet and began to run. Jake kicked up Sweetie to pursue him, dismounted, and grabbed him by the arm. "Why are you running? Where is Simon?"

"I's not do it, Mr. Jake! It Mr. Ben! He made me," said Nathan frantically as he struggled to pull away from Jake's grasp.

"Where is he, where is Simon?" asked Jake angrily as he tightened his grip on Nathan's arm.

"He in the overseer's house, there," he said pointing and cowering away from Jake. "Mr. Ben made me," he said as he tried to run again.

Jake stepped forward quickly to grab him. "Not so fast," he said as he grabbed the back of Nathan's shirt. He pushed him towards the overseer's house. "What is it you don't want me to see? What's going on in that house? Let's take a look."

Jake kept one hand wadded in Nathan's shirt and the other held tightly on his arm as he forced him ahead of him towards the house. They reached the door; Jake turned the knob and pushed the door open. The heat and smell inside the closed up house rushed out from the dim interior. Jake pushed Nathan in ahead of him. "Simon," he called, "Simon, where are you"?

Simon made a low moaning sound, "Mama, Mama?"

Jake saw Simon sitting in a chair with his head hanging low. He released Nathan and quickly crossed to the chair. He could see Simon was tied, his clothes, and skin soaked with sweat, and there was a strong scent of urine. Jake knelt beside the chair, drew his knife and quickly cut the rope binding Simon's wrist and ankles.

Jake grabbed Simon arm and shook it gently, "Simon, Simon its Jake. Can you hear me?"

"Where MaMa? I's wants MaMa," said Simon as he began to cry.

"Can you stand? Nathan help me get him up," said Jake.

"Owee! Hurts, my leg!" said Simon gritting his teeth and trying to stand.

"I's not doin' that, Mr. Jake. I's not hurt Simon, just doin what Mr. Ben say."

"Shut up Nathan, help lift him."

Simon was a big man and the strength of Jake and Nathan together could hardly lift his weight. "Just help him get his balance, Nathan. Give him a minute to stand and get his balance."

"Nathan yous tells Mr. Ben. Why yous tells?" said Simon as he looked at Nathan. "Yous not my friend no more."

"No, Simon. I's you friend. Mr. Ben makes me."

"What did you tell Ben, Nathan?" said Jake

"No," thundered Simon in a loud but quivering voice.

Jake looked from Simon to Nathan. "It's alright Simon," Nathan's not going to tell me anything."

"I's wants water, Mr. Jake," said Simon

"Nathan, go get water, and you come right back."

Simon was standing, but with support from Jake. Jake looked down and saw ligature marks on his wrist from where he had been tied. They weren't bleeding, but the skin was inflamed and raw. "Come on Simon; let's get you home so your mama can tend to you."

"I's hungry, Mr. Jake. Mr. Ben not gets me lunch."

"Your mama's got your lunch, Simon. She'll take care of you like she always does," said Jake as he walked with Simon out the door and into the sunlight and fresh air.

"Here Simon, sit down," said Jake indicating a chair when he realized Simon was unsteady on his feet. "We'll wait for Nathan to bring you water and then get you home. Does your leg hurt?"

"Mr. Ben hits me wiff his stick."

Nathan scurried around the corner of the porch carrying a bucket of water. Simon grabbed the bucket, brought it to his lips, and drank nosily tipping the bucket so water flowed sloppily down his shirtfront.

"Nathan fetch my horse, Simon can ride him home."

"Yes Sir, Mr. Jake."

Ben was returning to the overseer's house hoping Simon was now ready to talk. He came up short hearing Jake Sinclair's voice. He moved quickly behind the nearest slave cabin out of site peeking around the corner to see what Sinclair was doing. He could see Simon and Jake on the porch, Simon sitting and drinking from a bucket and Jake standing at his side. Nathan was leading Jake's horse towards the two.

He cursed under his breath. Why didn't Sinclair stay in the city where he belonged? Ben was prepared to deal with Roseanna; he felt no threat from her, but Sinclair's interference was different. Damn Simon for not telling him where the gold was. This whole business would be over with Sinclair none the wiser. He didn't want Sinclair to see him; he turned and quickly retraced his steps towards home. He needed to keep out of Sinclair's reach.

"Jane," he called loudly as he entered the house. "I'm going into the city."

"At this hour Ben? But why? It's late in the day to start. Can't it wait until morning?" she questioned as she came out of her sitting room and met Ben in the hallway.

"I've been putting it off. I need to see Lawrence and the banker. I can be at the bank before it closes and join Winston for dinner. I need to get things I've been neglecting taken care of."

"Then you'll be back tonight?"

"No, not if dinner with Winston goes late. I may stay over and be back in the morning."

"Well, if you feel it's necessary, I'll pack your bag."

"My toilet things and a clean shirt that's all I'll need. I'll saddle my horse if you bring my bag to the veranda that would save me time," said Ben as he turned to leave the house.

Jane hurried towards her husband, "Ben why are you rushing. Can't this wait?"

"I'm taking care of things while they're on my mind. Stop pestering me, do as I ask," said Ben testily turning to face his wife.

"But I just don't understand the urgency."

"Let me worry about the urgency. Do as I tell you and pack my things," said Ben as he stormed from the house to saddle his horse.

Jane watched him go and then quickly turned to the task. She didn't understand why this trip to the city was so important, but Ben never divulged any of his plans to her. His moods since the war were so hard to tolerate. It's best to let him do what he wanted rather than be a victim of his anger. No one tolerated Ben, Nancy avoided him since Roseanna's marriage, and he and Andrew were at each other's throats while she stood helplessly by trying to keep the peace with them all. The war, thought Jane, all because of the war.

CHAPTER 8

Simon's emotions were under control, his tears were dry but trails were left down his cheeks. He drank his fill from the bucket and complained his leg hurt. "Mr. Ben hits me wiff his stick, Mr. Jake, yous can't hits free man like me."

"He was wrong to hit you, Simon. Can you walk now or do you want to ride Sweetie?"

"Her name Sweetie? She be Sweetie?" asked Simon

Jack chuckled, "My mother named her Sweetie. She didn't exactly name her that, she just always called her Sweetie and the name just stuck. Unusual name for a man's horse."

"She not sweet, she not lets me scratches her ear."

"She wouldn't come when I first got her. She loved my mother. My mother would call her and say, "here Sweetie," and she would trot over to her and ignore me. Mother called her Sweetie, and she seemed to respond to the name so, I called her that too."

"Where yous mama?" asked Simon.

"My mama is in New York. Simon, your mama's waiting for you. Are you ready to go?"

"I's needs my mama," said Simon. As he remembered his circumstances, tears gathered in his eyes.

"You can hang on to me, or you can ride Sweetie," said Jake.

Simon shook his head no at the suggestion he ride the horse and began walking towards home.

"Nathan you come along and bring Sweetie," said Jake.

Jake walked by Simon's side to provide support if needed. Their progress was slow. Simon limped as they walked, but in a short time, they were at the kitchen house.

Mama Teal watched their progress and ran to Simon as they drew close. She wrapped her arms around him and pulled him close. "There my boy, Simon. Where yous been Simon? We look for yous. We scared."

Simon latched on to his mother nearly knocking her off her feet. He put his head on her shoulder and wailed as Mama Teal shushed him. Loretta threw her arms around her mother and brother crying as well.

Roseanna relieved that Simon had been found, stood with Jake looking at the trio unsure of what to do. At last, Simon seemed under control and released his mother.

Mama Teal wrinkled her nose as she looked her son up and down. "Simon yous dirty, and yous smell. We gonna gets yous clean up."

"I's want my lunch, Mama," said Simon.

"Yes, we gets yous food," said Mama Teal. "Come on now. Loretta gets to the kitchen and start supper."

"Mama Teal don't worry about that now," said Roseanna.

"Loretta knows what to do. She a good girl," said Mama Teal. "Miss Roseanna can yous help me with Simon?"

Roseanna didn't hesitate as she moved forward to help but she glanced at Jake wanting to ask him what had happened to Simon. "Of course I can," she said to Mama Teal.

"Miss Roseanna," said Simon, "I unhitch the Gig?"

"Mr. Jake took care of it, Simon."

Nothing was said as Mama Teal, and Roseanna slowly walked with Simon to Mama Teal's cabin, entered, and closed the door.

Jake had fetched water so Simon could be bathed and then stayed in the yard close to Mama Teal's cabin to be on hand if he was needed.

Occasionally the door to the cabin would open, and Roseanna would come out to attend to some errand necessary for Simon's care. She would tell Jake that Simon was settling down but was not talking about what had happened, only complaining about his leg hurting and wanting food. Mama Teal came out, went to the kitchen house, and returned with a platter of food for Simon.

Nathan sat with his head resting on drawn up knees across the yard. He raised his head whenever the cabin door opened hoping, Jake thought, for Simon to emerge. Jake felt pity for him and could see he was remorseful. Ben Ravenna manipulated Nathan and Nathan was afraid of the man, the mistreatment of Simon was wrong, but Nathan had been powerless to stop it, but was still at fault.

Andrew failing to find Simon after searching the grounds around the family burial plot and riding the boundary of the lake twice retraced his route and again searched the creek then returned to the kitchen house.

Loretta met him as he came through the door. "He's found, Andrew. Jake found him."

"Where, where was he?"

"He was at the overseer's house on Ben's property."

"Why was he there? He never goes on Ben's property. Why didn't he just come home?"

"I haven't gotten the whole story. We'll have to wait and see what Mama says. He was mumbling about Ben not letting him have lunch and hitting him with his walking stick. None of it made sense. But the important thing is he's been found. He's dirty and tired and said his leg hurt, and he's hungry but nothing more."

"Was Nathan with him?" asked Andrew.

"Yes, he's out in the yard," said Loretta.

"Where is Simon now?"

"Mama took him to wash him up and change his clothes because he soiled himself and he's afraid Mama will be mad. Jake and Roseanna went to help. We'll have to wait and see what they can find out.

'Where is Nathan?"

"Jake told him not to go anywhere, he's in the yard."

Andrew hastily left the kitchen house and went to find Nathan. Loretta followed.

"Nathan what happened to you and Simon. Why was Simon at Ben's?" demanded Andrew.

"Mr. Andrew, I's just doing what Mr. Ben say when I's tie Simon to the chair. Didn't want to but Simon wouldn't tell Mr. Ben what he wanted to know."

"You tied him to a chair?" exclaimed Andrew.

"Mr. Ben makes me."

"What did Ben want to know?"

"Can't say 'cause Simon he not let me say."

"You're not making sense. What are you not suppose to say?"

"Can't tell you, Mr. Andrew 'cause Simon wants it a secret."

"How did Simon hurt his leg?"

"Mr. Ben. He hit Simon."

"That no good man! He's not going to get away with this," exclaimed Andrew his hands clenched. He turned and angrily ran towards the bridge crossing the creek.

"Andrew wait! Don't go!" cried Loretta as she grabbed Andrew's arm to restrain him. "He's safe, Simon's safe. Please, Andrew, don't!"

Andrew pulled away. "Ben needs to answer for this!"

"Please Andrew," begged Loretta. "Let the authorities handle it. Go wherever you need to and report him."

"Report him for what? Mistreating a black man? Isn't that accepted in the South? Do you think anyone is going to come to the defense of a black man? Do you think anyone will care?" He jerked his arm free of Loretta's grip and continued quickly towards Ben Ravenna's house.

Loretta caught his arm again. "This isn't about Simon. It's about how much you resent and hate Ben Ravenna. Simon's fine. He'll forget all about this. He just wanted his lunch, and that's all he cares about. He'll eat and get cleaned up, and this will be over for him. We need to find out exactly what happened before you storm off and make things worse for yourself with Ben."

"I'm not letting him get away with mistreating your brother. Don't you care about your brother? Don't you want me to care about your brother?" said Andrew angrily.

"Of course I do. But he isn't hurt, Andrew. Let it go, I'm more afraid for you," pleaded Loretta.

"What could happen to me? Do you think I'm afraid of Ben Ravenna? Someone has to stand up to him. He needs to know there are consequences."

Andrew ran towards Ben Ravenna's home again. He stormed through the door yelling "Ben you bastard where are you? Ben Ravenna, show yourself you coward!"

"Andrew, for heaven's sake what's wrong with you?" said Jane running to intercepted her son as he went into Ben's office. "Stop yelling, Ben isn't here and watch your language in this house."

"Where is he? Where is Ben?" stormed Andrew ignoring his mother admonition.

"He's gone into the city. What's this about?" asked Jane in confusion.

"It's about Ben mistreating Simon, he hit him with his walking stick and injured his leg and tied him to a chair."

"Why would he do that Andrew?"

"That's exactly what I want to ask him, why?"

"Why are you listening to what a simple-minded black man said about Ben? Andrew this is nonsense. Besides, I just told you Ben isn't even here. He's gone to the city."

"When, when did he go?" asked Andrew excitedly.

"He hasn't been home, Andrew," said Nancy who had come to see what the commotion with Andrew and her mother was about. "I looked for him earlier and couldn't find him."

"Did you look in the overseer's house, Nancy? Because that's where this whole thing took place. When did he leave, Mother?"

"I don't know. I wasn't watching the time. Why don't you tell me what happened instead of storming in here and accusing Ben of some ridiculous nonsense," demanded Jane?.

"I just told you what he's done," responded Andrew.

"Andrew calm down. Explain this to me instead of making a scene," said Jane calmly as she walked towards Andrew and took hold of his arms.

Andrew shook off his mother's grasp and moved away from her. "There's only one thing on this plantation that upsets me, Ben Ravenna."

"You're being very harsh to a man who isn't even here to defend himself."

"Harsh? Did you hear what I said he's done?"

Jane was exasperated with Andrew. "Andrew I don't want you here anymore. This anger between you and Ben has to stop. In your eyes, Ben could never do anything that had merit. I don't want to hear any more of this."

"You would defend him to the death wouldn't you Mother. See what he can do? Now he's driven a wedge between you and me. You, who used to defend me to him, now take his side."

"I'm not taking sides, Andrew, but you need to see the truth about yourself. You have this hatred for Ben. He tries to keep the roof over our heads and food on the table. Is that so wrong?"

"It is when you take the roof and food from someone else and beat a defenseless black man. What's happened to your sympathy for the blacks? You used to care."

"It doesn't matter what color Simon is, he is simple-minded. Any accusations that come from him would be suspect."

"Someone tied him to a chair in the overseer's house. Jake Sinclair found him. Are you going to question Jake too?" asked Andrew pointedly.

"I don't doubt he was tied to a chair. Why blame Ben? Where's the proof? Taking the word of a simple-minded black man."

Andrew stopped pacing and stood still with his hand covering his eyes and his head bent. "I can't believe you don't see the Ben Ravenna I see, Mother. You're right; I can't see any good he has done. I no longer want to live in the same house with the cruel bastard. I guess you have no other choice than to stand by Ben, but I do," said Andrew as he turned and strode hurriedly from the room.

Nancy followed Andrew and tried to talk to him, but he dismissed her attempts with a wave of his hand and hurried away.

Jane now alone in Ben's office looked after Andrew with tears in her eyes. Ben didn't have business in the city; he left because of what he had done to Simon. He'd done precisely what Andrew accused him of doing. Andrew's disgust was now driven to new heights but to agree would certainly have made the situation worst. He needed to leave the plantation before he did something he would regret. She would leave, but she had to stay, she had no choice but to stand by Ben. She had created the whole situation with her decision to marry him.

Her good intentions for Andrew to take him out of London and away from the gossip about his father's suicide had been for her own escape from that very same gossip. She had been wrong about Ben stepping in as a father to Andrew. Ben married her for her money. Andrew had never been part of what he wanted.

She and Ben had gotten what they each wanted, and Andrew was suffering the consequences. Who would take her in if she turned against Ben? She needed to be here for her daughter. She had no family and no place to go. The Moorcroft name came to her head, the only family she had. Jane released a bitter strangled laugh, which turned into a sob. They would sooner see her dead than come to her aid. They wouldn't even respond to the letters she had written. What chance did she hope to have from them? Now she was losing the most precious thing she had in the entire world, her son, and all because of Ben Ravenna. Jane collapsed in the nearest chair, covered her face with her hands, and cried in earnest.

Roseanna came out of the cabin and quietly closed the door. "This is so strange, Jake. Simon isn't even talking about what happened, just talking to his mother and me as if he would any other time. It's as if he has blocked the whole thing from his memory. He keeps telling Mama Teal he's sorry he soiled himself and promising he won't do it again, then saying he's hungry, but he didn't catch any fish for his mother to fry."

"Perhaps he just needs time for it to settle in his mind," said Jake. "After some rest and food maybe he'll start talking then. That's essentially what he did, though, when I was walking with him when we came home. Nathan tried to tell me what had happened but Simon yelled at him and told him not to tell me. He just rambled on about everything except what happened."

"Do you think this whole thing affected his mind?" asked Roseanna.

"There's no way to tell, Roseanna. Maybe the doctor should come to look at him."

"Yes, I suggested that but Simon said he didn't want a doctor and Mama Teal agreed with him."

"It can be done later. We'll give it some time."

"That's best I suppose but I going to go against their wishes if I think the doctor should be called. He's having a bath now. I'm going to go and see about dinner for everyone. We're going to be hungry," said Roseanna.

"I'll tend to the horses, they need food and water, then come in and help you as best as I can," said Jake," but my cooking skills are not very extensive," he said with a smile for Roseanna trying to cheer her up. He gave her a quick hug and then sprinted towards the pasture.

Roseanna and Loretta busied themselves in the kitchen all the while watching for Mama Teal to come out of her cabin needing more help with Simon. The door to the kitchen house swung open, and Jake came in followed by Andrew.

"Jake we can't let this go unanswered," said Andrew. "I've been to look for Ben, and he isn't at home. Mother said he's gone to the city. Rather convenient if you ask me."

"We'll deal with it Andrew, but now our concern has to be Simon. Let's get the full story before we go off half-cocked," said Jake.

"I don't need to hear any more to know Ben needs to be dealt with," said Andrew.

Jake was going to reply to Andrew, but at that moment, Mama Teal came into the kitchen house. Everyone paused and turned to her.

"Simon be fine," she said with a smile. "He clean and happy like he always be. He gots a big place on his thigh that be sore. I's rub some grease then wrap it wiff a rag. He good now. Miss Roseanna he say he want you. Don't know why, but he say just Miss Roseanna."

Roseanna dried her hands and hurried to Mama Teal's cabin. She hesitated, and then knocked on the door. Simon responded to her knock, and she quietly opened the door and stepped in. The cabin was in semi-darkness as dusk had fallen. An oil lamp turned low barely dispelled the gloom. She could see Simon sitting on the edge of the bed, one her mother had given to Mama Teal years ago. Simon was almost invisible in the weak light. He had on a bright white nightshirt that glowed against the colors of a patchwork quilt covering the bed.

"Hello, Simon," said Roseanna. "How are you feeling?"

"I's good Miss Roseanna."

"Can I sit down?" asked Roseanna indicating a chair.

Simon jumped to his feet, lifted the chair, and moved it closer to the bed, then smiled at Roseanna and sat back on the bed.

"Your mama said you wanted to talk to me."

"Is I bad Miss Roseanna?"

"Simon no, of course not," said Roseanna her brow knit in concern.

"Yous not mad at Simon 'cause I not tell something."

"I'm not mad at anyone Simon. What did you not tell?"

"Mr. Ben say I's need to tell him, but Mr. James and Miss Annabel say no. Never, never tell Mr. Ben," said Simon shaking his head hard to emphasize what he had been told.

"What were you not to tell Mr. Ben, Simon?"

"Mr. James dead, Miss. Annabel. They both in the ground. That the truths?"

"Yes, Simon. You were there when they were buried. You remember don't you?"

"Mr. Edward and Mr. John they not in the ground."

"They are Simon, just not here at Pelicans Haven."

"Where they at?"

"Edward died in the war and is in the ground in Ohio. John died in the war too, but no one knows where he is buried, or in the ground."

"What's Ohio?"

"It's a state up north. We live in a state called Louisiana. There is a state called Ohio, too."

"They gone, they dead? Yous sure Miss Roseanna?"

"Oh, Simon, I wish it wasn't true, but I am sure."

Simon hung his head and stared at his hands lying in his lap. He looked up at Roseanna with tears in his eyes. "I's don't know they dead Miss Roseanna. They be here wiff they daddy and mama if they dead in the ground wiff them."

"Yes, they should be but sometimes things happen that don't seem right, and we can't do anything about. This is one of those times, Simon."

"I's tell you the secret Miss Roseanna 'cause they not gonna be here. Miss Annabel and Mr. James say to tell them but them not coming home."

"No. That's sad, Simon, but they won't be home."

Simon paused considering his next remarks. "Me and Mr. James and Miss Annabel buried gold in the rose garden. Mr. James say tells Mr. John and Mr. Edward where it be. Mr. Ben wanted me to tell him but yous the one I needs to tell if no one coming home. That the right thing to do?"

Shivers run up Roseanna's back, and she gasped at the words hardly believing what he had said. She finally found her voice, "Simon, that is the right thing to do." Tears came to her eyes, "you are a wonderful and trustworthy person. You are so brave to keep this secret and not to tell anyone."

"I is?"

"Yes, Simon. By far the bravest person I know. Mr. James and Miss Annabel would be so proud of you."

"I's get the shovel, and we go gets it now?"

"No, Simon. We'll go tomorrow or when you're feeling better. You need to rest tonight."

"I's do the right thing, Miss Roseanna?"

"Yes, Simon you did exactly the right thing."

"Yous not mad at Simon and yous my friend?"

"Friends don't get mad at each other, and I am your friend."

"Nathan my friend and I's mad wiff him."

"Maybe you and Nathan can talk and will make things better, and you can still be friends."

"Can we Miss Roseanna?"

"You can try Simon, but it's up to you if you want Nathan to be your friend."

"If Nathan not my friend who will fish with me?"

"Well, I know how you like to fish, and I know you like to fish with Nathan. Maybe you and Nathan should be friends again. You need to decide."

"Mr. Ben never be my friend."

"I'm sorry for what Mr. Ben did, Simon. It was so wrong, but I'm proud of you. You didn't give Mr. Ben what he wanted."

Roseanna got up from her chair, walked to the bed, and gave Simon a hug. "Everything will be fine tomorrow Simon. I want you to be the same Simon who has always been my friend and try to forget what happened to you. You should rest now. Do you want anything before I leave?"

"No, Miss Roseanna."

"Then goodnight, Simon."

Jake was close to the cabin door as Roseanna came out. She looked at Jake with tears in her eyes. "This is my fault. This wouldn't have happened if I had just thought about what I was doing."

"What do you mean?" asked Jake.

"When the question of the gold first came up, and I was spending so much time looking for it and finally asked Mama Teal to help and then Andrew. We took special care to not let Simon know what we were doing because we were afraid he would accidentally say something to Ben, Nathan or someone else. He loves to talk to people and sometimes doesn't realize what he says is inappropriate or not to be said at all. In the beginning, we didn't want Ben to know we were looking for the gold. All this time Simon was the only one who knew where it was. If I had only talked to him, he might have told me, it would have been found. I feel terrible for what he's gone through. How do I make it up to him Jake?"

"That's what this was about today, the gold, and Simon knew all along where it was?" asked Jake incredulously.

"Yes. Simon helped my parents bury it, and my parents told him never to tell Ben and to just tell my brothers."

"So he told you?"

"Yes. It's buried in the rose garden."

"What! Right there in the open in the front of the house?" said Jake gesturing in disbelief. "All this time that's where it was? But that's years ago, Roseanna."

"Yes. Simon thought that because John and Edward weren't buried in the family plot, they weren't dead. Once we talked about it and I explained they were buried somewhere else and he understood they were dead he wanted to tell me the secret of where it was."

"You had no way of knowing. Don't blame yourself. Even his mother kept the search secret from him. I'm flabbergasted," said Jake with a shake of his head. "It's buried right in the front of the house," he said in wonder gesturing in the direction of the garden.

"I can't tell you how many times my mother wanted me out there working in that garden. I wonder if she would have eventually told me the gold was there. She and Simon were out there all the time, but I couldn't be bothered. Simon is always so protective of the garden because occasionally I would ask Nathan to help me but Simon immediately said no he would do the chore himself."

"He was working hard to keep the secret," said Jake. "To bury that much gold would have been quite a task. Do you remember any time when both your mother and father were working in the garden?"

"I can't recall any time," said Roseanna wrinkling her forehead. "No, wait, I do remember my father digging to put the picket fence around the garden. He would have been digging to put in the post. That probably didn't have a thing to do with the gold."

"When was it, do you remember?"

"The boys had left by then I think, so after the start of the war. I don't remember the exact time."

"Maybe putting up the fence was a ruse to divert attention from what he was really doing. If your parents were concerned about Ben, the fence could have been the story they gave him. It would have been an excellent decoy to keep the Union Soldiers from finding it, too. People all over the South were burying their valuables to keep them from the Union Soldiers. Who would think to dig up a fence to look for valuables? Clever man your father," said Jake amazed at the simplicity of the idea and hardly hearing what Roseanna was saying in his wonderment about the hiding place. "Can't believe it, who would think to dig up a fence to look for gold or valuables?" repeated Jake as he marveled at the idea.

"I do remember the fence going in. Why didn't my mother tell me, Jake?"

Jake turned his attention back to what Roseanna was saying. "She didn't see the need, Roseanna. She was concerned about her sons not coming home, but she had no reason to believe your father wouldn't return. She didn't know he would be snake bitten and die. You must have been very young when they buried it. Not more than twelve or thirteen."

"Yes, of course, that would be right." Roseanna chuckled, "Simon wanted to get a shovel and go dig it up right away. I told him we would wait."

"This changes everything for you, do you realize? Now you could raise the horses."

"I hadn't thought about it, Jake. I'm still so overwhelmed with Simon. He is quite the man, isn't he? I mean who would have thought he could keep that secret," said Roseanna in wonder "My parents trusted him to stay silent. What a blessing to have someone that loyal."

"We still need to deal with Ben. Andrew is determined to see him pay for doing this to Simon."

"But what should be done, Jake?"

"I don't know what can be done. I'm more concerned how to keep Andrew from doing something he will regret."

CHAPTER 9

Jake blindly reached for Roseanna when he woke in the morning, but her side of the bed was empty. He lay in bed and gazed at the room. Gauzy ruffled curtains, pink flowered wallpaper, prints, and paintings of horses and riders on the walls, hats on hooks with ribbon streamers. A grouping of dolls adorned the bureau their faces painted with exaggerated eyes and bright rosy cheeks. They wore stiff satin dresses and large matching bonnets. Roseanna told Jake the night before the room had been hers since she was a little girl.

"We'll change to a different room Jake, and decorate with something that pleases you. This house has other bedrooms, you chose. It doesn't matter to me except whichever one you choose I agree it will be our room together."

"I insist on that. I want you with me. This one could be ours, but maybe different furnishings would be more, uh, pleasing to my taste."

Roseanna laughed as she cuddled close to Jake. "Are you saying you don't like my doll collection?"

"They're very nice but…" said Jake with a smile, "the room your father used gives a nice view of the pastures and the creek and is on the north side so will be cooler in the summer, but colder in the winter," he added.

"Then maybe a summer room and a winter room would suit you," suggested Roseanna.

"Or we could fill the rooms with other people," said Jake.

Roseanna looked at him puzzled, "What other people?"

"Children, Roseanna. You do want children, don't you? We've never talked about children. In fact, the circumstances under which we were married we never talked about a lot of things," said Jake thoughtfully.

Roseanna sat up and looked at Jake. "Of course I want children. It would be wonderful to see a little Jake running around. How many shall we have?"

"How many are you are willing to give me? I'm not getting any younger, so I should start thinking about that."

Roseanna rubbed her hands across Jake's chest and laid her head close to his heart. "I think there's plenty of time for you to father children. Mama Teal would be beside herself if we had a baby. She loves little ones. She was upset when Loretta lost her baby."

"Then we'd better work on making Mama Teal happy," said Jake as he gathered his wife in his arms.

Now, as Jake rolled out of bed, he thought about all that had happened with Simon and the discovery of the gold. First, he would deal with Ben Ravenna, and yes, Andrew, who was heading for trouble with his hatred for Ben.

Jake agreed with Andrew that going to the authorities would be a waste of time. They would minimize what had happened to Simon. They would listen but do nothing. The Negros were free, and the government was making overtures to them about how they should be treated and compensated for the years they were held in bondage, but that was the federal government. Locally the government was fighting the Negro's freedom by passing laws preventing them from gaining real freedom. It would take time to change attitudes about the Negros; resentment of any additional interference from the federal government would be unwelcomed by the locals.

Dressed and ready for the day, Jake left the house by the front door rather than go to the kitchen house where he was sure he would find Rosanna huddled with Simon being sure he had recovered from his trauma of the day before.

 He crossed the bridge and knocked at the door of Ben Ravenna's house, Cindy, the young Negro girl answered. Jake announced himself and asked for Ben. He was asked him to wait as the girl disappeared into the interior of the house.

Soon the door opened, and Cindy informed Jake that Mr. Ravenna was not at home, but Mrs. Ravenna asked would he come and speak to her.

Jake hesitated as he had nothing to say to Ben's wife, but out of politeness, he followed the girl to the dining room where Jane Ravenna waited. As he walked through the house, he admired the architecture with its soaring ceilings and marble floors in the entryway.

Jane rose as Jake came into the room. Her breakfast was on the table untouched. "Mr. Sinclair, good morning and thank you for coming to speak with me."

"Happy to oblige. I'm not sure we have anything to say to each other Mrs. Ravenna," said Jake.

"Perhaps not, but I do want to let you know I am aware of the incident with Simon. I had nothing to do with it and don't want you to think I had. I don't want to know any more of the details. I've been told by Andrew it was dreadful." Jane shook her head.

"That's why I'm here, I've come to speak to your husband, but I understand he isn't at home."

"No, he didn't return from the city last night."

"Oh?" said Jake.

"He told me his meetings might go into the night and he might stay over. My husband is not what I want to discuss. I want to talk about Andrew. Please, Mr. Sinclair, have a seat and coffee. I promise not to take up to much of your time."

Jake watched as his coffee was poured and the sugar and cream moved within arm's reach.

"You can call me Jake," he said. "We're not exactly strangers, and in fact related," he said with a smile as he stirred his coffee.

"I would like that," said Jane, "please return the favor and call me Jane. I want to thank you for giving Andrew a position with your company. He's excited to have the opportunity and quite capable, he'll be able to do any work you give him. He won't be happy I'm speaking to you; by the way. I would appreciate your discretion in keeping our conversation between the two of us.

To be frank, I have nowhere else to turn."

Jake gave a nod of his head as he took a sip of the coffee. "Tell me how I can help you."

Jane pushed her breakfast dishes aside and took a deep breath. "This is difficult, Jake, but you're aware of the tension between Andrew and Ben."

Jake nodded in agreement.

"I have no control over either of them, especially Ben. He is a different man from the man I married, especially since the war. I suppose I'm different as well," she said and then paused to reflect on what her next words would be. "Andrew is beginning to frighten me with his outburst and feelings towards Ben. I'm frankly concerned about where it will end. I was hoping I could convince you to somehow keep Andrew permanently at the site where you are building your business."

"There's no housing for anyone on the property."

"I assumed that, but I know this part of the country well. My daughter Nancy and Andrew and I picnicked quite frequently at a spot close to your site when the children were younger," said Jane smiling at the memory. "It was a favorite spot for others, too. It was so cool there on the banks of the river. Andrew loved roaming through the woods and swimming in the shallows, and Nancy is a gifted artist and spent hours sketching and painting wildflowers and insects while I sat in the shade under an umbrella with a novel.

"Andrew was very excited the first time he was there after you hired him. He told me about a tree he carved his initials years ago, and he found the tree. There's a house close to the site, possibly even adjoining your property. It sits abandoned and has for some time. I want Andrew to live in that house, so he is away from Ben."

"And how is it you would have Andrew move into the house?"

"With your help, I could rent the house, and you could tell Andrew you had rented it for his use and he needed to spend his time there to be closer to your project."

Jake mulled this over before he spoke. "There will be equipment and material there that needs to be watched so it isn't pilfered. I will need a watchman to keep an eye on things. Andrew though may not want to be that person. It would be convenient for him as he is to supervise the labor that will be clearing the property and would mean his time traveling to, and from the plantation would be less. Of course, there is also…," Jake paused.

"Loretta?" said Jane.

Jake raised his eyebrows in surprise at Jane's statement but then nodded in agreement.

"I'm aware of their relationship and the baby she lost. I led him to believe I'm opposed to Loretta, but in fact, I'm not. Ben is violently opposed to relationships between black and whites. We need not go into what the laws state. I let Andrew believe I was opposed in feeble attempt to dissuade him and to keep the knowledge from Ben. I was unsuccessful at changing Andrew's mind or feelings when it comes to Loretta. Would you consider my proposal?"

"I'll discuss it with my partner and give it some thought."

"Thank you. I love my son with all my heart. His life has not been easy having lost his father at an early age, and in truth, he and Ben were never close, no true signs of affection or bonding since Ben and I were married. That's my fault, but I won't bore you with the details because they aren't important. Since the war ended and Andrew returned home, the tension between them has intensified. Jane covered her mouth with her hand, drew a handkerchief from the sleeve of her dress, and dabbed at her eyes. "Forgive me. I will try to keep my emotions under control."

"Take your time."

"If you're not aware, Andrew's father, Malcolm Moorcroft, comes from a very wealthy family and as far as I know Andrew is the only Moorcroft grandchild even though my husband had two brothers, twin as it were. I have written to them multiple times without my husband's knowledge asking them to finance Andrew's return to London. They have ignored my request, not due to any fault of Andrew's but rather of mine. Ben has never consented to help

Andrew, but he wants to return to London, probably not for himself but for Loretta. Attitudes and laws regarding blacks and whites are different."

"Might I ask why your husband would not want Andrew to have his uncle's support?"

"Ben holds a grudge towards the Moorcroft brothers. I would be begging as he puts it. He feels my first husband's brothers treated me rather shabbily. That's the reason he gives, and I've never questioned him because he gets angry the moment I mention their name. Could we just leave it at that? I'd rather not air anything further, Jake. It's ancient history and really has no place in the conversation we have today."

"Of course. This certainly is taking a toll on you. I can't promise to help, but I will talk to Andrew without mentioning our conversation. Perhaps I can get him to see reason where Ben is concerned for his own good."

"I understand you can't promise. I'm desperate to protect my son from himself and perhaps hearing a warning from you would help. He thinks highly of you and would listen."

"There's still the business about Simon. There has to be a conversation with your husband about Simon's treatment."

"I know, and I understand. What Ben did was wrong, but I have no influence over him. He is my husband, and I don't wish to speak ill of him if I haven't all ready. Ben isn't my concern. It's my son."

The young Negro girl came to the door of the dining room and stood to wait for Jane to acknowledge her. "What is it, Cindy?"

"A man brung a letter. He says he needs an answer."

Jane held out her hand and took the envelope, sliced the flap opened with a knife and read the contents. "Tell him to wait, Cindy. I will be with him shortly."

Jane lay the letter aside. "Your confrontation with my husband will have to wait. His business in the city will take longer than he expected and he is asking me to send additional clothes for him. He will contact me later to let me know when he will return home."

Jane rose from her chair, and Jake followed. She stopped and turned to face Jake, "Thank you for hearing me out. I'll understand if there is nothing you can do. I had to try."

"I'll give it my consideration and speak with Andrew. If I may change the subject, the architect we hired to design our new building is Richard Philips. I thought you might like to know."

Jane threw her hands to her cheeks, a look of delight on her face. "Richard. Oh my goodness! A name I haven't heard in a long time. This house is a masterpiece thanks to him. He is a wonderful person as well as an excellent architect. Will he be visiting the plantation at any time? I would love to renew acquaintances."

"He will, actually, in the very near future. He mentioned you and your home, and I will make sure you get an opportunity to renew your friendship."

Jane impulsively reached and gave Jake a quick hug. "It would be delightful to see him again. Thank you, Jake, for listening to the pleadings of a mother."

"My pleasure. I hope I can help," said Jake.

Roseanna left the kitchen house searching for Jake. Simon had spent a restful night suffering no ill effects from the incident the previous day. Mama Teal made him breakfast, and he was happily eating until Roseanna came into the room. Seeing her, he immediately wanted to get a shovel and dig up the gold. Roseanna restrained him by asking him to wait until Jake could help.

She found Jake in the yard gazing at the rose garden. "Good morning," she said receiving his embrace and a morning kiss. "You've been to Ben's?"

"Yes, but he stayed in the city last night. A note came telling Jane business in the city would detain him. I think he's staying out of sight to avoid being confronted."

"I feel sorry for Aunt Jane. She's caught in the middle."

Jake nodded in agreement. "She's concerned about Andrew's attitude towards Ben, and I think she should be."

"I had the same conversation with Loretta. Andrew is upset at what happened to Simon."

"The relationship between Ben and Andrew was it ever good?" queried Jake.

"From my conversations with Andrew, no. Since the war, it is much worse. You're aware that Andrew deserted during the war. That was difficult for Ben to accept and strained their relationship further."

"Desertion wasn't unheard of during the war, men on both sides were guilty of leaving, and some were even executed for it. Many firmly stated it wasn't their war and they went home. Hard to live down and maybe to live with too if they lived to tell about it."

"Some men in Andrews's unit stopped at the plantation on their way home and told me the story of what happened with Andrew. Their accounts were very upsetting. He avoided all of us except Loretta. He found solace talking to her. That's how their relationship started."

"Jane is concerned enough about Andrew to want to discuss it with me. She feels there is nowhere else to turn and I could help somehow because Andrew works for me."

"What can you do?" questioned Roseanna

Jake shrugged, "I'm not sure. I'll talk to Randy. We'll see if we can help. I promised Jane I would keep our conversation in confidence. I will talk to Andrew, maybe I can make him see reason before this goes any farther."

"Yes, do Jake. The opportunity to work with you and Randy might be exactly what he needs to build his self-confidence and put the war behind him."

"Has Simon recovered this morning?"

"He has," said Roseanna with a smile, "and very anxious to start digging. I'm still amazed he kept this secret. He is bursting with excitement to show me the gold."

"Then we shouldn't keep him waiting."

"But Jake, before we start our search I've thought about what you said about the fence going up around the rose garden being a ruse to keep Ben from knowing what was going on. It's odd the fence was put up at all. The garden has been there for years, and there was never a fence. Then my father's warning to Simon telling him to tell no one, only my brothers. You were right from the very first; the warning in the letter you brought from my father was about Ben."

Jake shrugged, "He asked Randy and me to leave the first day we were here, and not in the most polite way. It could have been just lack of trust for strangers."

"I think he knew about the gold then. I'm so very thankful you stood up to him and stayed. I don't know what would have happened if you hadn't."

"Some other man who isn't nearly as handsome as me would have swooped in and taken my place," said Jake as he grabbed his wife and nuzzled her neck."

Roseanna giggled. "There's no such man," she said enjoying her husband's playfulness.

"We have work to do, let's go dig. You should be excited about this gold, Roseanna."

"Yes, Simon is chomping at the bit."

"If it's found it needs to be taken to the bank the minute it's out of the ground? We'll need to go back to the city."

"Yes, but Jake when is the architect coming?"

Jake rubbed his hands together thinking. "Could be anytime, he said he would send a note. Randy needs to be here, and Josh to execute a contract with Richard for building the property. Do you think they could all be here at the same time for a day or two?"

Roseanna looked thoughtful. "I don't know why not. I think we can accommodate everyone. Mama Teal, Loretta and I can take care of everything."

"Good," said Jake. "Lots going on, so we better get started."

Simon was excited to show Roseanna where the gold was buried that his leg if it hurt, was not impeding his movement. As he, Jake, and Roseanna walked towards the rose garden, he was talking excitedly, waving his arms in the air, running ahead of Roseanna and Jake, and then having to circle back as he waited for them to catch up.

"Here we are, Simon. Where do we start digging?" asked Jake.

"Can't dig Mr. Jake. Gots take down fence first."

"Simon most of the fence is already down. Are you saying we have to take down more?"

"Yes, Mr. Jake. Over the corner, fence not down," said Simon pointing to the back corner of the garden.

"We need hammers first Simon not shovels."

"I's gets it, Mr. Jake," said Simon as he ran towards the tool shed.

"Do you suppose he really knows where it is?" asked Jake.

"I think he absolutely knows where it is," said Roseanna. "It's etched in his memory."

Simon returned with hammers, and he and Jake carefully began removing the pickets of the fence, and then the railing. It wasn't long before the two started to sweat. The day was hot and humid, and even though they worked in the shade of the oak trees in the yard, their faces glistened with dampness and sweat saturated their clothing.

The fence down, Simon said, "We digs here, Mr. Jake," pointing to the last support post for the fence.

"How deep do we need to dig Simon?"

Simon touched his hand to his knee. "Mr. James say his knee. He say that's good Simon."

The two started digging, throwing the dirt in a neat pile. Roseanna stood silently watching. The soil was rich and moist making the task easy. They heard a ringing sound; Jake's shovel struck something. Jake looked up at Roseanna, "There's something here."

He tossed his shovel aside, got down on his knees, and began scooping dirt away with his hands. Soon the gleam of a gold bar appeared in the hole, and then more and more as he continued to widen the hole. He pulled one of the bars out, brushed off the loose dirt, and handed it to Roseanna.

"It's heavy and so shiny!" she said as she looked at the gold turning it over in her hands. "I had no idea what to expect." She grinned at Simon and Jake. "I don't believe it's really here. How much do you think its worth, Jake?"

"Jake watched as Roseanna examined the gold bar. "Mr. Cutler at the bank will tell us. I know the value fluctuates, but I don't know the details, Cutler will be able to tell us when he weighs it and certifies it. He'll have the records from when your father took it from the bank so he will be able to let us know if we've found it all."

Simon and Jake continued to uncover the bars, and soon a stack of forty bars was at Roseanna's feet. Roseanna and Jake stood alternately staring at the pile and handling the bars. "This represents a lot of money," said Jake. "Roseanna find something to put them in and Simon you hitch the wagon. Let's get it to the bank where it's safe."

As Simon and Roseanna went about their errands Jake shoveled the dirt back in the trench they had dug. Roseanna reappeared carrying an armful of flour sacks. "This is all I could find, Jake. Anything that makes sense was burned when the stable was set aflame."

"As long as it's hidden from view it doesn't matter what it is."

Roseanna and Jake started placing the bars in the bags being careful not to overload them. The rattle of the wagon told them Simon was coming to the front of the house. They placed the gold carefully inside, covered it with a canvas tarp securely tied. Jake wanted no risk of the gold rattling or bouncing.

"Simon and I could use a cool drink, Roseanna," said Jake as he wiped the sweat from his face with his handkerchief.

Once Roseanna disappeared, Jake hurried into the house and into the pantry where James Ravenna's shotgun was kept. He didn't expect trouble and didn't want to alarm Roseanna but wanted to be prepared. Ben Ravenna was ruthless and perhaps knew by now Simon had revealed where the gold was hidden. He was gone from the plantation, but Jake didn't know if he or his henchmen who had burned the stable could at this moment be watching as they unearthed the gold. The trip to New Orleans was two hours long; the shotgun would give him peace of mind. He secreted the gun in the wagon so it would be in easy reach if needed, and kept from view of the Union Patrol.

"Simon, I'll ride Sweetie, and you can ride in the wagon with Miss Roseanna."

"I's go Mr. Jake?"

"Of course you do, Simon. We're going to need you to help, and besides, you're the reason we found the gold, and it's right that you get it to the bank where it will be safe."

They reached the bank without incident as Simon sat proudly on the seat beside Roseanna and Jake rode Sweetie bringing up the rear.

 The gold was transferred into the eager hands of Arnold Cutler. He boasted to Roseanna again about her father's insight about the economy and how he had done precisely the right thing to hid the gold for safekeeping. He assured them the bar count at forty was correct and he would soon supply Roseanna with the exact value once it was weighed and certified.

Roseanna introduced the banker to Simon, explaining he had helped her father bury it and was the only one who knew where the gold was since that time.

"This will make you a very wealthy woman, Roseanna Ravenna," exclaimed the banker.

"Mr. Cutler, I'm no longer Roseanna Ravenna. This is my husband Jake Sinclair, and I want the gold in safe keeping under both of our names."

"It's a pleasure to meet you, Mr. Sinclair, and once again I will brag on Roseanna's father who was smart enough to see which way the wind was blowing during the war. He knew exactly what he should do and did it. I'm very happy for both of you," he said as he shook Jake's hand.

The trio left the bank and rode to the offices of Sinclair and Mason to summons Randy Thomas to come to the plantation for a conference to finalize the contract with the architect, Richard Philips. They then went to Josh Horn's office to include him in the meeting. Josh surprised Roseanna with the news that his work on the Wills of her parents was complete. He would bring the final documents for her signature when they met at the plantation.

CHAPTER 10

Nothing stirred on the plantation on a hot and humid spring morning. A fierce sun beat down as summer neared. Inside the house was alive with vigorous activity as Roseanna, Mama Teal, and Loretta were preparing for their guest.

"It's all men Roseanna. They're not going to notice if the silver isn't polished. You shouldn't fuss," said Jake as he trailed behind Roseanna as she moved from room to room making preparations.

His words to Roseanna and Mama Teal fell on deaf ears as the bedrooms were aired, linens washed, rugs beat and beeswax applied to every surface. "It's been a long time since we invited guests, Jake. I'm looking forward to this and want to do it as my mother would. Mama Teal is excited, too. She sent Loretta three times to buy this, that or the other she needs for the kitchen. Simon is digging clams and setting traps for blue crabs and has picked out the best of the hens so Mama Teal can make her Chicken and Dumplings."

"Men like to eat so focusing on food is wise especially because they're all bachelors."

Roseanna frowned, "Richard Philips isn't married either? How is it possible that none of them is married?"

"Don't know, I haven't asked," said Jake with a shrug. "Except Randy, there has never been a reason for me to know. Maybe the war has something to do with it."

"I would invite some young ladies to join us Jake, but I don't know who," said Roseanna, stopping her chores and looking thoughtful.

"Roseanna, this isn't a party it's a business meeting. Just concentrate on food."

"I want things to be pleasant, Jake. Would you look at the wine my father has and pick something that would be right for chicken and seafood and dessert? That's not fussing it's just part of the menu."

"Is there bourbon and scotch? They'll very much want that," said Jake pointedly.

"If not we'll get it."

"I feel like I'm in the way," said Jake as he watched Roseanna polishing a table.

"Jake, you're not. You're a married man who has a wife who wants to make him proud when she entertains his friends and associates. I'm a new bride, and this is my first time to entertain. I want to do it right."

"I appreciate that, Roseanna. Simon and I could get busy working on the fence, so we're out of the way. I could go to the building site and see if Andrew has made any progress with the hiring. I'll do that first; maybe give me a chance to talk to him about Ben."

Roseanna stopped polishing the table and put her arms around Jake. "All this is making you feel like you're in the way, but you're not. If this were your mother's home, she would be doing the same things I'm doing."

"Should I be helping? After all, this is about my business. There must be something I can do."

"Just go see about the property or work on the garden fence Jake. I think you'll feel better if you're not in the house."

Jake went to the yard, found Simon and after saddling the horses the two headed for the property. Jake admitted that Roseanna was right. What he saw as confusion evaporated from his mind, and he was more than content to be gone.

They reached the property and stood to watch Andrew and several men working among the trees at the river's edge. Smoke and flames rose from a giant pile of rubble that had been cleared filling the air with the scent of burning wood. Some of the trees close to the workers bore slashes of white paint, marked to be harvested for lumber. Andrew looked up to see Jake and waved a hand in greeting.

"You've found some of your work crew, Andrew. Will there be more?"

"I hope so Jake. More work to do than I thought. Two of these men work for the company that's going to cut your lumber. The trees they're marking will be knocked down so when the equipment arrives, they can start sawing the planks. I spoke to Reverend Rivers, and he's going to put the word out at church and post a notice. By next week, we should have more men coming out. We're making some progress."

"Once this is cleared," said Jake "we'll have to level the ground for the foundation of the building, should be right where we're standing," he said with a flourish. " Andrew, several of your new hires can be used at the plantation to clear the remains of the stable."

"Has Roseanna made up her mind about the horses?"

"No, but it needs to be cleared, and there's no reason not to get it done."

"She'll decide, she just needs more time," said Andrew.

"Yes, that's what she needs. You need to be at Roseanna's for a few days so you can sit in on the discussion about how we'll be proceeding here at the site."

"Jake," said Andrew with a grin, "I'm flattered you want me there."

"You're my foreman, Andrew. I want you to take an active part in the discussions. You need to meet the architect. He'll give you the guidance you need so you're doing the work in the most organized way to support him. The pilings for the dock and wharf will be the first order of business. Richard Philips should give us a time schedule for when that will start. Working where you are here on the riverfront is smart. Plan two days to be at these meetings so have anyone you hire start after that, so you're here to give directions."

"Will I meet your partner? I only met him briefly when the two of you first came to the plantation."

"Randy Thomas, yes he'll be there. By the end of these meeting, we should all have a clear idea of the direction we need to take. The architect will be in charge, Randy and I know our business but don't know anything about building. Could we discuss something else, Andrew?"

"Ben, I know it's about Ben. I've heard it all from Loretta," said Andrew with a frown. "Why isn't anyone concerned about what he did? Why not talk to him?"

"I intend to talk to him, but he's been gone from the plantation."

"Could it wait, Jake? I'm not in the frame of mind to hear any more about how I need to change my attitude about Ben."

"It can wait if you're not ready. But plan on taking the time for the talk while you're at Roseanna's for the meeting."

"I'll agree to that, but changing my attitude is not going to be easy," said Andrew pessimistically. "I need to get back to work, see you at the meetings. Thanks for hiring me Jake, if for no other reason, it keeps me away from Ben."

Jake watched Andrew as he joined the other workers. He had promised Jane he would help, and he intended to keep his promise, but for now, Andrew needed to accept the idea that the talk was necessary. Jake picked up an ax and handed Simon a shovel, "We may as well make ourselves useful, Simon. As long as we're here, we can lend a hand."

The preparations for the business meeting inside the house were at a fever pitch as the guest were due to arrive by early afternoon and things were not quite the way Roseanna wanted. Jake, to be out of the way of the activity gathered tools and with Simon went to rebuild the garden fence. They placed stakes at the boundary and tied string between the stakes to mark the boundary of the fence.

Jake could see Nathan as he loitered behind a tree watching them work. He had stayed away since the incident with Simon. Occasionally he would be seen lurking behind one of the buildings watching unsure of what his reception would be. Jake knew whatever part he had played in the torture of Simon was at Ben's instruction and that he had meant no harm to come to Simon.

"Nathan did you want to work today?" called Jake.

Nathan hesitated but then slowly ambled towards them casting sidelong glances at Simon as he came, but keeping the direction he walked close to Jake.

"I's do want work, Mr. Jake."

"Good we can use the help," said Jake

"Hey, Nathan," said Simon shyly.

"Hey, Simon," said Nathan returning the greeting.

The three worked in silence for a time until Nathan said, "Yous gots yous crab trap set Simon."

"Miss Roseanna has her party. She wantin' crabs and clam."

"I's help yous?"

"Yea we gets twice as much. Miss Roseanna be happy," grinned Simon.

"Miss Roseanna will be happy," said Jake, "let's get some work done on the fence first."

"Then we swim and catch crab," said Simon.

"That's a good idea," said Jake. "I think I'll join you at least for the swim. Great way to cool off."

Jake couldn't help noticing how beautiful the house and his wife looked as the time approached for everyone to arrive. Every room glowed. The dining room table was spread with a lace tablecloth and roses in a silver bowl graced its center. Delicious odors emitted from the kitchen house as Mama Teal put the final preparation on the food. The guests would be coming soon, and Roseanna was ready and eager, but a little nervous that everything would go smoothly. She was dressed in a lightweight pale yellow dress with her hair swept up on her head.

Seated in the dining room Jake, Randy and Andrew were laughing with gusto as Josh Horn regaled them with a humorous story, including a great deal of animation, about one of his clients and a stolen mule as they waited for Richard Philips to arrive. The sound of their voices reminded Roseanna of times long ago when the house would be full of guests; some for casual visits or dinner parties and at other times prospective customers who had come to look over the stock of horses. The laughter she heard was a sound that had been missing for a long time.

Mama Teal moved among the guest pouring coffee, sweet tea and offering slices of her savory spice cake. At a knock at the door, Mama Teal raised her head intending to put aside the coffee server and answer.

Roseanna quickly rose from her chair, "Finish what you're doing Mama Teal," she said, as she swept from the room.

Roseanna opened the door with a smile on her face ready to welcome the architect, but her smile quickly faded as she saw her uncle standing on the threshold. He was rumpled and looked as though he hadn't bathed or shaved for some time. His hat was in his hand as he leaned on his walking stick.

"Uncle Ben," said Roseanna in surprise, taking a step back, as the smell of the liquor on her uncle's breath reached her.

"I know I'm a sight, and not welcome. I've just returned from the city, haven't even been to the house yet, but could I ask you please to give me a minute of your time, and Jake too if he's here."

"Uncle Ben this isn't a good time, we're busy at the moment. I'm surprised you would just appear at the door after what has happened."

"That's why I'm here, Roseanna, to beg forgiveness and hopefully be allowed to explain myself."

"You need to beg Simon for forgiveness," said Roseanna testily, "and there is no explanation for what you've done. Now isn't the time," said Roseanna as she began to close the door.

"When would I be allowed to speak to you and Jake?" said Ben as he pushed against the door to keep Roseanna from closing it.

"You'll have to wait until a time when it's more convenient, but not now."

"I understand. I look forward to the opportunity. Good day, Roseanna," said Ben as he placed his hat on his head and turned to leave.

Roseanna returned to the dining room, and as she entered, the conversation ceased as everyone looked up expectantly for Richard Philips.

"Wasn't that him?" asked Randy.

"No," said Roseanna, "someone else."

The conversation resumed, and Jake gave Roseanna a questioning look, "Ben," she whispered.

"I see," said Jake.

Again, a knock at the door, Roseanna rose to answer, but Jake rose as well. "I'll go," he said thinking Ben had returned. This time the architect was admitted.

"Sorry, I'm late Jake. Didn't mean to hold up the proceedings but the team has arrived to sink the pilings for the dock, and they needed a few questions answered," said Richard.

Jake shook the architect's hand. "That's great news, sinking those pilings is the most important operation before the rest can be started."

Jake escorted Richard into the dining room and made introductions. "Richard you know Randy," said Jake, "and this is our attorney Josh Horn."

The two shook hands, and then Richard turned to Andrew, "I recognize this young man though you've grown quite a bit," he said as he smiled at Andrew. "You're Ben and Jane Ravenna's son."

"Yes, well partly right. It's Andrew Moorcroft. I am Jane's son from a prior marriage," said Andrew as he took Richard Philips outstretched hand.

"Jake told me he had hired someone to work at the site, but I just didn't place the name Moorcroft. Do you remember me, Andrew?"

"Of course, I knew you the minute you walked in. You built the house for Ben and Jane didn't you?"

"Yes, and you were right at my elbow most of the time. One of the best assistants I've ever had," laughed Richard. "You liked studying the blueprints and always had questions, intelligent questions."

"I must have been a nuisance," laughed Andrew. "But I remember the great tent you stayed in and wanted one for myself."

"Ah, yes," said Richard, "you did envy my tent, but you were never a nuisance. I enjoyed having you hang around, and you were never out of line. It's going to be a pleasure working with you Andrew. Jake tells me you studied engineering in school which will make you invaluable in assisting me."

"I certainly hope so, I'm looking forward to being part of the project," said Andrew, beaming.

"How's your mother, Andrew?"

"She's well, thank you. She would enjoy seeing you while you're here."

"I would enjoy seeing her again, and Ben as well, of course."

"It will be my pleasure to make that happen," said Andrew.

"What's this about a tent, Richard?" asked Randy.

"Been using a tent for years at the sites where I'm working rather than wasting time finding accommodations, which in most cases don't exist because I'm usually working in a remote area."

"Oh, Richard, there's no need to stay in a tent," said Roseanna. "You'll stay here with us for as long as you like."

"It's more than staying in the tent," said Richard. "It becomes my office complete with a work table for blueprints and a cot for sleeping and a small cook stove. Suits a bachelor just fine, it's quite comfortable and has everything I need. But thank you for your offer."

"At least promise that you'll share meals with us from time to time," said Roseanna.

"With pleasure. I would enjoy that and thanks for the invitation."

After several hours of discussion, everyone agreed to the workflow and scheduling for the new building. Jake felt confident that selecting Richard, as the architect had been the right decision as he sat back and listened to Richard explain the process and steps towards completing the project.

It was exciting to hear, and Jake and Randy eyed each other across the table nodding their heads in approval. They could almost visualize the finished building. When Richard had answered everyone's questions, they rose from the table to take a break. Jake could see everyone was as excited to move forward as he was.

Jake used this opportunity to talk to Roseanna about her conversation with Ben when he had come to the door.

"He looked very unkempt," said Roseanna, "and I could smell liquor on his breath. He asked if he could talk to the two of us. He wants to give us an explanation about Simon."

Jake frowned, "There's no explanation that he could give or that I want to hear."

"I told him that, and he needs to apologize to Simon."

"I want Andrew to know Ben has come home and talk to him before they come face to face. Josh needs to talk to you about finalizing the Wills. Let's get those things out of the way before dinner and then we can enjoy the rest of the evening. Randy can take Richard out to look at the stable and let him see about rebuilding."

"I don't know about the stable, Jake. There's always so much going on, I'm never sure what I want to do about the horses," said Roseanna.

"You don't need to decide, Roseanna, but what's left has to be torn down and cleared, and you want a stable for Moses and Sweetie don't you? Let's see what Richard would recommend."

"Of course, we can at least go that far with planning a replacement."

Jake and Andrew found a quiet place in the office for their talk. Andrew sat down and excitedly started talking about Richard Philips.

"I remember him so well, Jake. I was underfoot while he was working, I must have been in the way, but he was always patient with me and answered all my questions. He's probably the reason I decided to study engineering in school. I remember at night, I could see his tent from my bedroom window; we lived here with Uncle James while the house was being built. He had lanterns inside, and they would shine through the canvas walls. Sometimes he'd invite me to sit, and he'd cook for the two of us. It was a fun time for a kid."

"I can imagine, we all have great memories of things that happened when we were kids."

"I was looking forward to working for you Jake, but this changes everything now that Richard is here."

"Good, I'm glad you're looking forward to the work, and there's going to be plenty. Let's talk about Ben, he's back, that's who was at the door when Roseanna answered."

"That coward, he finally shows his face. I'll deal with him," said Andrew as he started to rise from his chair.

"Andrew sit down," said Jake sternly. "We need to talk about this before you go off with a head full of steam. Now, what happened with Simon was horrible, and it can't be minimized."

"I know, Ben is pretty low to treat a defenseless Negro man as he did," said

Andrew with disgust.

"Andrew, I can't tell you what to do, but there is a lot of concern over your attitude towards Ben."

"Jake, that's Loretta's brother and your wife. Think of what he's done to Roseanna."

"This goes beyond what has happened with Simon and Roseanna for you, Andrew. I handled Ben's involvement where Roseanna was concerned. I'm asking you to let me handle the incident with Simon."

"No, I can't do that. Ben deserves everything I can do to him."

"I won't argue with that, but I want you to leave it to me."

"Or else, Jake? What's the or else? Are you going to fire me?"

"This has nothing to do with your work. It has to do with your reaction to Ben."

"Who have you been talking to? My mother, Loretta? My mother defends Ben, she knows what he does is wrong, but she still sticks up for him. If you could ever get her to admit the truth she'd tell you that Ben is no good."

Jake knew when he talked to Jane she was not happy with her marriage to Ben and she had no concerns for him. She just wanted her son to be free of Ben's control.

"This is my own concern, Andrew. I'm not blind or deaf. I hear what you say and watch how you react whenever Ben's name is mentioned. He isn't worth all the emotion you spend on him. It's destructive to you while he feels nothing at all."

"You don't understand, Jake. I hate the man."

"Wasted emotion, Andrew. In the case of Roseanna, all that has happened is in the past. You've been at the property, so you've missed what's been happening the last few days. Simon knew where the gold was and told Roseanna. It's been found and is safely in the bank."

"Simon knew all along? The gold exists?"

"Yes. He kept a promise made to Roseanna's father not to tell. He was told never to tell Ben and only to tell Roseanna's brothers."

"Simon kept that secret?"

"Pretty remarkable. Simon didn't understand until he heard it from Ben that the brothers were dead; he thought they would still be coming home. Roseanna confirmed everything for him, and once he understood, he told her where the gold was hidden."

"And where was it?"

"Buried in the rose garden."

"We never thought to look there?" said Andrew in wonder shaking his head.

"Simon took Roseanna and me to the very spot where it was buried."

"Ben will never get his hands on it?"

"No, or anything else. One of the reasons Josh Horn is here is the finalization of Roseanna's parent's Wills. Ben's efforts to take control of anything or anyone are over. He doesn't benefit in any way."

"Good, he deserves nothing."

"So, you understand Ben has been rendered harmless. You can put all this aside."

"What about what he did to Simon? You expect me to ignore that? He's Loretta's brother."

"I've asked you to let me handle it. I agree with you that going to the authorities would never result in any action taken against Ben. No one in the south is going to come to the defense of a Negro man. Loretta understands your concern about Simon, but she wants you to leave it alone."

"You don't know all the things he has done. For years, I've put up with him. He was supposed to be a father to me, but never once acted like one. My mother used to defend me to him, but now she sides with him at every turn."

"Where does it end Andrew? You're a grown man now," said Jake spreading his hands in supplication. "Perhaps your mother doesn't side with Ben; she's just trying to keep the peace between the two of you."

Andrew sat quietly looking beyond Jake at the view outside the office window. "I'll try to handle myself better, but I can't promise."

"You don't need to promise me anything. You do this for yourself," said Jake rising from his chair. Let's go see what everyone is up to."

"You must be pleased this is behind you now, Roseanna," said Josh as he and Roseanna talked in the parlor. "The deaths of your family has been very tragic and in the case of your father much unexpected. You can put the business of your mother and father's assets behind you. Small compensation, but no more worry for you."

"I'm just glad it's over. I'm so fortunate it was Jake who found my father. I've thought that many times. What if no one ever found him?"

"I agree you should be thankful, and now you don't need to concern ourselves with any of this anymore. A few things to make you aware of and a signature or two and we'll be done. The plantation, at least that part that is in your father's name, reverts to you. You know what the other assets are, so we won't review that, and they are listed in the documents. You'll have inheritance taxes to pay and the property tax that is due. There were no debts owed by either of your parents, your father was very cautious about his finances. So, in spite of the difficulties you've faced, it's now resolved."

"I'm relieved. You've made it seem so easy. And there's nothing else to consider?"

"What about the gold that was supposedly hidden on the property?"

"Oh Josh, of course, you need to know about the gold. It's been found just a few days ago and is safely in the bank."

"Ah! We'll need to adjust the documents to reflect that and the inheritance tax. Do you know the amount?"

"No, I'm still waiting to hear from the bank."

"When you know, we'll make the changes. The other part of the inheritance that I need to make you aware of is the twelve thousand dollar IOU that your father signed with his brother, Ben. I wrote to him, but never received a response."

"I've promised my uncle that I would forgive that debt. He told me that the money wasn't an IOU, but money my father gave him to start some shared projects on the plantation."

Josh frowned, "The document you gave me doesn't bear that out."

"Please, just whatever you need to do, erase the debt, that's what I want to be done."

"I'll do that and notify Mr. Ravenna that the debt is free and clear. Now I need a signature where these documents are marked, and we are done."

As Roseanna signed, Josh handed each document to her. "I will send you copies of the letter and paid in full note to Ben Ravenna in the next day or so."

"Josh I can't thank you enough. You made this much easier than I thought it would be."

"I'll send you a bill," laughed Josh, "so no thanks are necessary. If I could, I'd like to ask you a question."

"Of course what is it?"

"Gwen Mason. What do you think of her?"

Roseanna stopped signing documents and looked intently at Josh. "I hardly know her. She's beautiful and stylish and seemed intelligent. I don't know what else to say."

"She thinks very highly of you."

Roseanna smiled, "How could that be? She hardly knows me. Are you asking for a particular reason?"

"I'm interested in what you think is all."

"I've answered your question the best I know how. Jake has only praise for her, and I trust his opinion. You should ask him."

"I know what Jake's opinion is. I wanted a woman's thoughts is all. She's invited me to come to New York and visit her."

Roseanna was surprised, "That sounds serious. Are you telling me that you have some shared feelings? I just had this conversation with Jake about all of you being bachelors. Could that be changing?"

Josh threw back his head with a hearty laugh. "That's exactly what I am hoping for, but can we keep it between the two of us?"

"You have my absolute promise." Roseanna was confused as she thought Gwen was interested in Randy but now her interest was in Josh. "I wish you luck and hope it works for you."

"Time will tell," said Josh. "I've known her since before the war. She's strong and determined, I like that."

"If we're done we should join the others," said Roseanna not wanting to continue the conversation about Gwen Mason.

Josh returned the completed documents to his case. "Will the next step for you be the horses, Roseanna?"

"Jake would support me, but I truly can't decide."

"Whatever your decision, I wish you well," said Josh as they left the parlor.

CHAPTER 11

Ben's decision to knock at Roseanna's door on his returned from New Orleans had taken a great deal of courage. He was no fool; he knew what his reception would be. It was necessary to be humble if the tables were to be turned in his favor. He was finally accepting the truth of his circumstances; he would never realize any gain from the estate of his late brother, and he would be the last person to benefit from any hidden gold. His niece was the help he needed, but between them stood Jake Sinclair. He would need to befriend Jake, a bitter pill to swallow, but it needed to be done.

Damn Simon. Had he told him the hiding place, the gold would be in his hands, and this would be behind him, and his departure to escape the consequences would not have been necessary. Jane would be particularly difficult to deal with; he had made her complicit in the falsehood of meetings that he needed to attend in the city. She would now understand what he had done. In time, she would forgive him, but now, other problems needed his consideration.

Reaching the city, his first thought was to go to the bank and again plead his case to Cutler for relief from his debts. He dismissed this as a waste of time. The prestige and influence of the Ravenna family name were gone. With every planter in the parish needing money, anyone in debt would be the last to be given consideration.

He went instead to the office of Lawrence Winston. The attorney was not receptive to Ben's visit since their last meeting had ended on such a harsh note, but after some terse words and grumbling, Lawrence had accepted Ben's apology.

The plain bold truth is what he once again heard from Winston, the value of anything Ben possessed had greatly declined since the war. His home and his acreage would create nothing more than a further glut of property on the market, and if it could be sold, would go for less than Ben would be willing to accept. Capital was what he needed, money to put a crop in the ground that would bring him the fastest relief. Most plantations were in the same circumstances, land rich, and cash poor.

Lawrence gave the same advice, "Go to your niece, Ben. Get on your knees if you have to, but go to your niece. She may not have the gold if there is any, but she has no debt, and she can borrow against her property."

Of all the men to find his brother as he lay snake bitten in the woods, why did it have to be Jake Sinclair? Any other man would take what was offered, the hospitality of a meal and maybe some small compensation. This Yankee would never admit he had come for what he saw as easy pickings, and he'd never get his niece to see the truth. Didn't matter, what had happened in the past, it didn't matter he needed to deal with the now.

Ben spent his time in the city in a cheap boarding house, sitting in a tavern drinking, and commiserating with other planters who were in his or worse circumstances. Several times, he was roused from a stupor when the bar was closing for the night. He gained some insight from one of the planters he spoke to; he had a chance of a resolution to his problems while most of them did not. He had his niece while the others had no one. He needed to get on his knees and beg.

Ben's return from New Orleans created a great deal of tension in his home. Jane would not condone Ben's treatment of Simon and his lie to her would not be forgiven. Her disdain was inevitable. For him to disappear for days and return with no explanation for where he had been in such deplorable condition, drunk and disheveled was unacceptable. Meals in the dining room were silent and stressed. Ben hardly touched the food, if he came for meals at all. He remained shut in his office with nothing but his liquor.

Jane had once defended Ben, not for his sake but in an effort to quell the tension between him and Andrew, but no more. Andrew was what mattered. He had regaled her with details of the meeting that he had attended with the architect, Richard Philips, and all that he would be responsible for on his duties working for Jake Sinclair. He was excited and looking forward to the work and learning the trade. Between Jake Sinclair and Richard Philips, Andrew had his champions and Ben's disregard for him no longer mattered.

Jane saw excitement and enthusiasm that had been missing since he returned from the war.

Ben's troubles and problems ceased to matter. Andrew was her only concern. She had brought her son to a new continent to protect him, hoping to replace his father with a man to act as his role model, and instead to her disgrace, she had created an entirely different cross for him to bear. She was responsible for what had happened between him and Ben Ravenna, but now she would do everything in her power to shield her son from harm.

Jake, Simon, and Nathan were making good progress on the rose garden fence. The troubles between Nathan and Simon had passed as they chatted as they worked. The meals that were served during the gathering to settle the final details of the new building for Sinclair and Mason were a great success thanks to their efforts digging clams and trapping Blue Crabs and the praise they received for their efforts had cemented their friendship back together.

The men who had come to the gathering were gone, and Jake was pleased with what had been accomplished. He and Randy were excited to see the beginning of the execution of the building. They congratulated each other on their selection of Richard Philips as the architect, and Andrew's interest had grown by leap and bounds as he renewed his relationship with the architect. He would give Andrew the guidance he needed to help move the project forward smoothly. Soon the pilings for the wharf would be sunk, and then work on the building could move forward rapidly.

The next step was hiring the men to help with the work and Jake was working on the repair of the garden fence while he waited to go to the church where the hiring session would be held. The response to the announcement that Reverend Rivers had made in the church had brought a crush of men back from the wars that were ready and eager to begin earning money again, and Jake would be at the church to help Andrew make the selections.

The weather was hot and the air heavy with humidity at this early time of the morning. Jake paused in his work to take his handkerchief from his pocket, remove his hat and wipe the sweat from his brow. He looked up to see Ben Ravenna crossing the bridge and riding towards him. "Simon and Nathan, you go find Mama Teal and have her give you a cool drink." Jake would take this opportunity to confront Ben, and Simon and Nathan need not be present as witnesses.

Jake stepped into the path of Ben's horse forcing him to stop. "Jake, good morning," said Ben, as he tipped his hat.

"It's time we talked," said Jake.

"I agree, and I came by the other day, but you weren't available. Just give me a moment to get off this dang horse. The old leg doesn't want to cooperate," said Ben, with a smile.

"Don't dismount, this won't take long," said Jake gruffly.

"Just bear with me Jake. I did have some things to discuss with you."

"No, I talk, you listen," said Jake. "What you did to Simon was inexcusable. It's a new low for you to torture a defenseless man, and you need to answer for it."

"There was no torture, he wasn't harmed," said Ben indignantly.

"The man was tortured, tied to a chair, and beaten with your walking stick. If the authorities would do anything, you'd be sitting in a jail cell now."

"That's harsh for what occurred. Simon is exaggerating," said Ben with scorn.

"Simon exaggerated nothing," said Jake. "He had contusions on his body and raw marks on his wrist where he was tied, put there by you."

"Jake he was not hurt, a few minor marks on his skin," said Ben. "You need to listen to what I'm saying. Simon knows where the gold is! He knows!"

Jake ignored Ben. "We just came out of a war where many of my friends from the north died as did many from the south. It was about the mistreatment and bondage of the Negros and yet you ignored that fact and held Simon captive and beat him."

"Jake you're not listening to what I'm telling you. This had nothing to do with Simon being a Negro. He knows where the gold is, I'm certain he does!"

"Which makes this more offensive because you would take something that doesn't belong to you?"

"I had no intention of keeping this for myself. I did this for Roseanna. She wants that gold. I'll talk to her; she'll listen to what I'm saying. Jake listen. Simon knows where the gold is! He knows I'm telling you he knows!"

"No, you listen and listen well. You treat anyone on this plantation with anything but absolute respect, black and white alike, you're going to have to answer to me," stormed Jake. "I will come after you, I will find you, and you will pay the consequences. Understand me, and understand me well, because there won't be another opportunity for you to get the message."

Ben backed his horse away from Jake. "You Yankees can't come down here and tell us what we can and can't do! Roseanna will listen; she wants to know where the gold is."

Jake stepped closer to the horse, grabbed the bridle, and jabbed his finger in Ben's face. "You leave my wife out of this," he said with a stony stare and clenched teeth. "This is between you and me. Don't you dare to go to my wife and tell her any of what you've done was for her?"

Jake stepped away from the horse, turned his back, and walked to the fence to resume his work. Ben sat astride his horse glaring at Jake's back. He was breathing heavily, and his hands where they clenched the reins were white.

"You're ignorant, Sinclair," he shouted. "Exactly what I would expect from a Yankee coming here and interfering in a situation he knows nothing about." He turned his horse and rode out of Pelicans Haven.

Roseanna took a deep breath and looked around her at the clutter she and Mama Teal had made in her parents' bedroom. All of the clothes had been removed from the wardrobes and drawers, folded, and neatly stacked waiting to be donated to the church.

The most challenging part would be going through their personal items. Roseanna and Jake had decided after giving all the bedrooms in the house equal consideration, this room would be theirs.

It needed to be cleared and the furniture removed so Roseanna could have new wallpaper installed. Roseanna had asked Richard Philips with his knowledge of merchants in the city for his recommendation on where she should buy the things that she needed, wallpaper, fabric for new drapes and new rugs for the floor. Jake needed to go to New Orleans, and Roseanna would go along to take care of the purchases.

It was a large room with two exterior walls each lined with windows and situated on the northeast corner of the house which gave relief from the effects of the hot western sun. It had been Jake's first choice, and Roseanna agreed that it would be perfect. She began sorting through the drawers in tables on each side of the bed. These were the very personal effects of her parents, small mementos that they had tucked away over the years for safe keeping. It was difficult for Roseanna as she fingered the items because so many things brought back her own memories.

The drawers she looked in first were her mother's. One drawer was stuffed with letters her mother had received from friends and family in her home state of Connecticut. Roseanna pulled one from its envelope and started reading. It shared news of a wedding the writer had attended where the bride, so overcome at the enormity of the ceremony, that everyone in the church needed to leaned forward to hear her whispered response when the vows were spoken. Roseanna smiled to herself remembering her wedding. The same could have been said of her. She stuffed the letter back in the envelope and laid it aside.

Her fingers touched a small cloth bag; she drew it from the drawer and opened the drawstring to reveal pearls, loose pearls. She remembered these from a necklace of her mother's she had worn at a dinner party her parents had held just before the war. The string had broken as they were seated at the table and the pearls had scattered everywhere, bouncing among the serving dishes, and even into the guest's plates. Some had rolled to the floor, and soon everyone was on their hands and knees scrambling to retrieve them. She had been so embarrassed to cause such a stir. It was one of the first times she had joined the adults, and she had disgraced herself to the point of tears. She remembered how forgiving everyone had been especially her mother, and she laughed at the memory.

"Here you are!" said Jake as he came into the room. "What's so funny?" he asked as he took her into his arms.

Roseanna smiled. "Nothing, just memories that I'm finding in this room. Some of it has been difficult, clearing out my parents' things, but some fun, too. There are so many memories."

"Maybe Mama Teal would do this for you."

"Of course she would but this is very personal, and she wouldn't know what to do with all of these things. What to keep and what should be thrown out."

If it's going to be too much for you we'll just stay in your room and sleep while all your dolls watch," said Jake with a grin as he pulled her close.

Roseanna laughed, "We don't need to do that Jake. No, I want this to be our room just as we planned. This house is like a museum, not only this room but also my brother's rooms. I'm just not sure what to do with it all."

"Let's just box them all up and put them in the attic. Later when all the memories aren't so fresh, you can take it out one box at a time and decide what you want to keep."

"That's the best idea, and Mama Teal and Loretta can help, and we can get it all done at the same time."

"Here's some good news for you, your garden fence is back in place. Except for some paint which I will mix for Simon and Nathan and then it will be done."

"Thank you, Jake, that means a lot to me but shouldn't you be on your way to the church?"

"Yes, in a minute. I wanted to tell you that I had a conversation with your uncle about Simon."

"Oh dear," said Roseanna, a look of concern on her face.

"It went fine," said Jake, at least from my point of view. Your uncle I'm sure wouldn't agree."

"What did he say?" asked Roseanna with a frown.

"I didn't give him an opportunity to say much."

"He did ask that we talk, Jake. I want to give him that opportunity. It would be nice to have all the bad feelings put aside."

"That has to come from your uncle."

"Do you think that will happen, Jake? He and Aunt Jane are the only family I have now."

"With no more nonsense from Ben, it can. I made that clear to him, maybe he understands. If you want to sit down and talk with him make whatever plans you want and I'll support you. I'll join you unless you would rather talk to him on your own."

"No, I want you there; I need you to be with me."

"Good, maybe I can mend a fence, too." With a final kiss for his wife, he left to go to the church hire a crew.

Roseanna, with the help of Mama Teal and Loretta, had finished clearing her parents' room then crossed the bridge to her uncle's house to make arrangements for sitting down for their conversation.

Nancy opened the door to her knock. "Roseanna how nice to see you," we just don't seem to see each other much anymore."

"We should do something about that."

"You seem to be busy and going to the city with Jake," said Nancy.

"We're going to the city again soon, why don't you come with us?"

"I don't know Roseanna. Maybe Jake would rather not have me go."

"Nonsense, he would love to have you come. We're only going for one night, and Jake will be busy with Randy at the office. We could browse through the shops. We could do anything you wanted just the two of us. Please say you'll come. I can use your help finding material for new drapes for a bedroom."

"It would be a relief to be out of this house," said Nancy with a sigh.

"Why, what do you mean?"

"My parents, things are not going well. Mother is upset over what happened to Simon, and she has dug her heels in until my father apologizes to her. She told everyone he was going to the city on business and she feels he deliberately did it so she would lie for him. They aren't speaking."

"That can't be very comfortable for you. Surely it will pass?"

"I don't know," said Nancy with a shake of her head. "I've never seen my mother be so rebellious. She is usually the peacemaker but not this time. She's never acted like this before."

"Come to the city with us. It will get you out of the middle of the battle. Please come"

"I will come, I would love to come," said Nancy with a smile

"Good! Now, I need to talk to your father. Is he here?"

"Yes, he's in his office. Just knock maybe he'll answer."

Roseanna gently knocked at the door, and her uncle answered her knock. "Roseanna, what brings you here?"

"You asked if we could sit down and talk so I've come to see when you would like to do that."

"Jake had his talk with me this morning," said Ben angrily as he turned and walked back to his desk.

"Uncle Ben would you expect him to just ignore what happened to Simon?" said Roseanna as she followed her uncle and took a chair before his desk.

"I would expect him to let me explain myself," said Ben heatedly. "But he wouldn't allow it."

Roseanna did not respond to this comment. "You asked to speak to us when you came to the door the other day. I'm here now Uncle Ben, it can just be the two of us if you prefer, but I would like Jake to sit with us. He's willing to do that."

Ben gave a hollow laugh, "Yes, why waste time with just the two of us. Jake Sinclair has so much influence over you nothing would be accomplished until you repeated all that I have to say to him. So, yes," said Ben distastefully, "by all means include Jake."

Roseanna tried to ignore the anger in her uncle's voice. "Would tomorrow suit you? You could come for lunch. Jake comes from the site each day for lunch. I'd like to include Aunt Jane."

"Tomorrow lunch will suit me. Your aunt doesn't need to be involved. You can invite her another time."

Roseanna stood from her chair, "I'm glad we're going to talk."

Ben looked at her for a long moment. "We'll see if it's possible to agree. Yes. It's important we talk if Jake is truly willing to listen. I have my doubts after this morning."

"He is, Uncle Ben. That's why I'm here now."

As she walked back across the bridge, Roseanna pondered if her uncle and Jake could sit down together and have a peaceful conversation? Was this the best time for this discussion? When if not now, the wounds would continue to fester and time would not heal the animosity, this needed to happen. She wanted a good outcome for everyone. If there had been problems between Uncle Ben and her father, it had been invisible to her, and there was no reason some long ago feud should continue. Pelicans Haven was built by family, and as part of that family, she wanted to make peace. They could all live in harmony, and the plantation could survive and be rebuilt.

CHAPTER 12

This lunch with her uncle and Jake could be a new beginning for all of them; they could heal, forgive, and move forward. They all needed to cooperate for this to work. Jake, for his part, had once again stated that he was willing to offer his hand in friendship, but he cautioned Roseanna to be slow in accepting any excuse of misunderstanding from Ben for all that had happened.

Roseanna felt anxious, she knew her uncle was angry with Jake for the words they had exchanged over the treatment of Simon. She somehow needed to keep the subject of Simon out of the conversation.

She asked Mama Teal to make a light summer meal, ham with her fluffy biscuits, several fresh vegetables from the garden and strawberry shortcake for dessert.

She set the table in the dining room with a crisply starched tablecloth and napkins, and as she placed the napkins on the table, she traced the initial stitched in the corner with her finger, an "R" for Ravenna, sad, there were no more Ravennas in this house. She vowed not to let this sadness ruin her day and decided this was another item to buy when she was in New Orleans, table linen so new napkins could be sewn with the initial "S" stitched in the corner.

Her favorite china was next; dainty florals ringed the edges of the plate on a cream-colored background. She wanted her uncle to feel like a pampered guest, so she added a bouquet of roses from the garden as a centerpiece. She dressed in a crisp summer dress of the palest pink with a stand-up collar. The full skirt was gathered at the waist, and the front button closure was accented by rows of tiny pleating.

Ben arrived punctually, and Roseanna ushered him into the parlor. Jake had promised to be back from the building site early so he would have time to dress for the luncheon, but the clock had struck noon, and he still had not arrived.

"I'm sorry, Uncle Ben. I can't imagine what's keeping Jake. I'm sure there's an important reason for his delay."

"Understandable, Roseanna. He has business to attend to, and sometimes business takes its own time getting done."

"Should we start eating and then Jake can join us?"

"I'm perfectly comfortable waiting; I have no plans for my afternoon. We can do whatever you prefer."

"I'd like to wait, I'm sure he'll be along soon. Did Nancy tell you that Jake and I have invited her to go to New Orleans with us? Jake has some business, and I've decided to go shopping."

"She told me you invited her. She doesn't get out a great deal, just with her mother for church, sewing circles and the ladies meetings that they attend. She needs to be with people her own age."

"I think so, too. It doesn't seem that life will go back to the way it was before the war, too much heartache, and problems."

"There's plenty of that to go around. It'll come if we're patient. Nancy is at an age when life should be carefree and gay. She is young yet, so I'm not concerned, but she does pout about the lack of social gatherings," said Ben

"I'm glad she agreed to go. We want to go through as many shops as we can. I need to buy some new things for the house and Nancy has a wonderful gift for color and style. I'm looking forward to her advice. We'll have a good time."

"I'll be concerned with the two of you wandering around the city."

"We won't be wandering far from the hotel. Jake has cautioned me about where I can and cannot go."

Jake hurried into the room with a strained look on his face. Ben rose to his feet and extended his hand. "Jake, good afternoon."

"Please, excuse my tardiness. I'm sorry for the wait," said Jake as he took

Ben's hand. "Unavoidable. We lost a man at the site today. Very tragic."

"Oh Jake," said Roseanna. "You mean someone was hurt?"

"No, Roseanna, much worse. One of the men working for the company that is sinking the pilings drowned. It happened so quickly. One of the cables used to support the post for the pilings snapped and hit him. He was on a boat and knocked overboard. He disappeared in the current, its running rapid, and he was carried away. We've spent hours looking for him."

"Tragic. What of the man's family?" asked Ben?

"He's from New Orleans, not a local man. Every man there was in the water, but we failed to find him. I shut the site down for the rest of the day."

"Jake, how horrible," said Roseanna.

"Andrew was the first one to attempt a rescue. He saw it happen and was immediately in the water. He made an extremely noble effort."

"Wouldn't his mother be pleased to hear that, her son a hero," said Ben, sarcastically. "The history of his behavior doesn't reflect heroism. He deserted during the war and came home with his tail between his legs. No need to explain to me how that wasn't an unusual circumstance," said Ben, holding up his hand to halt a protest from Jake. "I know there were others who deserted. Nevertheless, even before the war, he never showed promise. He shouldn't be blamed; his mother is more the reason. She was born to wealth, as was his father. Men were to become gentlemen and not accustomed or expected to dirty their hands in manual labor."

"Andrew has no problem doing manual labor and dirtying his hands. He has done more than his share. Richard Philips believes he shows a great deal of promise for architecture," said Jake.

"We're not going to agree on Andrew's merits. Perhaps he has found something that interests him. His mother has a whimsical notion that going to London and changing his environment will make his life better. She led him to believe that if he reconnected with his father's family, they would welcome him into their midst and help him establish himself."

"Perhaps a conversation about Andrew isn't where we should venture, Ben. One of the purposes of this meeting should be to try to put our differences aside. That's not going to be possible talking about Andrew."

"Should we postpone our meeting, Jake? This incident at the building site may have put you in a disagreeable mood," said Ben.

"It's the topic of conversation that's made me disagreeable. Let's change the subject and proceed as we planned. We're gathered at your request, Ben. You asked for an opportunity to talk to Roseanna and me. Everything was done that could be done for the man at the site today, but it's an ominous beginning for the project."

"Mama Teal has made a lovely lunch," said Roseanna, to break the tension in the room. "Shall we go into the dining room?"

In spite of what he said, Roseanna could see Jake was visibly shaken and was having a difficult time carrying on a conversation as they ate their meal. Ben started a discussion about the best strain of cotton to grow, and Jake out of politeness listened, but Roseanna could see that he was troubled about what had happened at the site. He asked questions of Ben that kept the conversation going forward, but his attention was not on what was being said.

Ben sensed Jake's lack of attention, "Jake, this accident at the site has you distracted. Maybe we should have this conversation at another time?"

Jake pushed his plate aside and sighed heavily. "It does, but that's no excuse for being a poor host. We made an agreement to talk, so why don't we stop with the polite chatter and hear what you have to say."

"I would agree we should. I assume, Roseanna, by now that your father's Will is settled," said Ben, "and there is no hope for the return of your brothers."

"There was never any question about John. Many men verified he was killed. As to Edward, we know what happened to him. I'm thankful the guard wrote and sent me Edward's few possessions. So, yes, the estates are settled, and both brothers are gone."

"You're a very fortunate young woman Roseanna. You inherit all there is of your father's estate."

"If you consider it fortunate to lose your entire family," said Jake angrily.

"That's not what I meant, Sinclair. Of course, that's a tragedy for Roseanna."

"I understand what he meant, Jake. You didn't mean any disrespectful did you, Uncle Ben," said Roseanna, trying to keep the conversation civil. Tell us what you want to talk about."

Ben paused to collect his thoughts. "I was wrong about some things that happened in the past," he said, pausing for Roseanna and Jake to deny his confession. When neither of them spoke, he continued, "Sometimes the advice from your attorney is not the path you should choose. At one time, I fired Lawrence Winston for what I considered very poor legal advice. To say I was misguided is an understatement. Things have been difficult. We were all foolish enough to think the war would be finished in no time. However, as you both know that was not to be. All I have left, along with others in the South, is our glorious past and memories of much better times."

"It's a start that you acknowledge you're not the only one to have suffered. You can do nothing but go forward as best you can," said Jake.

"Going forward is difficult. If I were younger, I would have the energy and the time to rebuild what I've lost. Your father and I spoke of that, Roseanna, starting over in our advanced age."

"You didn't seem to have a problem with your energy when you mistreated Simon," said Jake, sarcastically.

Roseanna gave Jake a shocked look. "Jake, let Uncle Ben finish what he was saying."

"You've never let me explain myself in that regard, Sinclair," said Ben testily. "That boy knows where that gold is hidden. I thought if I confronted him and asked him where the gold was, he would tell me and that would be the end of it."

"Please don't start arguing about the mistreatment of Simon," pleaded Roseanna, sensing that the discussion was headed for disaster.

"Could you explain to your husband, Roseanna, that it has never been the policy to mistreat Negros on this plantation? Simon had to be handled differently because of his reduced mental capacity. That's all that was happening."

"If you suspected that Simon knew the whereabouts of the gold you should have come to Roseanna and not taken it upon yourself to beat the information out of him," said Jake, with disgust.

"I resent that accusation. The whole affair was never about Simon it was about the damn gold, Sinclair," bellowed Ben.

The two men glared at each other across the table. "Stop, just stop!" said Roseanna, slapping her palms on the table. "The two of you stop. Put an end to this right now. Uncle Ben what you did to Simon was wrong. No one is ever going to believe otherwise. Now, that's the end of it."

A heavy silence followed as the two men continued to glare at each other. Ben took a deep breath and exhaled. "If that gold exists I could turn this whole plantation around, money will buy labor. Planting cotton would make the place profitable, and not in years, but in one or two growing seasons. The price of cotton has fallen but will come back in time. That dream you have of starting over with the horses is just that, a dream, and years in the making. Your father knew that, Roseanna."

"He never for one moment said that to me, Uncle Ben," insisted Roseanna.

"But he did to me, believe me, he did. He knew what a foolish notion the horses were. James was a good father to you, trying to appease your anxiety over the horses being gone because you were so attached and because you were too young to understand what the loss of the horses meant. We had many conversations about the best way to get both of us back to financial security and knew that planting cotton or sugar cane was the answer."

"I don't know if that's true Uncle Ben. I will admit that the time needed to rebuild a stable of horses would be years. I've thought about nothing else but how I would do it. Yes, it could be done, but how long would it take."

"I would just like to know how he intended to do it anyway."

"He had the money, Uncle Ben."

"But enough? How much would it take to replace those thoroughbreds?"

"He did have enough, but the time to accomplish what he wanted was probably why he would have ever considered raising crops," said Roseanna, "and Simon did know where the gold was."

Ben looked at Roseanna, stunned to learn that he was right about the gold. "So maybe by me pressuring Simon, he finally told."

"That's no justification for what you did," said Jake pointedly.

Ben was silent with his eyes downcast looking at his hands where he turned a spoon repeatedly in his fingers. "Could you share with me how much there was?"

"I had a letter from Mr. Cutler at the bank. It was the exact amount my father took from the bank. $287,000.00," said Roseanna.

Ben shook his head in disbelief. "My lands, how did my brother amass that money? Tell me that?"

"He invested all he had in the stock market," said Jake. "He didn't believe that the South would be successful in the war and never converted what he had in the bank to Confederate notes. He took what he had in gold and saved himself from financial ruin."

"John did say that he was concerned that the Confederate notes would be worthless, but why didn't he share his knowledge about the stock market with me? The knowledge he had could have saved me."

"Simple, he knew it wouldn't help you," said Jake. "That IOU for the twelve thousand dollars told him all he needed to know about your finances. You didn't have the money to invest."

"That IOU was not a loan. That was money to start rebuilding the plantation," said Ben. "I've told you that before, Roseanna."

"It doesn't matter, Uncle Ben. I've told my attorney that he should send you a letter that I consider the IOU paid in full."

"That's to everyone's advantage because we don't need to go to court to settle something that was never a debt in the first place. So, my brother had no trust in the South. He was a traitor."

"That's not true, he loved the South," said Roseanna taking offense. "But he didn't let his love blind him from seeing the truth that the South would lose."

"My brother always seemed to come out on top from the time we were boys. Unfortunate that I wasn't more like him, especially when it came to money."

"He was pretty progressive in his thinking about the market. Best thing he could have done to protect the money he had, and it paid off," said Jake.

"Nothing has paid off for me. I'm at the lowest I've ever been. I'm desperate, beyond desperate," said Ben with emphasis. "I'm going to lose my home and the land. I mortgaged everything, the house, and the acreage. When I bought into the Confederate dream of winning the war, I was sure I had done the right thing. I have no money to pay off what I owe. The whole of what I have will be auctioned off just to pay the taxes. I spent time while in New Orleans looking for a buyer or someone to lease the land, but there's too much acreage to be had. Selling or leasing won't be the answer, and the thought of some scalawag owning Pelicans Haven is very distasteful to me," said Ben casting a look at Jake. "The government is giving it away anyway. I'm stalling the bank off on the mortgage, but Cutler at the bank says no more. I need to ask you if you will share the money from the gold to help me get out from under the threat of losing my home."

"You should have told me sooner. I won't sit by and let you lose your home, Uncle Ben," said Roseanna with emotion.

"You pity me Roseanna?" said Ben softly.

"No, I care about you Uncle Ben and Aunt Jane, the whole family."

"If its pity you feel I don't deserve it. For generations, the Ravenna's have owned this plantation. Now more than ever because of the wars we need to hold this place together. But it's on the brink of being lost thanks to me," said

Ben, sadly.

"Uncle Ben, you didn't start the war."

Ben laughed without humor, "My problems with money started way before the damn war, Roseanna. The war just made everything snowball. It's been a lifetime for me and money troubles. You'd be mortified to know how and when my problems started, but I don't intend to share that with you. I'll take responsibility for it though, I brought it on myself," said Ben, as he rubbed his hands across his face.

Roseanna and Jake looked at each other, neither of them knowing how to respond to Ben.

"Of course, I'll help you, Uncle Ben," said Roseanna.

"I would be deeply grateful. I can't lose my home, Jane's home really. She loves that house. I will repay you, Roseanna."

"We're going into the city in the next couple of days, that is if Jake is still able to get away after what happened," said Roseanna turning to look at Jake.

"Yes, of course. I need to meet with Randy, and this accident at the site doesn't change that."

"Then Uncle Ben if you tell me the amount you need to bring the mortgage current and pay your taxes, I will go to the bank and have Mr. Cutler put the money into your account."

"Just a minute Roseanna," said Jake. "I think a breakdown in writing of where the money will go would be best, and what the terms of a loan should be," said Jake. "You can go to the bank and let Mr. Cutler know that you will take care of what your uncle owes. Then the two of you can meet with your respective attorneys and sign the papers. I'm sure your uncle wouldn't expect you to make him a loan without it being done legally."

"But Jake, I can't let him lose his home," cried Roseanna.

"I'm sure there's time, Roseanna. Isn't that right Ben?" said Jake pointedly. "We can visit with Josh Horn, and Ben can meet with Lawrence Winston and have the terms put in writing. Then the two of you and the attorneys can meet and finalize it all."

"Do you agree with that Uncle Ben?"

"I suppose Roseanna if Jake thinks that's best. I thought if we were family, we could do without the legal papers. There's not much time for hesitation. I need you to understand that."

"This can be done in a short amount of time. You're a businessman Ben, most times business and family don't mix. A legal agreement will protect you both," said Jake. "You understand this is the way it should be handled."

"Of course," said Ben. "I'm wondering, Roseanna, if you would extend the loan to allow me to get a crop in the ground? I could give you the figures for what I estimate it would cost. We could treat that as a loan to be repaid, and I could pay you a percentage of the crop yield."

"I think you would agree, Ben, that we should start just with the mortgage and taxes. Then we can discuss the money you would need for the crop," said Jake. "There's no rush on a loan for the crop. It's too late to put it in the ground this year. You'll have time for plowing and clearing before your ready to plant."

"Yes, there is work that needs to be done in the fields before planting. Jake's right, no need to rush. I would need money to pay labor to get that done. Been years since a crop was planted and the fields need plowing and growth needs to be removed. Can we agree that a loan can be made under those circumstances?"

Roseanna looked at Jake. "If you feel you want to loan the money for the crop to your uncle you should do so. A percentage of the yield plus interest could be very advantageous for you Roseanna," said Jake.

"Jake's right Roseanna this could be a perfect investment for you. Once the first crop is harvested, it will give me the money to replant and start getting myself back on my feet. The important thing will be that we saved the plantation from falling into the hands of someone who had no appreciation for what it has meant to this family."

"Uncle Ben, the important thing to me is that you don't lose your home."

Ben smiled, "Roseanna, you're more than generous. A thank you is certainly in order, and an apology for all that has happened in the past."

"I'll accept the thank you, Uncle Ben, but the apology will take some time. If you had come to me sooner with the truth…" Roseanna said, leaving the sentence hang.

Ben stood up from the table. "I need to earn your forgiveness, and I hope to do that, with you as well, Jake," said Ben as he reached to shake Jake's hand.

Roseanna and Jake walked with Ben to the door where Ben turned and shook Jake's hand again and gave his niece a hug. "You'll never know how this will relieve my mind. I'll be back with you soon with the figures you need. Jake sorry about the trouble at the site. Hope it doesn't cause any more delay. Could I ask a favor before I go? Nancy and Jane are unaware of the problems I'm facing. I would appreciate your keeping this in your confidence."

"Of course, we will, Uncle Ben," said Roseanna.

Roseanna turned to Jake as Ben left. "Jake, I can't let him lose his home. I think I need to pay what he owes while we are in the city. This explains so much to me."

"I don't believe there's any danger of that," said Jake, reassuringly. "Mr. Cutler will accommodate you in your request not to foreclose on your uncle's home."

"Jake, how can I not give him this money? Don't you want me to help?"

"You're using the wrong word, Roseanna. You're not giving the money, you're loaning the money. I'm advising you to make the loan a legal agreement. You should understand that the repayment of the loan may never come."

"Give, loan what's the difference. You would do the same for your family if it were needed. There's family history of this plantation that maybe you just don't understand and appreciate. I won't stand by and watch my uncle's home, and part of Pelicans Haven be sold to the highest bidder. You'd understand if your family was trying to preserve something that's been taken away from them because of the war."

"I think there was something in your uncle's past, not just the war that created this problem. He did imply something had happened. Your father managed to survive quite nicely during the war."

"And my father would share his wealth with his brother just as I'm doing," said Roseanna, heatedly.

"Roseanna, could I just point out to you that your uncle wants us to think he was acting on the advice of Lawrence Winston as he tried his best to take over your father's assets and this plantation. Think back and remember that Cutler is the one who told your uncle about the gold. So your uncle's claim that he had poor legal advice is not quite the truth."

"Jake, none of that matters to me anymore. It doesn't change anything. I still can't let him lose everything and watch some strangers live in my uncle's house."

"I don't trust your uncle. That's the plain and simple truth."

"That was before. I want all of that to be in the past. Ben needs me to do this for him, Jake. Uncle Ben is right, you're disagreeable today," said Roseanna, unhappily.

Jake laughed, "Disagreeable yes, especially where your uncle is concerned. The point I'm trying to make to you is that there has to be an end to the charity for your uncle. And yes, if it were my family, I would be doing the same thing you're doing. I just don't want you to be disillusioned into thinking that all will end well for your uncle because of this money."

"I'm not Jake, truly I'm not. I understand what you're saying, and I promise that I will let him know that there will be no more money until he begins to pay this back."

"Then we have nothing more to discuss except I would appreciate an apology for the remark you made about me being disagreeable."

Roseanna looked down her nose at Jake. "I do sincerely ask for forgiveness."

"That lacked sincerity, but thank you, and understand something, my opinion of your uncle won't change, and I'm quite sure he feels the same about me."

"Maybe in time things will improve between the two of you."

"Yes, perhaps they will, but not in the foreseeable future. I need to go back out to the site and see what's happened since I left. I think we've said all we need to."

"Good because my head hurts just thinking about the whole affair," said Roseanna. "I just want to get to the bank and to Josh and get my part of this settled."

"We'll leave in the morning if you and Nancy are ready," said Jake as he took Roseanna's chin in his hand and gave her a kiss.

"We will be," said Roseanna.

Ben walked back across the bridge towards home pleased and relieved that he had won the sympathy and support of his niece. Lawrence Winston had been right; down on his knees to his niece had worked. Now, at least, he would be out from under pressure from the bank for the mortgage and the parish for the taxes. He'd go to Lawrence first thing in the morning and have a document prepared for the agreement on the loan. Sinclair would probably demand an ungodly interest rate, but no matter, there may still be an opportunity to get him off the plantation and remove the influence he had over Roseanna. He was pleased, the plantation meant as much to Roseanna as it did to him. He could see that, and just maybe the Pelicans Haven had a bigger place in Roseanna's heart than Jake Sinclair did. He had no history here, and if Ben Ravenna had his way, he never would.

Early the next morning to escape the heat of the day Roseanna and Nancy trotted along in the gig towards New Orleans with Jake riding Sweetie at their side. The trip went slowly as slow-moving drays, and farm wagons clogged traffic on the road. By the time they reached the city the heat had soared along with the dust from the wheels of the vehicles. Jake and Roseanna wasted no time getting the details of the loan settled with Josh Horn and made their way to the bank to do the same.

Arnold Cutler was happy and relieved to have the news that Ben Ravenna's loans would be brought current. Roseanna was glad the matter had been settled. Jake had his reasons for not trusting Ben, but Roseanna vowed to go against Jake even though it would displease him. She needed to do this for the family and for the plantation.

CHAPTER 13

Storms from the Gulf of Mexico delivered days of continuous rain. Dark clouds edged with lightning illuminated the sky obscuring the sun as the storms moved towards the north. The creek on the plantation ran high and fast. The bridge that divided the plantation trapped debris against its foundation. Water stood in puddles, and runnels ran on the ground, the earth was wet and dripping. Work at the building site became impossible as the storms turned the ground into a saturated mire.

Jane Ravenna knew it was selfish to be glad of the weather, but it meant Andrew was home. He spent so many hours working for Jake Sinclair that she missed him. He was a breath of fresh air in the house where tensions between she and Ben had not eased. Ben's mood had unexpectedly changed. He was more pleasant than he had been in months and had stopped closeting himself in his office emptying his liquor decanter. He stayed in the barn doing chores, but Jane had no interest in asking what those might be. For her part, she was not ready to forgive him for the shameful thing he had done to Simon. He needed to ask for her forgiveness and apologize for involving her by having her lie to cover his wicked treatment of that poor man.

The stormy weather forced she and Nancy to cancel their usual gatherings with friends and women from the church. She was content at home, but a day away from the plantation would lift Nancy's spirits.

Now she stood on the veranda watching the rain and waiting for the mail carrier. She had done this since she had written to the Moorcroft twins in her attempt to claim any answer they sent before Ben found their letter. Today her persistence bore fruit. As the carrier rode towards her Jane smiled, "Miserable weather, you'll be relieved when this stops," she said indicating the darkened sky.

"It'll stop eventually," said Mr. Plumb. "Ain't got to build an ark yet, Mrs. Ravenna," he said with a chuckle. "Roads are flooded, and it's hard getting around; taking me some extra time for deliveries. You best stay close to home until it clears up." He tipped his rain-soaked hat and handed Jane the stack of mail.

Jane smiled "I won't be going anywhere, nothing important that I need to attend to."

She nodded her thanks as she glanced at the letter on the top of the stack. She felt a flutter when she realized the letter was from London. The Moorcrofts had answered. She quickly entered the house and hurried to her drawing room for privacy.

Sitting at her writing table, she stared at the Moorcroft letter, fingering the envelope, which was made of rich, thick vellum. She ran her finger over the engraved Moorcroft coat of arms she had once shared and allowed herself a moment to calm her breathing and say a silent prayer that the letter would be the answer for her hopes for Andrew.

Carefully slitting the seal with a sterling letter opener, she pulled out the creamy vellum pages and fingered a brooch at her throat, she began to read.

Dear Madam

You come with your hand out when in the past you have shown no consideration for the feelings of your family here in England. Your sudden decision to go to America took a devastating toll on our mother, depriving her of her only grandchild whom she loved with all her heart. The loss of his companionship certainly hastened her death. The support that you are asking for Andrew will be denied him due to your actions. You drove our beloved brother, Malcolm, to commit heinous acts, which caused him to take his own life…

Jane's forehead creased in a frown, and she stopped fingering the broach as her breath left her. A shiver passed through her body, and tears sprang to her eyes. She let out an agonized moan and the letter slipped from her trembling hands and fell to the floor. She dropped her head to her arms on the desk and began to cry, racking sobs shook her shoulders.

Andrew came into the room and hurried to her, "Mother, Mother, my God what's wrong," he asked with concern laying his hand on her shoulder.

Jane looked at her son through her tears, "Oh, Andrew I'm so sorry, so very sorry," she wailed. "They are so cold and hateful." She gave into a fresh bout of sobs turning away from Andrew and hiding her face in her hands.

Andrew was puzzled, "Who Mother? Who is hateful?" He saw the letter lying on the floor at his feet, picked it up, and began to read.

… To add to your disreputable behavior, you chose to marry a criminal who is wanted for murder in England. His illegal activities of kidnapping and transporting Negroes and selling them into slavery in America resulted in death to many of them. If you care for more of the facts of his crimes, you can investigate the fate of the slave ship, Helena, which was captured by the British government. You will see for yourself the fate of the Negros that were held captive. We have taken it upon ourselves, as our civic duty, to report to the British authorities your husband's exact whereabouts.

Now you come to us for support for Andrew, which tells us that Ben Ravenna married you for the inheritance you received from your parents and the monies left to you for Andrew's benefit upon his father's, our dear brother Malcolm's, death. Mr. Ravenna, who boasted of his prominence as a wealthy landowner in America, has apparently squandered all the money he possessed investing in the slave ship Helena. He had no care as doing so was against the laws of our country as well as his own. Now you're begging support for Andrew. History tells us that once again Ben Ravenna would squander those funds as well. There is no support or sympathy for you or Andrew from this quarter, Madam. Do not contact us in the future; your pleas will be ignored.

Reginald Moorcroft, Esq.

Andrew stared at the words in the letter not understanding what he was seeing. "This letter says Ben is wanted for murder, Mother."

"Murder, there was no murder." Jane had not read the entire letter but enough to know that the twins were still holding her responsible for Malcolm's suicide. "I did nothing to your father. You must believe me."

"No, Ben, not my father. This says he is wanted by the British authorities for murder."

Jane reached with trembling hands and snatched the letter from Andrew. "Ranting, they're ranting, Andrew."

Andrew turned and ran from the room. Jane wiped her eyes with a hankie. She was calmer now and started rereading the letter. Her hand flew to her mouth when she read that Ben was wanted for murder. It became clear after all these years, Ben had agreed to the marriage because he had lost his money in the slave ship. He didn't care for her or Andrew. This was nothing about a new start away from the horrible gossip about his father. He wanted her money. Yet they built this beautiful home together, they had a child together, and they had happy years. The war was what had changed everything. Ben hadn't squandered her money, it was lost to the Confederacy, and the slaves were gone because of the war. The twins had no right to judge Ben so harshly.

What if it were true. Ben wanted for murder? What a horrible secret to keep all these years. "The Moorcrofts are wrong Andrew," she said. "It's not true. Ben isn't wanted for murder."

She turned in her seat, but Andrew was no longer in the room. She must tell him the nastiness about his father and Ben wasn't right. Where had he gone? He had gone to confront Ben.

Jane panicked and jumped from her chair. "No, Andrew! No, no!" she screamed.

Ben was in the barn, and she ran to find him and her son. The front door gave a resounding slam as she left the house.

The sound of her mother's scream and the noise of a slamming door woke Nancy from her nap. She sat up in bed unsure of what she had heard. Rising from the bed, she looked out the window, which gave a view of the barn. She saw her mother running in the rain and calling for Andrew. She hastily pulled her dress over her head doing up the buttons as she sprinted for the stairs.

Andrew ran to the vast expanse of the barn. "Ben, Ben, where the hell are you? Come out and show yourself," he roared.

Ben limped from the tool room with Nathan at his heels and stared at Andrew. "What is it, Andrew? What's wrong?"

Andrew charged towards Ben with his fist clenched, "You! You're what's wrong with me and everyone else on this plantation. You bastard! Everything you've done to Roseanna and to Simon, me, and now my mother," said

Andrew gesturing wildly. "Now it all makes sense why you didn't want me or my mother to talk to the Moorcrofts."

Ben's face went slack with confusion and then his forehead furrowed. "Who's telling you this nonsense?"

"The only people who could tell, my uncles in London. It's all in the letter. The authorities know where you are and they'll come for you and good riddance!"

Ben felt sweat break out in his armpits, "You don't know what you're talking about," he said with scorn.

"You'd like to believe that wouldn't you, Ben," said Andrew in a cocky voice. "My uncles know, don't they? This time Ben you can't lie your way out of it."

"You're spouting nonsense," said Ben, dismissively, turning and walking away.

Andrew rushed after him and grabbed him by the shoulder spinning him around. "You don't want to talk to me, Ben?"

Nathan quickly stepped away from the two men as Ben angrily swung at Andrew with his walking stick, "Keep your hands off of me!" yelled Ben.

Andrew dodged away to avoid being hit. "I know everything. I know how you forced Lawrence Winston into lying about the guardianship for Roseanna making her marry Jake, I know how you beat Simon to get the gold that doesn't belong to you, and now I know how you treated my mother and stole her money and that you murdered the slaves on that ship."

"I did no such thing. The guardianship was to protect Roseanna. She did a stupid thing marrying that Yankee."

"But I was there Ben, outside your office on the veranda when you and Lawrence Winston schemed how you would take the whole plantation and the gold. I knew it all from the beginning. You forced her to marry, but it didn't work did it, Ben? She ended up making the best marriage she could have and snatched everything out from under you. Now the Yankee has it and you never will."

"Get out of my sight! You're babbling nonsense. You don't know what you're talking about."

"But I do! You deceived everyone, but most of all my mother and now it's all going to stop. You can't hide from murder. You married her for her money because you lost yours investing in that slave ship where all the Negroes died, and now you're wanted for murder."

"Ask your mother why she begged me to marry her, begged me in tears." stormed Ben."

"You married her for her money and squandered it all because you lost yours killing the Negros on that ship."

"You have it wrong. Your mother married me to get away from the gossip and talk in London about your father. Did she tell you about your father, how he really died?" spat Ben.

"You leave my father out of this. He has nothing to do with it."

"Your father has everything to do with this. Ask your mother how he really died. Do you have the guts to hear the truth?" spat Ben.

Andrew looked at Ben in astonishment. "Truth Ben, Do you even know what truth is?"

Ben ignored Andrew raising his voice in a shout. "Your father shot himself in the head, Andrew. Why, why do you think he would do such a thing? Because he liked men, more then he liked women, and he got caught in the act and killed himself in shame. Everyone blamed your mother. Your uncles told everyone she drove him to it. That Andrew is the truth!"

"That's a lie. You're not fit to even mention my father's name."

"Your father was a sodomite Andrew. He took the coward's way out. You know what it's like to be a coward don't you, Andrew?" You ran from battle and disgraced yourself."

"This isn't about me, it's about you Ben! Everyone knows about me, and finally, everyone will know about you and what you've done."

"Your mother couldn't stand the gossip about her and your father. She cried and begged me to get her out of London and offered all the money she had in the world just so I would take her and her pampered brat of a son away from the gossip."

"My mother did nothing except try to make a better life for herself and her child," said Andrew with a snort. "She just picked the wrong person to make it happen, she chose a murderer, a liar, an arsonist, a man who knows no shame when it comes to what he wants. A man who stops at nothing just takes what he wants."

Ben had heard enough. His face was red with rage and spittle formed at the corners of his mouth. He gritted his teeth, lunged towards Andrew and swung his walking stick striking a blow to Andrew's head.

The blow landed above Andrew's left eye and knocked him to the ground. He lay moaning and stunned, his hands grasped at his head feeling the blood from the wound.

Ben quickly limped towards the prone Andrew to take the advantage, raised the stick in both hands like a club, and swung it with all his might at Andrew's head.

Andrew, stunned from the first blow, rolled away to avoid the strike and grabbed the stick.

Ben pulled the stick to wrest it away from Andrew but succeeded only in helping Andrew regain his feet. Andrew grabbed the stick in both hands, and the two grappled back and forth the stick between them. Ben knew the younger man would overpower him.

"Nathan help me!" he yelled as he felt Andrew gaining the advantage.

Nathan watched terrified, undecided what to do. He heard Ben yell for him, and he took a hesitant step towards the two struggling men then turned and ran from the barn.

Andrew pushed the stick towards Ben forcing him backward. Ben lost his balance and fall heavily to the ground. Andrew threw the stick across the barn where it clattered as it rolled across the floor. He stood, his legs spread, breathing heavily as he stared at Ben.

"The British authorities will send for you now Ben. My uncles told them where you've been hiding. You'll be dragged to London in chains and tried for murder."

Jane ran through the wide door of the barn and saw Andrew standing with his legs spread wide looking at Ben who was on his back on the floor.

"Andrew, Andrew listen to me. Listen to me Andrew!" she yelled as she approached her son.

Ben lay spent, breathing hard and unable to get up. He reached quickly inside his coat for the derringer he carried and pointed the gun at Andrew.

Andrew flung himself at Ben grabbing the gun to wrest it from his hand. They wrestled with the gun between them. The gun went off, the sound reverberating in the barn.

Ben's eyes were startled wide. He froze, his mouth working to speak, but then he went limp under Andrews's weight.

Andrew rose to his feet, blood from the wounds to his head streaking his face and running into his eyes.

"No! No!" screamed Jane.

Ben lay on his back, a small hole in his chest just under his heart. He lay still his eyes closed, his breathing labored. He raised his hand to his chest and put his hand on the wound, and slowly pushed himself to a sitting position. He pulled his hand from his chest and stared vacantly at the blood on his palm. Blood suddenly bloomed like a flower on his shirtfront. He looked at Andrew his lips moving, but no sound came. He grimaced and just as suddenly, his face went slack. He fell back as a gush of air left his lungs.

Nancy followed her mother and was in the yard when she heard a shot and blood-curdling scream. She stopped, paralyzed in fear, standing in the rain uncertain of what to do. Her mother was screaming Ben's name. She ran towards the barn.

Andrew jumped away from Ben, watching in shocked horror, staring where Ben lay prone on the ground. Jane ran towards her husband, kneeling by his side, screaming his name repeatedly. Andrew stumbled unsteadily on his feet from the blow to his head. He moved backward away from his mother and Ben, a dazed look on his face, wiping at the blood that ran from his wound. He turned to see his sister.

"Andrew, Andrew what happened?" she said fretfully reaching for her brother when she saw the blood on his head and face.

Andrew stared at his sister, then wheeled, and ran out of the barn. He scrambled into the saddle, jerked the horse's head around, and spurred it into a gallop riding away from the barn. He was crying and the salty tears burned the open wound on his cheek. He wiped at the pain, and his hand came away streaked with blood.

Jerking the reins hard he pulled the horse to a stop, slid from the saddle, and fell to his knees in the mud beside the road and vomited into the tall weeds. The rain was coming in torrents. Using both hands, he scrubbed at his eyes to clear his vision and his chin to wipe away the vomit. Still, there was blood on his hands. He gingerly touched the wound and felt swelling, and then the pain and his head throbbed. He took his handkerchief from his pocket and wiped at the wound. More blood came, and he could feel it trickle down his cheek and neck and into the collar of his shirt. He pressed the cloth into the wound to stop the bleeding, clumsily remounted his horse, and kicked it into a gallop.

CHAPTER 14

Nancy was stunned to see the blood and wounds on her brother's face as she huddled in the rain at the entrance to the barn. She called his name and attempted to help him, but he ignored her, clumsily mounted his horse, and rode away. Nancy turned and went into the barn to find her mother crouched in the shadows over her father's prone form. She ran to her.

"What is it, what's happened? What's wrong? Is father hurt?"

"He's shot," cried Jane hysterically. "Andrew shot him. He's not breathing."

Nancy knelt in the dust of the barn beside her mother. She looked at her father's face, which was deathly pale. She hesitated a moment and then ran from the barn calling for Cindy the Negro girl.

"Cindy, my father's been shot," she yelled excitedly. "Go quickly, get Miss Roseanna, tell her to come to the barn." Then she turned and ran back to her mother.

Roseanna and Mama Teal stood looking at the yards and yards of fabric spread across the dining room table. The fabric was a rich pale blue satin intended as drapes for the bedroom for Roseanna and Jake. Roseanna stood with scissors in her hand and a measuring tape adorning her neck. She stared at the fabric calculating where the first cut should be. Richard Philip's recommendations for where the fabric could be found in the city were perfect. Roseanna, on the trip to New Orleans with Jake and Nancy, had found exactly what she had wanted in the fabric as well as wallpaper. The wallpaper was stripped in the same blue as the fabric with corresponding cream stripes.

Jake walked into the room. "This looks like a lot of work," he said as he surveyed the fabric flowing off the table and lying in puddles on the floor. "Is this what you and Nancy found in the city?"

"Nancy's choice and a good one. Don't you agree?" replied Roseanna. "She found the fabric for drapes and wallpaper to match. They'll go beautifully in our room. We're just making sure we cut it correctly, which is the hardest part. Do you like it, Jake?"

"Much more than the flowers and bows in your room," said Jake with a grin.

"I think you made your point about the flowers and bow and dolls in my room," laughed Roseanna.

"Have I mentioned that before?" said Jake with a grin.

"I's think yous cut where you gots that pin, Miss Roseanna," said Mama Teal, pointing to a pin as she smoothed the fabric with her hand, "it be fine."

"You've done this many times with grandmother and my mother, so if you're sure, I guess we could start to cut."

"You can just buy more fabric if you cut wrong can't you?" asked Jake, as he stood watching the two women with his hands in his pockets.

Roseanna and Mama Teal exchanged an amused look. "We'd rather do it right the first time," said Roseanna.

"If these storms ever stop I'd like to get back to the building site," commented Jake, as he walked to the window and stared out at the rain.

"Isn't there any work that can be done, Jake?"

"Not with the river flowing so high and fast. Putting the pilings in has become the issue. The flow of the water fills the holes with silt and sand faster than they can get it out. The men working to clear underbrush and trees are having problems with mud. It's above their shoe tops."

"It seems one thing or another keeps stopping the work," said Roseanna.

"It'll pass. The crew sinking the pilings isn't happy. They're all from the city and stuck in tents waiting for this to stop. I'm at least home where it's dry."

"Miss Roseanna, I's be getting you lunch now," said Mama Teal.

"I'll help, we can postpone cutting fabric until we're sure we measured correctly," said Roseanna. She removed the tape from around her neck and started out of the dining room.

A frantic pounding came on the front door. With a startled expression, Roseanna looked at Jake, and both hurried to the door to find a breathless, wide-eyed, and wildly gesturing Cindy.

Cindy blurted out her news, and Roseanna and Jake ran to the barn to find Jane crying uncontrollably as she knelt by her husband's inert form. Nancy, visibly upset, was trying to lift her mother to her feet and move her away.

Jake knelt beside Jane, laid his hand gently on her shoulder, and reached for Ben's wrist to feel for a pulse. After a moment, he turned to Roseanna and nodded to her to let her know that her uncle was dead.

"Aunt Jane, come with me now," said Roseanna in a quaking voice as she rushed forward and spoke to her aunt.

Jane stood and looked at Roseanna with blank eyes, her voice calm. "He's dead, isn't he? Andrew's shot him."

Roseanna was stunned when she heard what her aunt said. "Aunt Jane just come with me. We'll get the doctor to see to Uncle Ben."

Nancy, tears on her cheeks, clutched her mother to her. She understood her father was dead and she would need to care for her mother. "We need the doctor for Father. Can we send someone Jake?" she said knowing it was a false hope, as she helped Roseanna lead her mother from the barn.

"I will, Nancy," said Jake as he searched the barn for something to cover Ben's body.

Outside of the barn Jane suddenly stopped, "I can't just leave him there."

"Jake is with him, Aunt Jane," said Roseanna. "Come away now."

Nancy took her mother's hand trying to lead her away from the barn. "I'm here, Mother. Father needs the doctor. Jake is taking care of him."

"Your father, Nancy, I need to be with your father. Where is Andrew? He's bleeding, he's hurt."

Roseanna tried not to cry, but her voice broke as she spoke. "We need to get you both in the house out of the rain. We're getting soaked."

Jane's knees gave way, she collapsed in the mud of the stable yard crying and calling for her husband. Suddenly she stopped crying. "Where is Andrew?" she said wild-eyed. "He was bleeding. He's hurt we need to find him."

"We'll find Andrew, Aunt Jane. Just come with me, let me get you out of the rain. Come into the house."

Jane stood and walked slowly allowing Roseanna to lead her.

"I have to find Andrew," said Nancy. "Where is he?"

"Wait for Jake, Nancy. Let's get you and your mother out of the weather."

Jake hurried out of the barn and glanced at the three women as they made their way across the bridge. Seeing Nathan huddling close to a tree a short distance from the barn, he called to him, "Nathan we need the doctor. Take Ben's horse and ride for him."

"I can't go wiff Mr. Ben dead there," said Nathan pointing to the barn. "I hear the shot and see Mr. Andrew go way."

Jake ran back into the barn, and quickly saddled Ben's horse, led it outside and motioned to Nathan. "Go as fast as you can. Tell the doctor Mr. Ben has been shot and he needs to come quickly."

"He dead Mr. Jake?"

"The doctor will tell us, Nathan. Now go on," he said as he swatted the horse's flank.

Jake ran to saddle Sweetie to ride for the authorities and to see if Roseanna needed help. "Nathan he takes Mr. Ben's horse. I's see him rides away," said Simon as he ran towards Jake in the pelting rain.

"It's all right Simon," said Jake. "Where's Mama Teal?"

"She at the big house," said Simon, pointing.

"Can you saddle Sweetie, Simon, and bring her around the front of the house?"

"Yes, Mr. Jake."

Jake entered the house and followed the sound of voices coming from upstairs; he took them two at a time.

Nancy heard him, and ran to him, "Please tell me he isn't dead."

"I've sent Nathan for the doctor. We'll see when he gets here. How's your mother?"

"I don't know. She is asking for Andrew. He was hurt, his head was bleeding, a lot of blood. I saw him only for a moment, and then he rode away. Jake don't keep this from me. He's dead, I know he is."

"We need to wait for the doctor. I have an idea where Andrew has gone. Don't worry, we'll find him. I need to go to the authorities. We need to report this."

"What's going to happen to Andrew? Will he be charged with murder?" asked Nancy distressed.

"I can't answer that. We need to wait. I'm not sure if anyone knows what happened."

"Mother knows, she was there; at least when I heard the shot, she was in the barn."

"Your mother can tell us what she saw, and Andrew will tell us what happened."

"My father can't be dead, that can't be," cried Nancy as she clutched the lapels of Jake's coat in her fist, and buried her face against his chest.

"What can I do for you before I go?" he said, as he gently moved her away and stared into her face.

"Please tell me everything will be all right."

Jake hugged her and let her cry on his shoulder. "This is going to take some time to sort out. Where is Mama Teal? "

"She's with mother and Roseanna."

"Go ask Roseanna to step out for a moment and talk to me. You stay with your mother."

Nancy went into the room, and a moment later Roseanna appeared. She hurried to Jake, and he wrapped his arms around her.

"Jake, I can't believe this is happened."

"I've sent Nathan for the doctor to see about Ben and to help with Jane if she needs it."

"He's dead, isn't he? Aunt Jane needs the doctor, Jake. She's just moaning and crying for Andrew and fighting us trying to leave to find him. The doctor needs to give her something to calm her. This is horrible. Why did it happen, why, why?"

"Did Jane say anything about what set Andrew off?"

"No, she hasn't said anything. She just keeps calling for Andrew."

"I'm going to the authorities, and shouldn't be long. Mama Teal is here with you, and soon Loretta will hear about what happened. I don't want to leave you, but I don't have a choice. Will you be all right?"

"I'll do my best, said Roseanna, her face pale and drawn. "I didn't even think of Loretta. She's going to be upset."

"Can't be helped. Mama Teal will have to speak to her and let her know what happened and soon. What do you need before I go?"

Roseanna shook her head, "I was just sending Mama Teal and Nancy for dry clothes for Jane. She's soaked through and covered with mud, she fell outside the stable."

"Simon knows something is going on, he'll be upset. I'll have him saddle Moses and go with me."

"No, that will slow you down with the rain and the roads so bad. You go and please hurry. I need you back as quick as possible. Just go. I love you, and please be careful."

"I love you, too," said Jake and with a quick kiss, he ran from the house.

Roseanna went back into the bedroom to find Jane still agitated, and Nancy trying to calm her. Nancy too was distressed. Roseanna laid her hands on her shoulders. "Nancy, go with Mama Teal and get dry clean clothes for yourself and your mother. I'll stay with her."

"I can't leave her, Roseanna. She needs me. Did Jake leave?"

"Yes, now you go and when you get back maybe the doctor will be here to give your mother something to calm her."

"Come on Miss Nancy," said Mama Teal. "We be quick. Get yous, mama, all clean and yous too," said Mama Teal gently leading Nancy towards the door.

Jane, seeing Nancy leaving the room called out to her, "Nancy, Nancy find Andrew. You hear me, find your brother."

Roseanna sat on the bed beside her aunt, "She'll find him, Aunt Jane. Let me help you out of these wet clothes. Then we can talk about Andrew."

"It was because of the horrible letter, that's why Andrew shot Ben. It's not his fault. It's Ben's fault. Andrew should never have seen that letter, it's full of lies. He didn't mean to shoot Ben. Ben was going to shoot him, Andrew tried to stop him. That's what happened, I saw it all, and then the gun went off."

"All right, Aunt Jane," said Roseanna as she knelt to remove her aunt's mud-caked shoes. "Help me now with your clothes, you're wet and muddy."

"No, no, no. I can't do that now," said Jane fighting against Roseanna. "Let me go and find Andrew. I don't care about the wet clothes," she cried trying to stand.

"Roseanna, how are you and Jane my dear, how are you?" said Doctor Olson as he came into the room. "Nancy told me to come on in," he said by way of explanation to Roseanna. "I passed her as she was leaving the house, Roseanna," he said studying Jane as he talked. "Now Jane let's get you calmed down."

"No doctor. Ben's dead," said Jane. "I need to find Andrew."

"We'll find Andrew in due time," said the doctor as he opened his bag and studied Jane. "Roseanna, can we have some water for Jane?"

Roseanna left the room and came back with the water. As she was entering the room, Nancy and Mama Teal came up the stairs. "Here Nancy, take this to your mother. I need to talk to Mama Teal."

Roseanna took Mama Teal by the arm and drew her aside. "Mama Teal you need to go and talk to Loretta. She's going to be upset about this if she doesn't already know. No one knows where Andrew is. Could he be with her?"

"I's talk to her Miss Roseanna, but Andrew and Loretta done with each other. I's knows he not be wiff her."

"I'm, I don't understand what you're saying Mama Teal," said Roseanna with a frown. "Could you just go and be sure and ask her if she knows where he may have gone?"

"Yes, Miss Roseanna, but Loretta she done wiff him, she done," she said as she went down the stairs.

Loretta was no longer involved with Andrew. Roseanna didn't give it more thought as she hurried down the stairs to watch out the rain-streaked window for Jake's return.

Richard Philips sat in the opening of his tent staring at the falling rain deep in thought about the next project he was scheduled to complete. While the weather was preventing him from working on the project for Jake Sinclair, he had work to keep his mind occupied. As was his habit, he awoke early to find yet more rain that would prevent work at the site. He sat at his worktable putting the final changes on the drawing for a future project.

Content with what he put on paper, he donned his rain gear, grabbed his fishing pole, and persuaded a beautiful fish to be a part of his leisurely breakfast. After years of being away from civilization due to his occupation, he knew how to cope with the weather, and lack of conveniences. He was a resourceful man, tall and distinguished with a full head of snow-white hair and deep blue eyes. He was deeply tanned from his time working in the sun and muscular from the physical aspects of his profession.

After breakfast, and with a cup of freshly brewed tea, he sat watching the rainfall. He heard the pounding horse hooves and was startled to see Andrew riding towards him. Andrew brought the horse up short, clumsily dismounted from the saddle, and fell to the ground.

Richard Philips ran to him, "Good god, Andrew," he said taking in the blood and wounds, "What's happened to you?"

Andrew didn't respond, but looked at Richard with pain-filled eyes and gasped for breath. "You're bleeding! Come out of the rain, get in the tent."

Richard lifted Andrew to his feet. Andrew staggered, but with help from Richard sat in the chair by the tent opening.

Richard crouched by the chair, "Let me look at your face." He grasped Andrews chin in his fingers to examine the wound. "Did you fall from your horse?"

Andrew did not respond. Richard went to a table in the tent and retrieved a basin and cloth. He poured water from a tea kettle into the basin and came back to Andrew's side. "This is going to hurt."

Richard carefully swabbed at the wound wiping away the blood. Andrew's eye was swollen until it looked like a plum had been forced under the skin. Richard pressed the cloth to the wound. Andrew winced and pulled away from his ministering. "Be still Andrew. We need to stop the bleeding. Are you hurt anywhere else?"

Andrew reached his hand to the top of his head as he stared intently at Richards' face. "Here," said Richard taking Andrew's hand and placing it on the cloth he held to the wound at his eye, "hold this while I take a look. A nasty gash, not bleeding, but needing stitches. I'm more concerned about your eye," he said, as he gingerly removed the cloth from the wound. "It's not going to stop bleeding; you're going to need some help from a doctor," he said, as he studied Andrew's face. "Hold this while I get something to bind it."

Richard found a shirt and ripped strips to use as binding to hold the cloth in place. "Tell me what happened."

Andrew nodded his head and covered his face with his hands. "I think I killed Ben." He then started to sob and shake uncontrollably.

"What? Andrew stop crying and tell me what happened," said Richard as he shook Andrew by the shoulders.

Andrew looked at him with unfocused eyes. "You're soaked to the bone," said Richard grabbing a blanket from a cot and wrapping it around Andrew's shoulder.

"I think he's dead. I didn't mean to kill him. We argued I remember he hit me with his stick; he pulled his derringer and pointed it at me, the gun went off, and Ben was lying on the floor. There was blood and... I don't remember."

Richard stared intently at Andrew, "You don't know if he's dead, just wounded perhaps."

"I don't know. I don't know. My mother was there," said Andrew, as he suddenly lurched from his chair, fell to his knees outside the tent, and vomited in the mud.

Richard followed and helped him to his feet and brought him back inside the tent. "You need dry clothes, and then we need to go to the plantation."

"No! No! I'm not going back. Oh! God! My mother! I can't face my mother."

"Son, you need to go back and see how Ben is."

"I can't. I just can't."

Richard stood looking at Andrew trying to make sense of what he had told him. Could it really be that he had killed his stepfather? What must Jane be going through? Who was there for her? He needed to go the plantation and help in any way that he could. The authorities needed to be summoned, and Ben, did he need a doctor?

Richard rummaged through the meager wardrobe he kept at the building site and found clothes for Andrew. "Put these on Andrew. They'll be too big, but at least they're dry and clean. We're going back. You need to go back."

Andrew stood and began disrobing. He was unsteady on his feet, and Richard helped him dress. "Richard do you believe me? I didn't mean for him to be shot."

"I know, Son. Just get the clothes on and then we can find out how Ben is."

"Richard my mother was there! I didn't mean to shoot Ben! Richard, do you believe me? I didn't mean for him to be shot."

"I know, Son. Just get the clothes on and then we can find out how Ben is."

"Richard my mother!" moaned Andrew. "I didn't mean to shoot Ben!"

"Andrew stop! You're rambling and asking questions I can't answer. You need a doctor to look at your head. Now get dressed, we have to go to the plantation. That's where we'll get answers," said Richard sternly.

CHAPTER 15

Roseanna paced the floor of the parlor as she watched the rain-streaked window for Jake. The house was quiet save for the steady sound of the rain on the roof. Whatever the doctor had given Jane had calmed her and her keening and calling for Andrew had stopped.

A shiver passed through Roseanna, as she suddenly comprehended her uncle's death. She wrapped her arms around her body to stop from shaking. The sight of Jane on her knees in hysterics beside Ben's body begging him to speak replayed in her mind. Uncle Ben dead. Where was Andrew? What would happen to him now?

Roseanna heard a noise behind her and turned to see Nancy coming down the stairs. "Is she better, Nancy?"

"Quieter," said Nancy her face lined with tension. "The doctor sent me out. He thinks she'll calm easier if I'm not there. He'll stay with her until she sleeps. Is Andrew back?"

"No, Jake isn't back either."

Nancy started to cry. "Oh, Roseanna! What happened between my father and Andrew? Why did Andrew shoot him? Now, what will happen? My father is dead, what will happen now?"

Roseanna moved to Nancy's side and took her in her arms. "I can't tell you what will happen. The shock is too much. Things will change, and all you can do is face them as they come. I'll do whatever I can for you and your mother and so will Jake. Try to think about what is happening now and where Andrew has gone and how badly he is hurt."

"Oh, Andrew. He was bleeding, Roseanna. My father has a temper, always with Andrew; I know they must have argued. They always argued. Andrew must know what has happened or he would have stayed. Why would he shoot my father? I can't believe he left. I don't understand."

"We'll talk to him, Nancy. He'll tell us what happened. Your mother talked about a horrible letter, but it didn't make sense. Do you know what she meant?" asked Roseanna as she stroked Nancy's back to calm her.

"What letter? What letter was she talking about?"

"She said a horrible letter," said Roseanna. Then to distract Nancy, "We should change; we're both wet and dirty. We'll feel better if we put on dry clean clothes."

"Roseanna wait! What did she mean about a letter?"

"That's all she said. She said it was a horrible letter full of lies, and Andrew should not have read it."

"Where is it," asked Nancy?

"Honey, I don't know. I'm telling you what your mother said to me. Let's get dry clothes for the two of us. Are you hungry? You must be hungry."

Nancy grabbed Roseanna's arms. "Roseanna I want to see the letter. Help me look for it?"

"Let's wait for Jake; he'll find it. It may not be anything, just your mom rambling because she's so upset."

"It must mean something or have something to do with what happened. I need to know. Please go with me and help me look. It would be in my mother's drawing room. I need to see that letter."

"Nancy, I don't want to miss Jake when he returns." Roseanna looked towards the lane where Jake would be arriving as she considered what she should do. "We'll go, but we have to hurry."

The two women ran across the bridge in the rain making a wide path around the entrance to the barn, entered the house, and went immediately to Jane's drawing room. Nancy grabbed a letter lying on her mother's desk and started to read.

"What does it say Nancy?" asked Roseanna trying to read over her cousin's shoulder.

Nancy fell into the chair at her mother's desk with her hand covering her mouth. "It says my father is wanted for murder in London for the death of Negroes."

"Let me see," said Roseanna.

Nancy visibly shaken handed the letter to Roseanna and began to cry again. "What does it mean? Murder. My father wanted for murder."

"The person who wrote this letter, Reginald Moorcroft, is that Andrew's uncle? I know your mother wrote to ask for help to get Andrew to London. Nancy, we must go back and wait for Jake and Andrew. I don't want to miss them. We'll take the letter with us to read and show to Jake."

Roseanna pushed the letter deep into her pocket as the girls hurried back to the house. The doctor was in the parlor watching at the window.

"She's calmer now," he said. I dosed her rather heavily, and she'll sleep for some time and be able to cope better when she wakes. Nancy, you can go and sit with her now if you want. She's not going to know you're there but you'll feel better knowing she's sleeping and maybe sleep yourself."

Nancy hesitated for only a minute. "Roseanna, keep the letter for me," she said and hurried up the stairs.

"You need to see to Ben now doctor?" asked Roseanna.

"Ben's beyond anyone's help. The Negro man, Nathan, told me where he was. I was there first and sorry to say he is gone."

"I can't believe this."

"Death is no stranger here as you can attest," said the doctor patting Roseanna's shoulder. "I've heard that you lost both of your brothers to the war, and I've also heard the news that you were married," he said on a happier note. "Guess congratulations are in order. Do I know the young man in question?"

Roseanna smiled, "No, but you'll like Jake. He's a good man. He's gone for the authorities to report this."

"Where is the boy, Andrew?" asked the doctor.

"No one knows," said Roseanna. "Nancy saw him leave the plantation, and she said he was bleeding from his head, but he hasn't come back. I just wish Jake would come home."

"Weather has the roads flooded, they are hardly passable in quite a few places," said the doctor as he looked out the window, his fingers hooked in his vest pockets. "Not so easy getting around out there so it may be taking longer than you would expect. Who is this coming into the lane?"

Roseanna swiftly turned to follow the doctor's gaze. "Jake," she said with relief seeing him with two other riders. "He's back." She hurried out the door to the veranda with the doctor at her heels.

As the riders came closer, Jake directed the two men with him towards the barn on Ben's property then came to the veranda and quickly dismounted. "Are you all right, Roseanna?"

She nodded her head and gave him a small smile as she reached him, "Jane is sleeping, the doctor gave her something, and Nancy is with her. Who are these men?"

"Federal authorities," said Jake. "Has Andrew come back?"

"No, and Mama Teal said Loretta won't know where he is as they're apparently not together any longer."

"Doesn't matter, there are other matters to deal with. I'll go and see what's going on over there. I'll be back as soon as I can."

"Jake!" exclaimed Roseanna pointing at the lane. "Look, it's Andrew with Richard Philips!"

Jake hurried from the shelter of the veranda to meet the riders as they approached. "Andrew, are you all right?" he asked as he saw the bandage on Andrew's head.

"He needs medical attention," said Richard as he dismounted and went to help Andrew from his mount.

The doctor came to Andrew's side. "Let's get a good look at you, Andrew," he said studying Andrew's face. Are you in pain?" he said, as Andrew was settled into a chair on the veranda.

"My head, it hurts," said Andrew, as he reached towards his head.

"Sit still and let me look at you," said the doctor, and then reached into his medical bag.

"Couldn't get the bleeding to stop, and had no idea what to do for his eye," said Richard. He, Jake and Roseanna watched the doctor attend to Andrew.

"Where is Ben," asked Andrew excitedly.

"Andrew son, Ben is dead," said the doctor clasping Andrew by his shoulders.

"Oh god," said Andrew as he lowered his head and covered his face with his hands. "I can't believe this happened. He's dead! I didn't kill him! He tried to kill me, and I was just trying to defend myself. Where is mother?"

"Your mother is fine, Andrew," said the doctor. "I gave her something to make her sleep. She's quite upset, but she'll be better when she wakes. Be still now so I can stitch your head."

"Andrew, what happened in that barn? Did you and Ben argue?" asked Jake.

"We did, but I don't remember, it's a blur, something about my father and my mother. He was angry and hit me with his stick," said Andrew. "He took his gun from his pocket and pointed it at me. I grabbed it, and it went off."

"Andrew did you read a letter from your uncle in London?" asked Roseanna.

"What letter? I don't remember a letter."

"He's not well," said the doctor. "This blow to the head has caused some memory problems."

"I need to see my mother and Nancy. Where are they?" asked Andrew.

"Andrew, listen to me," said Jake. "Try and remember what happened. The authorities are here, they've gone to the barn to see what's happened to Ben. They'll want to talk to you."

As Jake was talking, the two federal authorities came to the veranda. "Is this is the other party that was in the barn with Mr. Ravenna?" he said to Jake.

"Yes. I'm Andrew. I was there."

"Are you responsible for that gentleman in the barn being shot?"

"Yes," said Andrew hanging his head.

"Where did you get the gun?"

"I didn't have a gun. It belongs to Ben. He had it in his hand, I tried to take it away."

"The gun isn't in his hand now," said the federal authority

"I don't know where it is. I could hardly see, and I just ran."

"This injury to your head was caused by Mr. Ravenna?"

"He hit me," nodded Andrew.

"Why did you run?" asked the authority.

"I was scared. I don't know," said Andrew confused.

"I need to take you in. A judge is going to have to sort this out," said the authority. "Do you have a weapon on you," he asked as he patted Andrews's pockets.

"Can't you see that he's not himself? He needs medical care. Leave him here with me, and I'll bring him to the judge along with his attorney," said Jake.

"Can't do that, sorry. Are you through with your treatment, Doctor?

"Yes, but he'll need further care and be watched for a concussion."

"We'll see that he sees a doctor and gets the rest he needs. We have to take him, Mr. Sinclair, whether he remembers or not. That man in the barn is dead and certainly didn't shoot himself. This young man, Andrew, says he's responsible; he'll have his day in court. I can't leave here without him. If he is to be set free until his trial, have his lawyer go before a judge. What the judge decides makes no difference to me. Andrew is saying it was self-defense and he just tried to take the gun away. I can't decide if that's the truth, it's not up to me," said the man with a shrug. "I must bring in who is responsible."

"Give me time to speak with him and help him with this as much as I can before you take him then."

"Take a few minutes to talk to him but be quick. I'm only performing my duties. You understand that."

Jake turned to Andrew, "They're going to take you, but don't worry I'll leave for the city and get your attorney and get this straightened out. Is Lawrence Winston who I should see?"

"No," said Andrew emphatically. "I don't want him. He's trouble. Him and Ben from the beginning with Roseanna. Ask Josh Horn to help me?"

"I'll go right away. Josh can start the process of getting this resolved. You just take care of yourself and let me handle things here. Is there anything else?"

The arresting officer ambled towards Jake and Andrew, "We have to go now. You can see Andrew at the lock-up, but I need to take him in now."

Jake stepped aside, and Andrew stood up, the authority grasped his arm and led him off the veranda, and assisted him onto to his horse. They turned their horses toward the road away from the plantation. Jake walked beside Andrew's horse as the trio of men rode down the lane. "Andrew," he said laying his hand on Andrew's leg, "don't get discouraged. This is only temporary. I'll go to Josh right away."

"Just take care of my mother," said Andrew. "Tell her I didn't mean it to happen. I love her and don't want her to hate me because Ben is dead. Tell

Nancy I love her."

"I'll see to things," said Jake reassuringly. "Take care of that head of yours. We'll all be here waiting for you to come home."

Richard Philips trotted along beside Jake. "We believe in you Andrew," he said. "We'll take care of your mother."

Jake and Richard stopped as the men reached the end of the lane and left the plantation neither of them aware that the rain, for the time being, had stopped. They stood silently watching as Andrew was led away.

"I hope you'll let me help," said Richard. "I can spend time with Jane if she'll let me. Years ago when I built the house for her and Ben, Andrew and I got to know each other very well. I've taken a liking to Andrew and want him cleared of this. Just say what you need me to do, let me help in any way that I can."

"There's a lot to do, and I'm glad you're here. I have to go to the attorney. While I do that, would you help with Ben's burial? Arrangements need to be made, and we'll need a coffin?"

"Of course. I can build one. Plenty of what I'll need at the building site. I'll go right away," said Richard as he started to move away.

"Wait up, Richard. Something else needs to be done first. The Negro man that works for Ben, Nathan is his name, was there when this happened. I want to know what he saw. Come with me as I talk to him."

They hurried towards Ben's property, both eager to get on with the task that lay ahead of them and to have Andrew freed from any charges that would be brought.

"Jake," said Richard, "do you think Jane will recover from all of this?"

"I certainly hope so. She was quite distraught, enough so that the doctor saw fit to give her something to make her sleep. No one has had a chance to talk to her and get her side of the story."

"She has to be able to tell what she saw. She's a wonderful woman. Building the house, we spent so much time together. Ben was never interested or involved; it was always just she and I. Over the years no matter where I went or how many other women I met, she was always in the back of my mind with her grace and politeness. I can't imagine her any other way and probably why I never married even though I always blamed my lifestyle of moving from place to place. Then when you hired me and told me you were married to Roseanna Ravenna, my first thought was I would see Jane again. This isn't the time to be talking about this, but I hope she will at least give me an opportunity to help her."

Jake stopped and stared at the other man. "I can't respond to that, Richard, except to say we all need to do what we can to help Jane and her children. That's what we should be thinking about."

"I know, Jake. Forget I even mentioned any of this to you."

Jake and Richard, after a brief search, found Nathan in the overseer's cabin where he had been hiding to stay away from the activity in the barn.

 "Nathan, you tell me what happened between Mr. Ben and Mr. Andrew. They've taken Mr. Andrew because he shot Mr. Ben. You were there, so tell me what went on."

"I's don't see nuthin Mr. Jake."

"You were there Nathan; you had to see what happened."

"I's gone Mr. Jake when Mr. Andrew kilt Mr. Ben. I runned."

"What did you see before you ran Nathan?"

"They yellin' and Mr. Ben he hit Mr. Andrew in the head and he gots blood."

"What else Nathan? What were they yelling at each other?"

"Don't know 'cept Mr. Ben talkin' bout Mr. Andrew's father and bout Miss Roseanna. Then Mr. Ben hit Mr. Andrew knocks him down. Then they fights with Mr. Ben stick, and Mr. Ben he say Nathan help me, but I's afraid and runs out the barn."

"Did you see Mr. Ben with the gun?"

"No such. I never see that but I's hears the bang after I's leave the barn."

"You didn't see Mr. Ben with the gun?"

"Sometime I's do, he always has it here," said Nathan patting his side to show where Ben kept the gun.

"Did you see Mr. Andrew with the gun?"

"No 'cause Mr. Andrew he not have a gun like Mr. Ben."

"To be clear you did not see Mr. Andrew shoot Mr. Ben?"

"No sir, but Mr. Ben dead and Mr. Andrew shoot him."

Jake nodded his head, "Yes that we are sure of, Ben is dead. Nathan, you need to help now. Find Simon and fix a place for Mr. Ben in the plot. You hear me, can you do that?"

"Yes, Mr. Jake, I's be doin it."

CHAPTER 16

Richard Phillips delivered a hastily made, but serviceable coffin and now the task of preparing Ben Ravenna's body for burial could be done. Mama Teal advised the funeral be held quickly and the body put in the earth so the smell of death would not linger in the parlor of Jane's house. Nathan, with a note from Roseanna, went to request that Reverend Rivers come to the plantation, but she gave no explanation to avoid the spread of gossip through the parish. Jane still slept from the dose of medication given her, and Nancy, through her tears, made the necessary decisions for her father's funeral. The funeral would be postponed a day to secure Andrew's release. When Reverend Rivers arrived at the plantation, he was shocked at the news and promised discretion. Nancy asked that only close friends of the family be notified.

Mama Teal, wise in many ways, gave Roseanna the strength and the guidance she needed to face the task of preparing Ben's body.

"I don't know what to do Mama Teal," said Roseanna, her eyes wet with unshed tears and her stomach queasy. "I'm thankful you're here."

Mama Teal gave Roseanna a reassuring hug. "Yous let me and Loretta do this child, yous sad 'bout yous uncle."

Roseanna emphatically shook her head. "No, no Mama Teal. Aunt Jane was there for my mother and my father. I must do this for her."

"Here are what we be doin'then," said Mama Teal as she ticked the details off on her fingers, "we need to gets him wash up right where he lay, stuff the wound so they no more blood, and bind it good. We gets the best clothes, scrap his face of whiskers, comb his hairs nice. Get herbs and spice from the kitchen, and flowers from the garden to lay wiff him for the smell. Mr. Philip gets him in the box and into Miss Jane's parlor. It be done fine."

"Is that all Mama Teal? Nothing more?" said Roseanna as bile rose at Mama Teal's words.

"Gots to set the house to rights for a wake wiff black over the mirrors and closin 'the curtains. 'Cause of the smell we needs more flowers and spices in the parlor. Nathan and Simon gets pine boughs from the woods, so theys smellin' good in the parlor."

"Nancy wants extra time for her mother, and Reverend Rivers can't come for at least one more day."

"It be done fine Miss Roseanna, you see. Don't you's worry none," she said as she reached for a basket and headed out the door of the kitchen house to the garden. Roseanna and Loretta close on her heels.

Daylight was fading when the burial details were completed. Roseanna was ashamed that several times she needed to step away from the body to regain her composure when her stomach began to churn. Now it was over, her uncle's body was laid in his parlor.

No one had eaten throughout the day, and with Jake, Josh, and Andrew returning to the plantation soon, Mama Teal and Loretta went to the kitchen house to prepare food while Roseanna, doing her part, went into the dining room to clear the table. She stopped in astonishment as she entered the room to see the fabric for the drapes just as she had left it. It seemed hours ago when Cindy had knocked to summons her and Jake to the barn.

She set about carefully folding the fabric to save for another time. As she worked, she remembered the day she had sat with her uncle and Jake in this very room talking about a loan to pay Ben's mortgage, and working with him to start planting cotton and now he was dead.

Roseanna stopped her task with a gasp, everything had changed. She realized her aunt would not only face her husband's death and her son arrest, but also the debt due at the bank, and the threat of having her home sold to the highest bidder at auction. She sank into a chair as she thought how she could get to the bank and pay the debt so that Jane would not lose her home. Jake would understand and go with her, they would do this together, but it had to be done and soon.

She was startled to hear a sound behind her; she turned to see her aunt in the doorway watching. Her hair was mussed from her slumber, and a crease ran along her cheek where the bedding had pressed against her face. "Aunt Jane, you're awake. How are you feeling?"

Jane looked pale, and her eyes had a lethargic look. "Andrew? Is he here?"

"He, he isn't here Aunt Jane," stammered Roseanna. "He came back, but the Federal authorities took him to the lock-up."

"No!" thundered Jane in disbelief. "That should not have happened. I must go to him."

"No, no Aunt Jane wait," Roseanna reached to restrain her aunt. "Please wait! Let me explain what happened. Come and sit in the parlor."

Jane reluctantly allowed Roseanna to take her by the hand. Then she perched on the edge of her chair as though poised for flight. Roseanna knelt at her feet. "Andrew came back; he had gone to Richard Philips at the building site. He was hurt, Richard helped with his wounds, and the doctor was here and treated him. Jake did what he could to keep the authorities from taking him, but they insisted. Jake has gone to the city to get Josh Horn to help Andrew."

Jane clenched her hands into fists. "No! He should not have been taken. He was defending himself from Ben. Ben was going to shoot him."

"We know Aunt Jane," said Roseanna in a soothing voice. "Jake tried to stop them from taking Andrew, but they said it was up to a judge to decide what had happened."

"I need to go to him Roseanna," said Jane with desperation in her voice. "Ben did horrible things. I know he did. There is a letter from Andrew's uncle telling me what Ben has done in England. He's to be arrested for murder."

Roseanna took her aunt's hands. "Aunt Jane," said Roseanna very calmly and slowly, "you know that Uncle Ben was shot, you know what happened?"

"He's dead, Roseanna," said Jane her eyes filling with tears, "but Andrew didn't murder him," she said with sudden clarity, "and I can't let this happen to my son, I can't lose both of them."

"We know Andrew was defending himself."

Jane searched Roseanna's face. "Where is he? Where is Ben?"

"Home, at rest in the parlor just as he should be, Aunt Jane. Mama Teal and Loretta with help from Richard Philips, who built a fine coffin, took care of him."

"Has Reverend Rivers come?" asked Jane as the thought came to her.

"Yes. All is ready, and you would be so proud of Nancy. She was so brave and told us exactly what should be done for her father."

"What should I do Roseanna? I need to see Andrew. You understand. He can't be accused of murder when he was defending himself. I need to go to my son!"

The sound of voices announced the arrival of Jake and Josh Horn.

Jane sprang to her feet. "Why did you let them take him, Jake? You should have stopped them!"

Jake strode quickly to her side and took her hand. "I did what I could. They understood that Andrew was defending himself, but they had no choice. Andrew admitted he shot Ben. They had to take him."

He turned to Josh Horn, "This is Josh Horn, an attorney. Andrew asked for him, and he will do everything in his power to set things right."

Jane vigorously shook her head. "No. Lawrence Winston is our attorney. Ben would want…," she stopped, "It doesn't matter what Ben would want, does it?" she said as she collapsed in a chair.

"Andrew asked for Josh," said Jake.

Jane frowned then turned to Josh Horn. "How long will this take, Mr. Horn? You must fix this."

"Tomorrow first thing we will go to the courts; Andrew hasn't been booked, just detained. I will go and petition for his release. First, I should introduce myself, as we have never met. I am Josh Horn," he said extending his hand. "I have been the attorney for Jake and his partner, Randy Thomas, for some time and have also represented Roseanna. I know your son; I met him a while back, and he is a fine young man. Jake hasn't had a chance to tell you that the two of us stopped at the lock-up to see Andrew. He's fine Mrs. Ravenna and very much concerned about you and his sister."

"He was hurt," said Jane. "I saw the blood on his head myself. What about his wounds?"

"A doctor was called for him. He's resting and recovering from his injuries, and his memory is quite clear about what happened."

"I'm sure you are a fine attorney Mr. Horn, but Lawrence Winston, he needs to be here."

"I will see that he comes," said Jake reassuringly.

Josh gave Jane a feeble smile. "Mrs. Ravenna, Andrew requested that I act as his attorney when he was taken and again today when I saw him at the lockup. I intend to do that," he said firmly.

Jane frowned wringing her hands. "He can't be charged with killing my husband. Why was he taken?"

"Tomorrow we will get him released, and he will be home with you, for now, tell me about the letter from Andrew's uncle in London," said Josh.

Roseanna quickly withdrew the letter from her pocket and handed it to her aunt. "It was in your drawing room, Aunt Jane. You told me about it, and Nancy and I went to find it. I didn't have time to talk to Andrew about it, everything was happening so fast when the authorities were here."

Jane smoothed the creases from the letter. She shook her head sadly. "Andrew came into my drawing room as I was reading this," she said waving the letter. "It had just come with the letter carrier. I was so upset and overcome by what Reginald Moorcroft had written. I didn't mean for Andrew to see it, but he did and then went to find Ben. There are things in this letter that have been secret for so long, but if it means getting Andrew free, I don't care about secrets."

"Andrew told Jake and me about the letter. He said that Ben would finally be seen for the kind of man he is," mumbled Josh.

Jane stared at the letter in her lap not hearing what Josh had said. "I begged Ben to marry me. First, he turned me down, but very shortly and suddenly, he changed his mind. I thought that he cared for Andrew and me and wanted to take care of us, but it was for my money." She hesitated a moment, then blushing she continued, "I must tell you about Andrews's father and what happened to him…"

Josh laid his hand on Jane's shoulder, "You don't need to say anymore. Andrew gave us the details."

Jane's face reflected her sadness, "Andrew shouldn't know how his father died. I hid it from him for years." She covered her eyes and bowed her head.

"That isn't what started the fight," assured Josh. Ben began beating Andrew. He struck the first blow. Andrew wanted Ben to face up to all he had done to Roseanna, trying to take the plantation and the gold from her, and then beating Simon. The money he took from you Jane, and the reason he took it, that was the final straw. Andrew had enough and stood up to Ben in that barn today."

"I wanted to get Andrew away from London. I knew nothing about Ben being wanted for murder or about investments he made in some slave ships. He used me, and I not only allowed it, but I also begged him to marry me and promised him my wealth, which was considerable. Now I know why he so suddenly changed his mind about marrying me, he found out about the slave ship being captured and lost all his money." Jane lowered her head and wiped tears from her eyes, "He used me and treated my son horribly. He never cared for anyone but himself."

Nancy ran into the room from the hallway where she had been listening. "That's not true, Mother. He loved me and always took good care of me! I read that letter, Mother. If what this…this Moorcroft person said in that letter is true, and father tried to kill Andrew, I understand why you're angry but he loved me."

"Of course he did Nancy," said Jane. "I'm as guilty in this as your father. But

Nancy, Andrew did not kill your father. He defended himself."

"I'm not angry with Andrew, he was badly hurt by my father, today, and not just today but all of his life. I saw it, but I didn't care because I was clearly his favorite, he spoiled and pampered me. He may not have cared for Andrew, maybe from the very beginning, but he loved me."

"Andrew and I must have been a constant reminder to Ben of what had happened in London," said Jane. "Through my own well-intentioned but poor decisions, this has come to consequences I never foresaw."

"You couldn't have known," said Roseanna. "You did what you thought was right for Andrew."

"And maybe too much for myself," said Jane, tearfully.

A knock at the door sent Mama Teal to answer. "It be Mr. Philips," said Mama Teal.

"Aunt Jane do you want me to ask him to come at another time?" asked Roseanna.

"No, please ask him to come in. I need to thank him for all his kindness," said Jane.

Richard came into the room with greetings for everyone, but eyes only for Jane. "Rain is over thank goodness, and now we need to get this nightmare with Andrew resolved."

"Richard, I'm glad you've come," said Jake greeting him with an outstretched hand. "There's good news for Andrew. His memory has returned, and he is quite well. Josh will go to court to have him released tomorrow."

Richard hurried to Jane's side and took her hand. "My sympathies for all that you are enduring and my help in any way that I can."

"You've been so kind," said Jane with a sad smile. "Roseanna has told me how helpful you were especially with Andrew. She tells me you nursed his wounds and brought him back to the plantation."

"He was so distraught over what had happened. I did what anyone would have done. I'm glad he came to me."

"Everyone has been so helpful. There aren't enough thanks to go around," said Jane looking around the room. "Richard, he thinks so highly of you. These last few days when the weather has been so horrible because of the rain and the storms he has talked to me about how you have inspired him for this work."

"Did he also tell you that I have invited him to work with me on some of my other projects?"

"He did and thank you for that."

"No need to thank me. Andrew is a natural for this trade, and I'm pleased to see his interest. I need him back on this project, and so does Jake."

"Mr. Horn assures me that this will be settled tomorrow and Andrew will be home. I am already in your debt and so is my son. Thank you," said Jane.

"No thanks are needed," said Richard.

"Sorry to interrupt," said Roseanna. "Mama Teal has prepared food for us. We all need to eat, and Richard, please join us."

It was late and after midnight before everyone was settled for the night and the house was quiet. Jane and Nancy stayed the night, as did Richard Philips and Josh Horn. Exhaustion settled on all of them, but restful sleep would elude them as each struggled with their own thoughts and problems.

Jake and Roseanna climbed the stairs for the last time that day and once behind closed doors fell into each other's arms. "Jake, what a horrible day. I still can't believe he's dead," said Roseanna with her face buried against Jake's chest.

"We've known your uncle and Andrew shared this dislike, but this is beyond what any of us could have expected," said Jake, as he absentmindedly rubbed Roseanna's shoulders.

"Will there have to be a trial, Jake? It just seems so wrong when Andrew was defending himself."

"We need to trust that Josh can prove to the court that Andrew needed to save himself and will be home where he belongs," said Jake stifling a yawn.

"Jake I know how tired you are, but there's something important," said Roseanna anxiously. "The bank, I have to go and pay off Ben's debt so the property won't be sold at auction."

"I understand, I think it's the right thing to do. We'll go after the funeral in a couple of days."

"Aunt Jane has been through enough. I don't want her to know she's at risk of losing the house. This can't wait, I promised Uncle Ben I would make it right so the plantation would stay as Ravenna property. I can't leave this for Aunt Jane. Remember Uncle Ben said not to say anything to Jane or Nancy, they don't even know there is debt. I want this done before the reading of Ben's will because it will all come out then. Jane doesn't have to know if I go to the bank and take care of the debt. I can't leave my aunt with this burden."

"Roseanna, sweetheart, I don't have time," said Jake as he pulled the tie from around his neck and unbuttoned his shirt. "I've promised Jane to go to court with her. I also need to go to my building site and get the work started again. With the weather being so bad for all this time and now with my foreman in lock-up, I need to be there. I have to do this for Randy because every day there is a delay it costs both of us money and Randy worked hard for this and I can't let him down. I'm sorry that Ben has died, but please understand the importance of this. I actually wish Randy were here, he could help."

Roseanna paused with a hairbrush in her hand and whirled around to face Jake. "I can go to him. I can go to Randy and the bank. There's no reason I can't. I have to see the banker, and we promised Aunt Jane that Lawrence Winston would be sent for. I'll go to New Orleans see Mr. Cutler at the bank and then go to Lawrence Winston's office and then for Randy."

"No, Roseanna, no. There's every reason you can't," said Jake shaking his head negatively. "The roads from the storm are worse than you can imagine. I've been out there today, and they are horrible. It has to wait. I can't expect

Richard Philips to run the workers. That's not what he was hired for."

"But one of us has to go. We promised Aunt Jane, and I won't let her down. I'll take Simon with me so I won't be alone. I'll see Randy and let him know what has happened."

"Roseanna you can't. These storms may not be over yet, and the roads are in deplorable condition. I know we promised your aunt Lawrence Winston would be told. I can be at the site by dawn and send one of the workers for Randy and Winston. I'll start the workers and then be back to go with Jane and Josh to court. Randy needs to know what's happening" Jake paused and ran his fingers through his already mussed hair. "Dammit Roseanna, I don't want to agree, but one of us does need to go."

Roseanna went to his side, "It will be fine. Randy will come, you know he will."

"Yes, he would. That's what we should do, go to Randy, he needs to know what's happened. I worry you going, Roseanna. Take the gig and Simon. He is so strong he will be able to help if you get stuck." Jake laughed as he climbed into the bed, "He could carry you, Moses and the gig out of harm's way if you needed him too."

Roseanna laughed. "I can just see him trying to do that. Good, it's settled. I'm glad you agree," said Roseanna as she finished dressing for bed.

"I can't stop thinking of Simon carrying Moses and me," laughed Roseanna as she climbed into bed and turned to Jake. He was asleep, and she kissed him lightly, blew out the lamp, cuddled close, and in minutes was asleep herself.

CHAPTER 17

Roseanna's intention of an early departure for the city was not to be. There were countless details needing her attention. Jake was again giving his opposition to her going to the city. He followed her from room to room, as she did her chores. He blocked her path as she attempted to enter the parlor.

"Now listen, Roseanna, this business at the bank can wait."

"I have listened, Jake. I know the dangers, and I'm taking Simon. Didn't you want to go to the site this morning to get the work started? You best hurry so you're ready to go with Josh and Aunt Jane.

"Where is Nathan? Why don't we send Nathan for Randy with a note asking Randy to notify Lawrence Winston? Then we'll go to the bank after the funeral."

Roseanna fluffed the pillows on the sofa in the parlor, "Nathan is gone."

"What do you mean gone? He was here yesterday."

"He apparently told Loretta goodbye and then left. Richard brought two men from the building site to help dig the grave for Uncle Ben because Nathan is gone." Roseanna paused and placed her hands on Jake's shoulders, "I'm going. I want this debt of Uncle Ben's settled before the Will is read and that will be done when Lawrence Winston comes."

"Your uncle always said you were stubborn," said Jake sighing heavily as he embraced her.

"I won't be long and will probably be home before you finish in court. What should I tell Randy?"

"Just send him out to the site. Richard will get everything going again now the weather has finally cleared, but supervising the workers isn't his job."

Leaving the responsibilities of the household in Mama Teal's capable hands, Roseanna, with help from Simon, climbed into the gig. Moses stomped impatiently, and when Roseanna snapped the reins, he bolted out of the lane.

The storms had passed, and the sun and blue sky had returned, but the saturated earth had only begun to dry. Damage caused by the torrents of water that came with the long-lasting storms had altered the roads leaving ruts and gullies. In places, puddles the size of small lakes formed and completely obliterated the roadway. Roseanna carefully guided Moses around fallen trees and other debris slowing his pace. Her pale blue dress was wet and splattered with the mud flying from the horse's hooves and the wheels of the gig, while her straw bonnet slipped from her head and dangled down her back by the ribbons tied under her chin.

As she drew closer to the city, the traffic of coaches, wagons, drays, and horseback riders grew thicker, and the road became a churned mess of mud from the wheels of the vehicles and the hooves of the animals. Roseanna stood in the gig concentrating on the road and the traffic in front of her.

Suddenly a rider in the uniform of a Union soldier grabbed Moses' harness and guided the gig off the road. Another soldier held up his hand as a signal for Roseanna to stop. She pulled hard on the reins to bring the gig to a halt as other uniform-clad men fanned out around the gig. Moses pranced nervously at the close proximity of their mounts. Simon swung his head from side to side staring open-mouthed at the men as they formed a ring around them.

"Good morning, Madam, I'm Sergeant Warren of the Federal Patrol. Where is it you're headed this morning?"

An astonished Roseanna could only stammer, "I'm, I'm going into New Orleans. What is it? Why have you stopped me?"

"Your name please."

"Mrs. Roseanna Sinclair. Why have you stopped me?" she demanded as she eyed the men circling the Gig.

"What brings you to the city today Mrs. Sinclair?"

"Errands, I have errands," said Roseanna. "Is something wrong?" she asked.

"Your name sir," said the man speaking to Simon and ignoring Roseanna's question.

Simon overcome with the shock of the men surrounding the gig did not answer but stared fixedly, his eyes wide with fear.

"Son, what's your name," repeated the sergeant leaning closer to Simon.

Simon moaned in discomfort and fear. "Yous not take Simon. Simon not kilt Mr. Ben," he said as he sank lower into the seat and wrapped his arms around his head.

"Simon," said Roseanna laying her gloved hand on Simon's arm, "tell the man your name."

"I's be Simon," he shouted jumping nervously and looking behind him as one of the horses standing close to the gig nudged him and exhaled a loud snort.

"Simon where are you going today?"

Simon stared at the Sergeant his eyes wide with fear. "I's goes with Miss Roseanna 'cause she say," he said in a quaking voice.

"Do you want to go with Mrs. Sinclair?"

"No," said Simon vigorously shaking his head. "I's want MaMa!"

"Simon," said Roseanna with concern, "It's all right. He's confused by your question Sergeant Warren. He doesn't understand. He knows me only as Miss Roseanna. He is a free man and worked for my family for years. Simon don't be frightened," she said reassuringly.

Simon was now crying openly, "Them takes Simon! I's needs my mama," he wailed as he crouched into a tight ball on the floor of the gig and covered his head with his arms.

"Oh, Simon! No, no! They won't take you," said Roseanna realizing Simon believed the men would take him as uniformed men had taken Andrew.

Puzzled the sergeant asked, "What ails this boy Mrs. Sinclair?"

"You! You've frightened him! I ask you again, why have you stopped me?"

"There's no reason for Simon to be so alarmed Mrs. Sinclair, and you've done nothing wrong. The patrol must see that everyone is safe and I noticed you seem to be having some difficulty with your gig due to the condition of the road and the amount of traffic. Might I have one of my troops ride with you and take control of the reins? Simon here can then take the trooper's horse."

"I think you've done quite enough, Sergeant Warren," said Roseanna as she laid her hand on Simon's shoulder. "I'm quite capable of handling this gig provided you and your men would move aside so I can continue on my way," said Roseanna tersely.

The sergeant tipped his hat, "As you wish, Ma'ma, just trying to help. Fall out men and let the lady continue her journey."

The troops quickly moved away from the gig and Roseanna maneuvered it back on the road and into the stream of traffic.

"Simon, come up here now and sit on the seat. That man is gone, and no one is going to take you," said Roseanna, carefully keeping her eyes on the traffic. "We are going to see Mr. Randy now. You know him; he's Mr. Jake's friend."

"I's want Mama," cried Simon.

Jane was anxious to go to court and for the horror of Andrew's incarceration to be over. When Jake announced, it was time to leave she hurried out the door with Nancy close on her heels. Josh mounted his horse to follow on horseback, confident Andrew would be seated in the carriage with his mother and sister on the return trip.

Their journey would take them away from New Orleans to the Circuit Court north of the plantation. Jake swore under his breath, his apprehension growing as the road turned into a quagmire. How foolish he had been to agree to let Roseanna go to New Orleans alone. He drove slowly over the debris, ruts, and puddles trying to put his concern for Roseanna out of his mind as he concentrated on the road ahead.

The news of Ben Ravenna's death, a member of a prominent family, created quite a stir in the parish. Sketchy details reached every ear causing tongues to wag with truths and half-truths. Andrew arrested for killing Ben, and Andrew severely injured. Ben Ravenna wanted for murder in England. As a result, when Jake escorted Jane and Nancy into the courtroom, which would typically be empty for this type of proceeding, they were stunned to see a contingent of neighbors from the parish in the courtroom come to witness the drama.

Josh pushed through the swinging gate in the rail and nodded a greeting to the prosecuting attorney, Fred Monroe. Josh knew him to be fair, reasonable and well liked, and he felt confident that the proceedings would go smoothly.

Jake escorted Jane and Nancy to seats in the gallery behind the defense table. They sat alert grimly waiting, staring straight ahead, as the buzz in the courtroom grew. A door opened, and a uniformed officer of the court led Andrew to a chair beside Josh. Jane's face relaxed in a smile when she saw her son, she blew him a tender kiss.

Shortly the bailiff instructed those in the room to rise as Judge Dennis Post entered the room.

Andrew gripped Josh's arm and whispered, "Jake I know this man."

"How do you know him?"

"He was in my regiment."

"Was he there when you deserted?"

"I don't remember, but I think yes."

Josh exhaled; concerned the Judge would know Andrew's military history. The judge took the bench glaring at Andrew, as a frown wrinkled his forehead.

Andrew's case was the first to be heard. "Mr. Monroe, the floor is yours, sir," instructed Judge Post peering down from his chair above the court.

Those in the courtroom from the parish craned their necks to get a better view and to hear what had occurred at Pelicans Haven.

Prosecutor, Fred Monroe, rose to his feet, "Thank you, your honor. Your honor, after reviewing the reports of the arresting officials, in this case, this morning I have filed charges of Involuntary Manslaughter against the defendant, Mr. Andrew Moorcroft. I waive filing further charges until I have an opportunity to review the case more fully. I apologize to the court, I received the case late yesterday, and I was detained on another matter."

Josh was not surprised at the charge against Andrew and was immediately on his feet. "Your honor, at this time I would request bail be set for my client. I think Mr. Monroe's further inquiries into this matter will satisfy the court that this was, in fact, a case of self-defense on the part of my client."

Fred Monroe rose to his feet, "I have no objection to bail being set, your Honor."

"I believe," said the judge, "we should allow Mr. Monroe the time he requires to gather information and set a later time to discuss bail for your client Mr. Horn."

"Your honor, if it pleases the court, my client, Mr. Moorcroft, is here today only because of his ability to fight off an attacker and save his own life. We appreciate Mr. Mason's lack of time to review the case and know that when he does, he will reach the same conclusion. I object to bail not being set at this time."

"Your objection is noted, Mr. Horn, but we will give Mr. Monroe time for his inquiry. We have a death of one of our citizens, Mr. Horn, and I'm not apt to grant bail. Mr. Monroe may find that he will need to adjust the charges against your client and then having to issue an arrest warrant will not be necessary."

Jane, unable to control her emotions, began to cry silently as Nancy tried to console her. Andrew, bandages covering his head and injured eye, shifted in his seat to look at his mother distress showing on his face.

Josh took several hurried steps towards the judge's bench, "Your honor, I appeal to you to set bail at this time. I ask you to let this man go back to his family and his job as the foreman of a building crew until such time as Mr. Monroe has concluded his inquiry."

"Mr. Horn, I've ruled on this, Sir. We will allow Mr. Monroe the time he requires. These proceedings are dismissed."

"All rise," intoned the bailiff and the judge exited the courtroom through a doorway behind the bench.

Roseanna, angry at being stopped by the patrol, had only a short distance to go to reach the offices of Sinclair and Mason. Pulling the gig to a stop, she turned to Simon, who was still visibly shaken, "Simon, stay with Moses. I'll see Mr. Randy and then we'll go home."

Simon huddled in the seat, "They gonna take Simon, Miss Roseanna?"

"No, no Simon," said Roseanna, patting Simon's hand to reassure him. I'll only be a moment."

She jumped from the gig, hurried through the door of the office and ran up the stairs to the second floor. She burst through the door of Sinclair and Mason startling Randy Thomas.

Randy jumped to his feet. "Roseanna! What a surprise. Why are you here? Where is Jake?"

The full impact of all that had happened at the plantation and the difficulty of the trip into the city took its toll on Roseanna. "Oh Randy, thank goodness you're here," she said tears streaming down her face as she hurried towards him.

Randy, shocked at the outburst, gathered her into his arms "My god, Roseanna. What's happened? Where's Jake? Are you hurt," he asked taking in her disheveled look, her clothes wet and spattered with mud, her bonnet hanging down her back and her hair a wild tangle lose from its pins.

"So much has happened, Randy. Please help me with Simon. He's downstairs in the gig," She broke free from Randy and hurried back the way she had come while gaining control of her tears.

Randy still puzzled by Roseanna's appearance, followed to find Simon sitting in the gig crying and nervously looking around. He waved his arms excitedly when he saw Randy. "Mr. Randy yous not let them take Simon."

"Simon, no one is going to take you," said Randy. "Roseanna, what the hell is going on?" he said in frustration helping Simon from the gig.

In a rush, Roseanna told him all that had happened at the plantation. Simon was upset because the patrol had stopped them and they were in uniform like the men that had taken Andrew because he had shot Ben Ravenna and how she needed to see Lawrence Winston, and she needed to go to the bank, and she needed to get Simon home so he could be with his mother.

"Damn," cursed Randy. "Ben Ravenna dead by Andrews's hand? We need to get to the plantation now! Why isn't Jake with you Roseanna? You never should have done this alone."

"He didn't want me to, Randy, but there was no other way to get this done. I'm just thankful you were here," said Roseanna. "It was the patrol, that's what caused the problem."

Randy quickly escorted Roseanna and Simon back up the stairs to the office where he supplied Roseanna with paper and pen so she could write to Lawrence Winston telling him of Ben's death, the time of the funeral and that Jane was requesting that he come to the plantation immediately. A messenger was sent to deliver the message. Back to the gig with Roseanna and Simon, Randy mounted his horse, and they headed across the city to the bank.

Randy stayed with a calmer Simon as Roseanna entered the bank to speak to Mr. Cutler. Roseanna gave no explained why Ben's debts were to be paid immediately with money from her account, and that all debts be canceled.

Cutler was surprised at Roseanna appearance and her brisk attitude. She was brief with an explanation saying it was a private family matter, and the details would be heard soon enough.

Documents were prepared and signed, and Roseanna left the bank with the canceled notes in her reticule satisfied that her Aunt Jane and Cousin Nancy would now be able to live peacefully in their home with no threat of eviction.

As soon as the judge left the courtroom, everyone began talking at once. Jane, who had been crying since the judge had denied Andrew bail, jumped from her seat, reached across the rail, and clung to her son while Nancy and Jake tried to restrain her. As Andrew was removed from the courtroom, Jane turned to Josh angrily shaking her finger at him, "You told me he would come home today. You promised. What happened, why is he still being held?"

"I know Jane, stay calm and give me a moment to talk to Mr. Monroe and then I will speak with you. Jake, help Nancy and Jane to a seat."

Josh turned to Fred Monroe. "How well do you know this judge, Fred?"

"Quite well and I'm somewhat surprised that he would not grant a request for bail. If I as the prosecution didn't object, why did he?"

"My client was a deserter during the war, and the judge was in his regiment and may know of Andrew. If that's the reason, the judge needs to recuse himself immediately."

"What! You must be mistaken he wouldn't do that. We need to speak to him in chambers," stammered Fred Monroe in astonishment. "He shouldn't have been on this case if what you're saying is true."

"Possibly he looked at the case just before the court and didn't recognize the name, Andrew Moorcroft, but when he saw him in court remembered him. He studied Andrew rather thoroughly several times."

"I did notice that, thought it odd," nodded Fred Monroe. "I'll send a note and ask him to see us. He'll be expecting it, I wager."

"I understand you have to look closer at the case, and the women with me are Andrew's mother and sister. The mother is the only one who actually witnessed the shooting. You should talk with her, and you'll see that my client shouldn't be charged. The only other witness is a former slave, and of course, he can't testify against a white man, but someone did speak to him, and he told them he ran from the area before the shot was fired."

Fred Monroe looked across the room at Jane. "Her husband killed by her son, how tragic," he shook his head in disbelief. "Are you aware the gun was not in the barn when the authorities arrested your client, they had questions about your client's guilt because of the missing gun? That's why I asked for more time to review the case."

"It's been recovered. A well-meaning doctor took it, as I understand, and he turned it in. The gun didn't belong to Andrew, it belongs to his stepfather, who is the victim. What you hear from Andrew's mother will settle this. Andrew should be set free; this is clearly a case of self-defense."

"My offices are across the street, bring his mother to tell me what she witnessed. We may get this resolved before we hear from the judge."

CHAPTER 18

The events of the day along with the heat sapped Roseanna's energy leaving her feeling like a wilted flower. She found a seat in the shade of the veranda to catch her breath before helping Mama Teal and Loretta with the chores and meal preparations necessary for the remainder of the day and for her uncle's funeral tomorrow. Life would cease to be hectic. Andrew would be home, the funeral over and life would be bearable again.

Returning from the city with Randy had been trouble free. He took Moses' bridle and led him through the severely damaged areas in the road, and Simon was calmer knowing they were going to take him to his mama. As they traveled, they come upon Sergeant Warren and the patrol going towards the city. The Sergeant smiled broadly and tipped his hat to Roseanna, but she turned her head with her nose in the air refusing to acknowledge him and patted Simon for reassurance.

 Roseanna fanned her face as she slowly rocked in her chair thankful the whole affair was behind her. Randy had gone to the building site to join Richard and help where he could and had promised to keep the details of her unsuccessful trip to the city from Jake to save him needless concern. After all, there was no need for him to know. She stretched and yawned. Andrew was coming home, time was wasting; they should be back from court very soon.

As they left the courtroom with Fred Monroe leading the way, neighbors from the parish, who had been in the courtroom, tried to gather around Jane out of curiosity or to express sympathy. Jane, upset from the court session, began to cry uncontrollably as they approached her. Jake and Josh shielded she and Nancy and ask everyone to stand aside and give them privacy.

Once seated in Fred's office, Josh cleared his throat, took both of Jane's hands in his, and said as gently as he could, "Jane, I can't truthfully tell you why the judge denied bail for Andrew, but Fred and I suspect that the judge knew Andrew from the past."

Jane wiped her eyes with a hankie and sniffled. "What do you mean, how would he know Andrew?"

"The judge was in Andrew's regiment when he deserted. Andrew told me he recognized him."

"No, no! This is all Ben's fault. Tell them Nancy, tell them how your father forced Andrew to go to fight and how Andrew refused, Ben called him a coward. Tell them, tell them," she wailed.

"Mother please, this isn't helping," said Nancy reaching to pull her mother to her in an embrace.

Jane pulled away, "Ben Ravenna even in death causes trouble for my son. How could I have been so blind that I didn't see? Ben berated Andrew and told him repeatedly that he needed to fight for Louisiana and the South, but Andrew would never fight for people to enslave Negroes," wailed Jane flinging her arms in the air for emphasis. "Ben said Andrew would disgrace us if he didn't fight. He pushed Andrew until he joined, but he never wanted any part of the war. He did it to please Ben."

Nancy clutched her mother's hand and pressed a wadded handkerchief to her mouth to stop her own sobs. Jake sat helpless with his jaw clenched as he watched Jane and Nancy.

"Jane, if what we suspect is true, we'll get it corrected," said Josh. "Fred sent a note to the judge asking that he meet with us. In the meantime, you talk to Fred and tell him what you saw in the barn. I think we can have all the charges against Andrew dismissed once you tell your story, and Fred understands what happened."

Fred Monroe leaned close to Jane and spoke to her in a soft voice. "Mrs. Ravenna, if we go to court, the court will hear your testimony in order to determine the guilt or innocence of your son. That would be a formal examination. Here you just need to tell me what you saw. I understand you're emotional, but take a deep breath, compose yourself, and perhaps we can get your son home where he belongs."

Jane wiped her eyes and then started to speak. "I came into the barn, and they were struggling over a stick, my husband's stick," she said. "He walked with a limp, you see, and used the stick to help him. Ben fell to the floor, then reached into his coat, and drew out a gun. Andrew saw the gun, and he ran to try and take it away, but it went off." Jane sobbed, and she stuttered as she tried to speak. "Ben was shot, and Andrew left the barn. No one was there but me and Nathan."

"Nathan is the Negro you spoke of before, Josh?" asked Fred Monroe.

Josh nodded.

"Nancy, can you add anything to what your mother has said?" asked Fred Monroe.

"No, I was outside the barn when I heard the shot. Andrew came out with his head bleeding, I tried to help him, but he rode away."

A clerk from Fred Monroe's office quietly came into the room and handed Fred a folded note. Fred opened the paper. "It's a reply to my note to Judge Post. His schedule is full, and he can't see us until tomorrow before the court."

From the weariness of the last several days, Roseanna had drifted into a light sleep as she sat on the veranda. She woke with a start at the sound of the carriage making its way up the lane and hastened from her chair to greet Jake, her aunt, and cousins, but stopped short when she realized Andrew was not with them.

Jane immediately and tearfully began to tell Roseanna what had happened in court. "Ben, once again, Ben, that's why Andrew isn't with us. I'm exhausted, Roseanna. My strength has ebbed, and I feel as if I can't go on. Why are they doing this to my boy?"

"Aunt Jane, I'm so sorry, come, let me help you. It's sweltering, you need rest and to refresh yourself. Tomorrow will be a long day for you and Nancy. Come into the house where it's cooler."

Roseanna and Nancy guided Jane in the house to the coolness of the parlor where Nancy removed her mother's bonnet and gloves while Roseanna fetched cool drinks. Roseanna studied her aunt, the strain showing so vividly in her face. She was always so controlled and elegant, but now a shell of her former self.

Jane calmed as they sat quietly, but suddenly she turned to Jake, "Will you take me tomorrow to see that Josh and Mr. Monroe get to see the judge so we can bring Andrew home?"

"Jane, there's nothing we can do and Ben's funeral is tomorrow morning. I'm certain Josh and Fred Monroe will be successful with the judge, and Andrew will be on his way home. Josh promised he will ride to the plantation immediately if anything changes."

"No, Jake. I want you to take me to court tomorrow."

"Mother, please. Listen to yourself. Daddy's funeral is tomorrow, and you must be here."

"I don't want to be here. I want to be with my son."

"Jane, Josh is meeting with the judge in his chambers, not in court. We won't be included in that meeting. We need to stay here and wait. I'm certain Andrew will be here by early afternoon," said Jake.

Jane ignored Jake and turned to Nancy, "You saw all those horrible people from the Parish in court trying to find out what happened between your father and Andrew. Gawking and whispering about us, they'll be here tomorrow just to gossip. I don't want that. I don't want them here."

"There's no way we can prevent it, Mother. There's nothing we can do. I told Reverend Rivers only close friends should come, but we can't turn people away."

"Jake can stop them, can't you Jake?"

"I think anyone who was in the court today and has heard the gossip, has put together what happened between Ben and Andrew. Roseanna and I will make your excuses to anyone who comes and tell them you are indisposed. You don't have to see anyone unless you want to."

Jane sighed, "If that is the best we can do," she said as she leaned her head back and closed her eyes. Shortly she was asleep.

CHAPTER 19

Roseanna woke to the sound of thunder; she had slept fitfully, dreaming about her uncle. It was hot and still at this hour before dawn. She lay tangled in the bedclothes. She threw them off and eased from the bed so as not to wake Jake. At the window storm clouds, gathered and faint flashes of lightning lit the horizon. Rain could fall before her uncle's funeral, perhaps a good thing, it would keep the curiosity seekers away, and Jane would be granted her wish that no one attend the funeral.

Roseanna sighed and hoped all would go well on this day. As she descended the stairs, the clock struck the hour of five. It was quiet in the house, no one was stirring, but she knew Mama Teal would be in the kitchen house with the beginnings of breakfast. A warm bath would help her wash away the fatigue and face the events of this day.

She entered the kitchen house, surprised to find her aunt sitting at the table sipping a cup of tea, the pot by her elbow waiting to serve her again. She was dressed in a black dress; a matching bonnet lay in her lap. She smiled, but lines of fatigue showed on her face.

"Aunt Jane, good morning. You're up early."

"Couldn't sleep, Roseanna. Rather than fight it, I readied myself for the day. Will you have tea?"

Roseanna took a chair at the table. "That would be lovely. This will be a hard day, Aunt Jane. I want to make it easy for you."

Jane reached across the table and firmly grasped Roseanna's hand. "Nothing you can do, Roseanna, nothing you can do. I want to assure you I have passed through the sorrow and tears. I'm ready to put my life together as best I can. I will attend to my husband's burial today, and my son will come home, and I will apologize to everyone for my emotional outburst."

"You don't need to apologize, Aunt Jane."

"Everyone has been so caring, you and Jake. My poor Nancy has been so helpful. I must make things less demanding for her. She must feel I don't care about her, or her father. I've been so concerned about Andrew."

"She understands, everyone understands."

Jane shook her head negatively, "No, she can't understand. She must see me as so uncaring and what I said about keeping people away from the funeral was nonsense. Anyone who comes is welcome; Ben had friends who of course would want to be here. We'll turn no one away."

The storm that had threatened earlier arrived with rain coming steadily as Randy and Jake hitched a wagon and led the horse to the door of Jane's house. With the help of Richard Thomas, Ben's coffin was placed in the wagon. Reverend Rivers, and his wife, Evelyn, arrived and stood on the veranda waiting for the storm to pass. Those few who had braved the weather stood in the yard sheltered by the trees, some huddling under umbrellas and some in rain gear. They all waited for the signal to begin the walk to the family burial plot.

Reverend Rivers stood in whispered talks with Jane and Nancy. He gave each of the women a brief hug, and then he nodded a signal to Jake, Jane was ready to start. Grasping the bridle of the horse, Jake, moved the wagon slowly forward.

The group that followed the wagon was solemn, the rain serving only to darken the mood. Jane was composed as she faced the burial of her husband; she walked with her arm linked through Nancy's, sharing an umbrella. They bowed their heads close together watching their footing to avoid puddles and the ruts made by the wheels of the wagon. The Reverend Rivers followed and then Roseanna, escorted by Randy. Richard Thomas and the few in the Parish who had braved the weather followed, and last came Mama Teal, Simon, Loretta, and the Negroes, including Cindy, who served at the Ben Ravenna home.

The wagon reached the burial plot, and the men stepped forward to assist Jake as the coffin was lowered into the waiting grave.

Reverend Rivers stepped to the grave, "We're here today to seek comfort and understanding. Our hearts ache over the tragedy of this death, and the heartache for this family. Gather close as we prepare to place our brother, Ben Ravenna, in his final resting place."

He read scriptures selected by Nancy, and then directed all to bow their heads in prayer.

The upheaval of the past days etched deep lines in Jane's face, but she shed no tears, and as the Reverend finished his prayer, she scooped a handful of mud from the ground and threw it atop her husband's coffin. Nancy followed her mother's example; the two women shared an embrace, wiped the mud from their hands, turned from the grave, and retraced their steps to the house.

Obeying the Judge's summons, Josh Horn accompanied by Prosecutor Fred Monroe approached Judge Dennis Post's chamber door. Josh glanced at Fred, who nodded in assent, and Josh knocked.

"Come in," came a response.

Josh opened the door to find the air in the room filled with the blue haze of smoke from the Judge's cigar. The judge sat at his desk in his shirtsleeves, the offending cigar in one hand, and a sheaf of papers in the other. He laid the papers aside and rose to face the two men.

"So, you want to talk about this Moorcroft case. I figured you would when I ruled from the bench. My apologies, Fred, for ignoring your motion to approve bail for this defendant."

"It came as a surprise, Your Honor."

"There was a reason, I had concerns. As his attorney, Josh, you may know Andrew Moorcroft was a deserter during the war and as it happens, from my regiment."

"Your Honor, you know you can't use that information against my client."

The Judge held up his hand to silence the attorney. "I damn well know what I can and can't do. Of course, I can't, but there are other considerations. I recognized his name from the reports I read but wanted to be sure. The minute I saw him sitting in my courtroom, I knew him for the coward he was. I read the reports of the arresting officials, he confessed to shooting Ravenna, and he left the scene. With his background of deserting, I certainly could not agree to allow bail as Fred admitted in court he needed more time to examine the evidence. For all I knew the charge might well change to murder, I didn't want to free Moorcroft in that event."

"You're biased against this man, Your Honor," said Josh.

The judge ignored Josh's remark. "Did you know any of this information, Fred?"

"No, Your Honor, I didn't know he was a deserter until yesterday, Josh, here told me. But that's not why he is in court now."

The judge nodded in agreement. "Let me finish explaining myself. In the arrest report, they noted the weapon was missing. Moorcroft should not have had a gun; it's against the law which might have meant more charges would be filed against him."

"It wasn't his, Your Honor; it belonged to the deceased. His wife told me, Ben Ravenna, carried it since the beginning of the war, and refused to obey the law and turn the gun in when the war was over," interjected Fred.

"Well, where the hell was it, if Moorcroft didn't have it?" asked the Judge.

"There was a doctor at the scene; he did a foolish thing, he took the weapon before the authorities arrived. He turned it in the next day at the lockup when he went to treat Moorcroft's wounds," said Josh.

"How serious are the wounds?" asked the Judge.

"He isn't out of the woods. He may lose vision in one eye. There are multiple wounds to his face and head where he was struck.

The Judge leaned back in his chair and rubbed his face with his hand, then struck a match to the cigar, which had extinguished itself. "Seeing him sitting in my courtroom made me angry," said the judge with a tensed jaw. "He left the scrimmage we were in, threw down his weapon and left. He disobeyed a command to pick up his weapon and fight, everyone else was fighting, and men were dying around him, he turned and walked away. Someone should have shot him in his cowardly back."

"I understand how you must have felt, you and the entire regiment, Your Honor," said Fred Monroe.

The judge nodded his head with a great sigh. "You have no idea how that felt, Mr. Monroe. I watched men die, and he walks away," said the judge angrily. "Mr. Horn, I understand I must recuse myself from any further proceedings. I'm very bias against your client."

"Your Honor, perhaps it won't be necessary," said Fred. "Since we were in court yesterday, I've had the opportunity to review all of the information and talk to the defendant's mother and the wife of the deceased. This is a horrible tragedy for her, but she is the only witness. This is clearly a case of self-defense. Moorcroft, if he had not tried to take the gun away from Ravenna, he would be the victim, and Ben Ravenna would be on trial. Your Honor, I'm filing a motion to drop all charges against Moorcroft; he should be released."

"I'm sure you agree with this, Mr. Horn," said the judge as he frowned at Josh.

"From the very beginning, you're Honor."

The judge drew on his cigar, "Give me the motion. I'll sign it."

CHAPTER 20

Only time could heal the tragedy of Ben's death, but a small degree of peace and quiet had returned to the plantation as summer descended. It brought with it a monotony of heat and humidity making everyday chores and routines unbearable. Andrew was home, cleared of all charges, and back as foreman at the work site. Nancy and Jane were adjusting but learning a different life now that Ben was gone.

Roseanna and Jake sat over breakfast in the dining room with the windows thrown wide to catch an early morning breeze.

Jake topped toast with jelly, licking his fingers to catch the sweetness. "Bring a lunch when you come to the building site today with my bags. You'll see how close we are to finishing. The warehouse is ready, and soon the living quarters. I'll be in New Orleans by evening helping Randy empty the warehouses and getting our inventory up river to our own warehouse. If all goes well, I'll be home in two days, and Sinclair and Mason will be here permanently."

"It's exciting, Jake. You and Randy have worked hard for this. When you're back home, we can move the furniture from the attic to the living quarters. Mama Teal and I will finish with the supplies for the pantry and kitchen while you're away."

"Randy and I would fumble the whole business of setting up house if not for you and Mama Teal. Tell me, could you give up Simon?"

Roseanna paused; her teacup held in mid-air and gave Jake a puzzled look. "Give up Simon? What do you mean?"

"He loves the warehouse, Roseanna, and wants to be there. He can't do all that needs to be done, but there are things he does extremely well. I promised to buy him a horse to travel back and forth. Would you agree to let him work for me part-time?"

"Of course I would agree, but have you talked to Mama Teal; is she going to let him? Wait, Jake when did all this happen?"

"Each morning Simon brings Sweetie saddled and asks can he come with me. Will you talk to Mama Teal and work out something for him?"

"I'm not sure she would; she worries about him, Jake, especially after the incident with Ben. If he would be with you and Randy that would be different. He misses Nathan. There's no one to fish with, and there isn't enough work for him."

"I told him I would get him a horse. He wants to name it Moses," chuckled Jake.

Roseanna sat thinking how genuinely attached Simon was to Moses, so much so that if he had a horse, he would name it Moses. She would miss Simon; he had been by her side since she was a little girl. This was his decision to make. He was a free man. If he wanted to work at the site, no one should keep him from doing so.

"He can have Moses. He needs a safe horse, one he knows. He helped train Moses and loves him. I'll find another."

"Roseanna, are you sure? But maybe a young mare could be a start with the horses for you. Richard could build the stable."

"No, just a saddle horse, I need time to find the right mare, the bloodlines are too important. We do need a stable for the horses and equipment, though."

"Richard's work at the site is about done, he has other projects scheduled, but would build for you first."

"I need to decide, but I'm too undecided to decide," laughed Roseanna, wiping crumbs from her mouth. "I sound silly."

"What keeps you from doing this?"

"I don't know, Jake, just confusion if I should."

Jake shook his head, "I'm not confused. Read the letter I wrote for your father. It's there, Roseanna, you are to rebuild the Ravenna stables. That's it, no confusion."

Roseanna sighed in exasperation, "Something keeps holding me back."

"The foolishness Ben Ravenna put in your head about plowing up the whole place for cotton. Something your father never intended. If you want, go back to the plans you had with your uncle and finance cotton on his side of the place, but you go back to raising horses. There's money enough for both ventures."

"I'm waiting for a sign or something," said Roseanna with a shrug.

Jake eyebrows shot up in surprise. "A sign? What sign, Roseanna? Your father's letter was quite clear about what should be done and who should do it. Sweetheart, don't wait so long that time slips away and it's too late."

Mama Teal came into the room with the mail. "Here the envelope, Mr. Jake."

"Mama Teal, has Simon told you that he wants to work in the warehouse with me?"

"That all he talkin' bout, Mr. Jake. He just awaitin' 'cause me and Miss Roseanna needs to say."

"I want him to do this, Mama Teal," said Roseanna.

"He gots chore here."

"We'll manage; Simon should be happy."

"If yous say he can, I's happy, too.

"Good it's settled," said Jake looking through the stack of mail. "One for you Roseanna."

Roseanna studied the envelope. "It's from Gwen Mason. Why would she write to me?" She began to read the letter. "Gwen and Josh are getting married. Why didn't he tell us?"

Jake gave Roseanna a smug look. "I've known for some time, but Gwen wanted to tell you herself."

"She's asked me to stand up with her, but I hardly know her?"

"She likes you and wants a pretty girl to brighten up her wedding."

Roseanna frowned. "I don't think that's why."

"Roseanna she likes you. I'm standing up with Josh."

"She didn't say when the wedding would be."

"They haven't set a date. Josh has several cases in court and can't take time. Gwen, showing her usual lack of restraint, is planning the world's most elaborate honeymoon to Europe, so timing is an issue. The wedding will be in New Orleans, Josh insisted."

"I'd be honored to do this," said Roseanna hesitantly, "but Jake …"

"But what? It would really please both of them."

Roseanna's shoulders drooped, and she sighed. "Josh wanted this; he told me weeks ago. I'll write telling her I will."

"Good. Now when you come to the site today with my bags would you bring a picnic?"

"I'll work in the garden, it's ragged after the storms, then I'll bring a picnic and your bags, and see you off to New Orleans. Then it's time to go back to making the drapes for our bedroom," she said with a smile and a kiss for Jake as he left the house.

Before the temperature rose, Roseanna gathered the tools needed in the garden. She surveyed the ruined plants and debris that littered the garden enclosure. The rose canes were broken, overgrown, and damaged from the storms. Her mother would be distraught to see the plants looking so neglected. Pruning would set the bushes back, but it was needed. In time the plants would regain their growth. She worked collecting the debris from the ground and stacking them in a pile for later burning, and then trimmed the plants of broken canes, and overgrown foliage.

Nancy, coming into the garden carefully stepped around the pile of damaged plants. She was dressed in a casual pale green dress with a narrow skirt with a bonnet tied under her chin. Gloves covered her hands.

"Good morning," she called. "Where is Simon this morning?"

"He has a new job working for Jake, and because he needs a horse to go back and forth I've given him Moses," said Roseanna.

"Roseanna, he's yours since he was a colt," said Nancy in surprise.

"It's safer for Simon on Moses. He is lonely now that Nathan's gone, he needs something to do, and working for Jake is perfect."

"Nathan will come back, Roseanna. Where would he go?"

"He always talked about going north."

"I guess with Daddy gone, there's nothing to hold him here."

"There's exciting news, Josh Horn is getting married."

"Josh? But he's never mentioned it."

"It's been a secret between the men. I wasn't to know until Gwen, Gwen Mason, that's who Josh is marrying, told me and asked me to stand up with her."

"The woman from New York, Jake's partner? When will this be?"

Roseanna shrugged, "It hasn't been decided, but I don't know if I can stand up with her."

"Why?"

Roseanna hesitated, and then took a deep breath. "Mama Teal thinks I am going to have a little one."

"What! Roseanna! When tell me when!"

"Mama Teal's not sure she's just seeing signs."

"What signs?"

"I'm tired, sleepy, and sick to my stomach. No appetite. Mama Teal is so clever, she may be right because I do feel different, I can't explain it."

Nancy grabbed Roseanna for a hug, "The baby will call me aunt. Aunt Nancy, I like that," she said laughing.

"Of course you'll be Aunt Nancy. I don't know when the wedding is, but she doesn't want someone who is going to have a little one standing in her wedding," said Roseanna using her arms to show how round her body might be.

"Tell her you will. You don't know for sure, right? Roseanna how exciting. I so envy you, married, and having a little one. A boy, let's hope, and he should look exactly like Jake."

"We have to wait, it may not be, and don't envy me, your time will come."

"I hope so, Roseanna, I truly hope so. But it's so exciting for you."

"Tell me, how is your mother?"

"Better each day. Mother, Andrew, and I spend time talking about everything. Sometimes we laugh and sometimes cry. Andrew feels guilty. He blames himself for father's death. He never should have gone to the barn that day. That letter made him reach a point where his anger at father exploded."

Roseanna's breath caught, "Poor Andrew."

"He wants to write to his uncles in London and tell them about my Father's death and how horrible they are to blame my mother for his father's death. Mother doesn't want that, but he hasn't said he won't. Mother blames herself for everything that has happened."

"Why? What she did was for her son and a better life. That's what any mother would do."

Nancy nodded, "I've told her that. Mother and Richard are becoming closer; Andrew is happy, but I don't know how to feel. I want Mother to be happy, and I like Richard, but it does seem disloyal to my father?"

"Years ago, your mother and Richard were close when he built your house. It's not as if he has come along and your mother started caring for him. They're renewing a friendship."

"I know. Between the war and the troubles for Andrew and my father's death, she deserves to be happy. I'm not sure she was happy with my father, not since the war began. Somehow I see her relationship with Richard as wrong. I come upon the two of them sitting together over a cup of tea, they're laughing or talking in low voices. It takes me by surprise, and I feel betrayed."

"I don't think he needs to be encouraged to stay. Jake wants him to build the new stable when he's finished at the site. We can put it off if you like, and then he'll go work someplace else."

"Mother would be unhappy, and Andrew would probably go with Richard. If they were both gone, mother would be miserable. Roseanna you should let the stables be built. Now that the gold has been found and you have the money.

Jake said the same thing. I need to decide. Maybe I can't raise horses by myself."

"Roseanna that's nonsense. You did this all day every day with your father and brothers, and your father always said you were better than he and your brothers."

Roseanna looked thoughtful and then shook her head with a sigh. "Let's change the subject. What of Andrew's injuries?"

"The doctor has yet to say if they will heal completely. Andrew can see shadows, dark and light, but not clearly. There's going to be scars."

"If I know Andrew that isn't going to stop him from doing what he wants, which is to work with Richard."

"Roseanna, my father's Will left everything to my mother, and then to me if she passed before him with Lawrence Winston as my guardian. Father never mentioned Andrew, he hated him."

"Nancy, there was tension, but he never hated Andrew," said Roseanna. "I saw that only after the war started and especially after Andrew deserted."

"Maybe hated is too strong a word, and what I saw was resentment. It did get worse after Andrew deserted. I never stood up for him, and I should have. I talked it through with my mother after the funeral."

"What did she say?"

"That it was her fault. Her dream for Andrew was he would be of the gentry like his father and uncles. She begged my father to marry her so she could take him away from London and the gossip about his father taking his own life. From the very beginning, father wanted to adopt Andrew, but mother refused; she would not let her son be the son of a Louisiana cotton farmer. She wanted him to carry the Moorcroft name. My father felt he wasn't good enough. The outcome was that she drove a wedge between them."

"How sad, but the war caused a lot of problems, too," said Roseanna.

"It made the problems worst. I love Andrew, he's a wonderful brother, and I have to make this up to him. My father paid more attention to me, but what child would admit that they were a parent's favorite?"

"This happened before you were born, Nancy. Your father didn't spoil you and treat you different; he couldn't treat Andrew as a son, he was treating him the way your mother wanted."

"Andrew was defending himself in the barn that day, and if the tables were turned, he would be dead instead of my father. I feel like my loyalties should be with my father, but Richard Phillips is the first truly wonderful thing to happen for Andrew."

"What about Andrew and Loretta going to London?"

"When Loretta lost the baby, everything changed. She only wanted to go to London because of the baby, and when the baby died, she broke it off."

"Are they both satisfied, Nancy?"

"Yes, they are. Loretta wants a man who can give her a home and children close to her mother and her brother."

"I'm glad for them if they're content."

"Roseanna, there is something I need to say, and my mother wants to talk to you, too. Mr. Winston knew father was in debt at the bank, but neither of them told my mother. Mr. Winston went to the bank, and they told him you had paid father's debts. He gave us the documents he had prepared for my father's signature for a loan that you were going to make. The two of you were going to start raising cotton together. Is that true?"

"Yes, we did plan that."

"Mr. Lawrence also told us that the property would have been sold at auction."

"Oh, Nancy, that won't happen."

"I know, now it won't, but Mother and I want to sign the documents and somehow pay the money back to you."

"No, no. I don't care about the money Nancy. I want Pelicans Haven to stay with the family. I don't want strangers here, living in your mother's house."

"Roseanna that money should be used to start raising the horses again.

Roseanna chuckled. "Maybe I won't raise the horses. Maybe I don't feel the urge, or I have no confidence that I could. I don't care about the money. Your father repeatedly insisted the horses were a dream, a childish dream. He said my father agreed, but I'm certain my father didn't. Maybe father was a dreamer, too. It would be hard to rebuild something that took a hundred years to create. Your father was right, cotton and sugarcane will make money. Since the war, there isn't much cotton being planted." Roseanna turned and looked out across to the acres and acres where the cotton used to grow. "Remember seeing the fields of Pelican Haven with cotton growing?"

Nancy frowned and nodded her head, "I more remember the thrill of seeing the beautiful horses and being at the stables and watching your father and brothers work with the horses, but most of all watching my cousin, Roseanna, and wishing I could be just like her."

Roseanna smiled at her cousin. "I want the plantation to be like it used to be, before the war. We can do this, Nancy. We're strong, we survived a war, and we can do this."

"But the horses are what built Pelicans Haven, not cotton, horses, Roseanna, and I have no money to plant cotton."

"But I do. There's enough to hire the labor for planting cotton, and in time, maybe the horses. Jake says we can do both. We can work out how to share what we earn."

Roseanna grabbed both of Nancy's hands in hers, "Nancy, we're the only Ravennas left. There's no one else, no man to carry on the family name, no fathers, no brothers, just you and me. We have to keep this land together so Pelicans Haven will be here for our children, the ancestors of the Ravennas. We need to do this for the generations to come just as it has been for years. Do it with me, Nancy; tell me we'll rebuild it together."

"I will Roseanna, but bring the horses back."

"I'll decide, there's time for that, but first the cotton."

After a busy, hot day, though exhausted, Roseanna couldn't sleep. She sat in the dark at the open window staring out at the moonlit pastures and listening to the sounds of the night. A light breeze stirred bringing the sweet smell of blooming flowers. She missed Jake in bed beside her. Now that his business would be out of the city, he would always be here with her. She smiled to herself, he would only be gone for two days, but she couldn't remember her life without him.

She caressed her stomach, feeling for anything that would tell her a baby was growing there. Maybe there was a baby, and that was why she couldn't make a decision about the horses. Jake, and Nancy, too were telling her to decide. Jake was suggesting there was something in her father's letter and she should reread the letter.

She sat thinking about her father's letter and then lit a lamp and carried it down the stairs to his office. Taking it from the drawer of his desk, she smoothed the creases and began to read. Jake's bold, heavy handwriting was familiar to her now. He had written the letter for her father when he lay on his deathbed. She could see nothing different or revealing in the letter that she had read so many times before. What had Jake meant that her father's letter was clear about who should rebuild the stables? Suddenly Roseanna understood, she was to rebuild the stable. Her parents were confident John was dead when her father left, and her father had been unable to find Edward and expressed little hope in the letter he would be found. Her father was dying when the letter was written, he knew he was dying, but he still told Annabel to proceed with the plans they had made, and the plans were to rebuild the stables. Then she was the only one in the family who could do it, the only one left. That's what Jake meant. It was her; she was the one to do it. Her father knew this, and no matter what happened, the stables were to be rebuilt. Her parents must have spoken of her taking on the responsibility in the event no one else was left and if her father didn't return. She would be the only one left. That was the plan, for her to build the stable again. Her parents planned that.

Roseanna cried out, gripping the letter tightly in her hands as she leaned closer to the lamp to reread the words. Tears blurred her vision; she angrily wiped them away. There was a message in the letter, a message for her, and only her. Why had she never realized it before now? Her parents knew before her father left that she would possibly be the only one to carry the dream of the stables forward. That was her answer; she had always had the answer. She needed to follow her parent's plans.

Tears stained her face as she looked at the letter again. "I'll do it, Daddy. I promise, just like you wanted," she said aloud.

But how? How would she begin?

Coming soon Pelicans Haven – Book Three – *And So It Shall Be*

ABOUT THE AUTHOR

Cecelia makes her home in Springfield, Missouri with her husband, Chip, cat, Aslin, and pup, Babette. She devotes most of the days to writing, reading, playing Scrabble online with friends and family, and hunting for antiques.

Currently, many writing projects are keeping her involved including book 3 of *Pelicans Haven –And So It Shall Be*, which continues Roseanna and Jake's story and presents different characters while answering questions readers are asking. She is also working on a novel set in Pennsylvania shortly after WWII titled *Age of Consent*.

Cecelia has co-authored a nonfiction book, *To the Glory of God: Pioneer Churches in Springfield, Missouri* about churches in Springfield that were established and still in existence some as early as 1833. This book will be published in the fall of 2017.

Cecelia would enjoy hearing from you. You can find her on Facebook (Cecelia Marriott Chittenden) or Email her at seemcapril@gmail.com.

Made in United States
North Haven, CT
22 March 2025